The Watcher Bee

Mary Melwood

ANDRE DEUTSCH

First published in 1982 by
André Deutsch Limited
105 Great Russell Street London WC1

Second impression 1983

Printed in Great Britain
by Ebenezer Baylis and Son Limited
The Trinity Press, Worcester, and London

British Library Cataloguing in Publication Data
Melwood, Mary
  The watcher bee
  I. Title
  823'.914 [F]   PR6063.E46/

  ISBN 0-233-97432-6

' . . . for what has gone before is dreaming to waking, ashes to fire.'

From a poem by Joanna Justice

ACKNOWLEDGEMENT

For his never-failing interest and encouragement my love and gratitude, as always, to Morris Lewis, and for his admirable typing of a far-from-perfect manuscript, my most heartfelt thanks and appreciation.

For my sons
Bob and Rod
with love

Chapter One

I can't remember life before Charlie. We met when we were two and loved each other at once, our contentment with each other so complete we needed nobody else. The grown-ups thankfully left us alone most of the time until the day we went into the wood and stayed too long searching, we tried to tell them later, for a marvellous bird which alighted before us and charmed us away. We lost the bird and were lost ourselves, grew tired and fell asleep and were discovered just before the summer nightfall lying cheek by cheek upon a bed of wild strawberries. So touching, so pretty, leaf-stained and strawberry tinted, dear little Charlie, sweet little Kate, innocent as angels and in those early years as amiable with each other as angels are supposed to be.

I grew to hate him and he to loathe me but that was after we had begun at the Little School and rivalries and odious comparisons spoilt the harmony between us.

Charlie's house was next to ours, had once been ours, in a way was ours still. My uncle had let it, not sold it as I was always ready to remind Charlie when he boasted about its superior size, its many rooms and passages, its back stairs and front stairs, apple chambers and boot-holes, all perfect for our games of hide and seek. It was a farmhouse, though the farm part was several fields away, and its delightful advantages would have been mine if my father hadn't died soon after, and because of, the first world war.

'He joined up straight away,' said my uncle, 'couldn't wait to be a hero, much good it did him and you too.' The way he looked at me always made me feel to blame. He made things worse, did my father, by not getting a scratch on him during the war and then coming home in the spring of 1919, sick and thin like a ghost, but eager to marry my mother, Uncle's sister. He saw the summer out, stayed long enough to ensure my appearance in the world and died in the autumn. My mother died of influenza soon after I was born in April. It was a wonder, said my uncle, I didn't follow them, being so puny I could be put into a quart jug.

So there I was, a war legacy of doubtful value bequeathed to Uncle Ben, my mother's brother, who lived at the farm with Granny, and Aunt Beth, my father's sister, who lived next door, my double aunt and uncle who married to make it more convenient for them to bring me up. 'Not that we hadn't always got on well enough,' said my uncle, 'we were relations anyway, some sort of cousins, second or third, don't ask me which, but I doubt if we'd have married, except for you.'

'Some sort of cousins' – for years I couldn't understand the complicated cousinships in our family. I was bestowed with such an extraordinary number of second, third, fourth, step, foster and courtesy cousins that I began to think I was cousin to everybody in the world. Some were very old and appeared only at weddings or funerals, paying calls of politeness at our house and giving me fusty kisses I longed to wipe from my face. Some were of a different feather, being newer, brighter and more familiar to me by their regular appearance on Sundays in our pew at church. Amongst them I was gathered like a fledgeling into the ancestral nest. The pew had been inhabited by our family for so long, I had been familiar with it since I was so young, it seemed almost a second home to which I was attached with historic strings, for like all the other pews in the church it had been made by my grandfather when he was a young man.

After my parents died Uncle Ben let the house and farm and sold the stock to Charlie's father who, with the other livestock, took over Granny as well. She was old and had wept at the thought of leaving her home so she stayed in the four bay-windowed rooms at the front of the house with her cumbersome old furniture and Charlie's mother to keep an eye on her. Uncle Ben, who had always hated farming and missed my father who would have been his partner, married my aunt, moved into her house next door, then proceeded to create an orchard, our orchard, which became his vocation, the passion of his life.

It wasn't an orchard like Charlie's. There the trees looked as if they had survived the ice-age and against sensible expectation bore fruit every autumn whose original names were long forgotten, but to which we gave our own evocative ones. 'Katie's downfall', from the tallest tree, owed its name to a particular painful moment in my history.

Charlie and I had climbed every tree in the orchard by the time we were four except this, a tapering pear tree. One day as if propelled by a force underneath me I scurried up the trunk. At the same time, inside myself, I was feeling the exhilaration of going up, but also seemed to be with Charlie and some other children who were admiring and envying me. I was both going up and watching myself go up amongst the leaves and shadows. Nothing stopped me until I reached the top, from which immediately without a moment's contemplation of the view or enjoyment of my triumph, I crashed to the ground. In the same flash of time as the earth came up and struck through my body into my head I knew I must get on to my feet and not look a fool in front of Charlie. I was inside myself with the pain and shock and outside myself with Charlie, watching myself being brave. I saw Charlie's mother running through the orchard. I saw myself as I held my head and moved it from side to side and heard a wavering voice which I knew was mine saying, 'Don't worry, people, I've only shaken my dome.'

So it gave me a shock the first time Charlie called me a coward and a double shock when he allied the word with "girl". He was in the back-yard pumping water into a bucket, his baby cousin tottering in the background. Neither Charlie nor I was taking much notice of the baby though we were supposed to be keeping an eye on him. We were arguing – and it was a dangerous place to have an argument, especially for me as I was getting the better of it. Exasperated, Charlie suddenly lifted the bucket of water, in the same second I snatched the baby into my arms and Charlie soaked himself instead of me. 'Coward,' he yelled, 'just like a girl – only a girl'd think of a rotten trick like that.'

I held the baby until I got to the gate then put him down and bolted for home, dry but guiltily turning over in my mind the connection between "girl" and "coward".

That was the first time the word "girl" had been flung at me as an insult. I was puzzled and disturbed. Charlie and I had seemed the same kind of creature with differences certainly, he was in breeches, I was in short frocks, he could send a jet of water from his trousers almost over the hedge. I couldn't but it had never seemed to matter. We both had strong bare legs and healthy appetites. We could run equally fast, climb the same trees, turn somersaults, play leapfrog and jump ropes with equal agility – moreover, I was the one regarded as clever. I was quick with an answer while Charlie still struggled with the question. I could talk fluently to anybody willing to listen while Charlie was awkward, as if embarrassed by the feeling of words trying to struggle from his tongue.

We gradually moved into a period when the emotions between us became a mixture of hate, venom and rage and frequently shouted all three at each other across the farm-track which struggled downhill between our two orchards. Boys were vile, girls rotten. The sex war flared between us. Through this weak spot in the walls of our early paradise other troubles of the jealous world worked their way in, year by year, until by the time of the trench digging we were more like enemies than friends.

There was a pile of war books on the shelves of our dining-room and sometimes on Sundays after tea Charlie liked to look at them. He was fascinated by pictures of soldiers in the trenches at the Front. One night when he was ready to go home he asked if he could borrow a book. Surprised, but ready to encourage his first sign of literary interest, Aunt immediately gave him permission, and he went home with several volumes under his arm. It was some time before I saw him again. I did homework most nights because it had been decided I should sit for a scholarship to a girls' high school and I had less time to play.

One day, as I was sitting on our orchard wall looking across to Charlie's place waiting vaguely for something to happen and wishing it would, I saw Charlie come out of the small outhouse we called the boot-hole. He was carrying a spade and garden fork and looked determined to be busy. He saw me, said nothing, but spent some time inspecting the ground near the wall, selected a site and began to dig. I couldn't see what was happening but I could hear the sound of the spade and see occasional clods of earth flying about. I was quiet for a time then asked in a civilised way what he was doing.

5

'Scrubbing the floor.' He laughed briefly at his own humour then ignored me until I was almost ready to give up my vigil and go away. It was irritating to wait without being able to see what he was doing behind the wall. Suddenly his head appeared over it, he looked across at me and said, 'Can't you see I'm digging a trench, you idiot?' then went on digging.

Next day there was a gang of diggers who worked steadily, disappearing at mealtimes then coming back to work with renewed vigour, exchanging virile conversation and taunting remarks I was meant to hear. I was both impressed by their exploits and despondent at being left out.

'Charlie's digging a trench,' I said indoors.

'What on earth for?' asked my aunt.

When I asked Charlie the same question he said, 'What does anybody dig a trench for, stupid?' and his unpleasant gang of sycophants laughed amongst themselves and the word "girl" was flung across the wall more than once.

'I'm sick of hearing about Charlie's trench,' said my aunt. 'If he's so fond of digging why doesn't he dig the garden?'

'Why don't you dig one yourself,' asked my uncle, 'if you're so interested in trenches?'

This seemed so obviously sensible I immediately provided myself with tools, went to our orchard wall, chose a site opposite Charlie's and began to dig a trench of my own. It was hard work and lonely, especially as the labours on Charlie's side were going on in such invigorating company from which I was excluded, for nobody spoke to me, only at me.

The next day I invited some of my friends to help. They didn't enjoy digging and weren't much good at it, they were inhibited by worries about making their dresses dirty and disliked worms, but we exchanged some spirited remarks with Charlie's gang and so enlivened the monotony of shovelling. Every now and then members of both gangs stood on the walls and hurled insults and clods of clay at each other. That cheered us all.

Deeper and deeper we probed into the earth, each gang watchful of the other, each determined to out-dig the rivals. Sometimes I let a fanciful report of our progress be overheard on the other side so that Charlie was unable to contain his curiosity and demanded outright how far down we had dug, saying he bet it wasn't very far, girls were no good at digging.

Down, down we dug. At first my enthusiasm was strong enough to keep my auxiliaries from flagging, then one by one they lost interest and faded away. The same happened across the wall with Charlie's gang until at last only we two remained doggedly delving, deeply entrenched in determination and thick clay.

I put an old rag rug on the floor of my trench and some orange boxes for stools and a table. I arranged bricks to make a fireplace and burned twigs, hoping their spiralling smoke would inform Charlie of the superior amenities on my side of the walls. I had ambitious ideas of sleeping out, it looked such a true to life dug-out, secure against attack and cosy as well. I wished Charlie could see it and thought of inviting him in, but knew he would ask me to see his trench and it might be better than mine. I decided not to risk exposing myself to his superior remarks and let myself be seen with books and pens and exercise books as if I were taking up residence for a long time. Then it rained for a week, the pit half filled with water, Aunt said the cat would drown in it, and I would have pneumonia; so Uncle filled it one day when I was at school. I cried when I came home and saw what he had done, it looked like a newly filled grave,

7

more soil had come out than had gone back, the ground wasn't even though Uncle jumped on it wearing his big boots and said it would be level in time. He decided to plant an apple tree in it and thanked me for digging it.

The end of my trench was ignominious for me and a triumph for Charlie and his gang who, hearing of my demise, returned to gloat. They whooped and yelled, made derisory remarks about girls being stupid enough to think they could dig trenches, and performed celebrative dances along the top of the wall, shrieking with pride and making hubristic remarks about the superiority of boys until one of them fell on to the track below and broke a leg. Rumour said Charlie had a good hiding from his father. I hoped it was untrue – if true it wasn't fair.

This concluded the trench war after which Charlie and I became absorbed in our own affairs for a time. Peace or indifference reigned between the orchard walls, there was no more flying ammunition of little green apples or pebbles and lumps of clay, no more rivalry, no more boasting. I was too busy working for my scholarship and feeling important for trivial hostilities with Charlie and didn't bother to find out what he was doing.

Chapter Two

The ancient maniac whose rule of terror the Big School had endured for thirty years at last relinquished his desk and stool in their grim corner of the main classroom, broke his last cane on his last shivering victim, for the last time struck the tuning fork on his awesome desk, presided over the last hymn of his reign then faded from our lives, though none of us, not even he, knew it at the time.

The children in the Little School dreaded crossing the road – a crossing symbolic as well as practical – to the Big School. Their fear was no disgrace, generations of children had feared Old Billie who had ruled like a demon for years. Children of the past who had become parents shuddered at the memory of his cane and beard, still talked of the agile step which enabled him to be in half a dozen places at once and the paralysing glance of his eyes, especially of the one at the back of his head. Little School children heard and trembled. When my turn came to "go across" Aunt reassured me. She and my mother had been young teachers on his staff and had liked him well enough once they had learned to turn their heads while a caning was going on. Old Billie wouldn't harm me, promised my aunt, I was a good child as well as her niece. Charlie was neither. She looked dubious and I was apprehensive for him.

But nemesis overtook Old Billie who was put into an asylum late one Friday night. When his former pupils heard the news they said they knew he had always been mad, hadn't they called him Mad Billie behind his back? Their only regret was that he hadn't gone off his head when they could have had the benefit of it. A new lightness touched the hearts in the playground on Monday morning. Even the ex-infants from the Little School skipped and hopscotched as if they were not new little things expected to quiver in corners.

In Old Billie's place came a young man who had no beard, who used no cane and terrifying glances, who had modern ideas about education, even used the word enjoyment in connection with it and made jokes in class, real jokes which caused proper laughter not polite smirks. He had about him the mystique of having been a soldier and mentioned in dispatches. He smoked cigarettes as soon as lessons were over, turned the pages of exercise books with nicotine-stained fingers and smelt of smoke mixed with something fresh and pleasant. He taught the rudiments of Latin to promising pupils like me and introduced amongst faded books whose antiquated pages were always falling out, new brightly coloured ones with entertaining stories or excerpts from Shakespeare and the classics. He made us mobile, helped to shove the ancient forms to make space for acting. In the middle of the rough-floored classrooms we made unaccustomed gestures and wondrous sounds as we orated passages from *Macbeth* and *Julius Caesar*. 'I'd rather be a dog and bay the moon,' we cried in heartfelt throes, or 'Tomorrow and Tomorrow and Tomorrow' in voices sombre with mystery, the mystery heightened because we read no further than the extracted passages and knew little of what came after. It was then I heard the first faint playing of the theme I was never to forget.

It was Mr Pinder who encouraged me to write short stories and little pieces to be acted in concerts at end of term. It was he who suggested to Aunt and Uncle the idea of my sitting for a scholarship to Fulford High School where several of my older "cousins" had been, and where one was even then in the leaving form. It wasn't a new idea that I should go there, what was new was that I should try to win a scholarship and go for nothing. I was excited and began to talk of the Hockey School and saw visions of myself running about with a hockey stick like the illustrations of girls in the pages of popular weeklies.

Charlie's parents, caught in the general enthusiasm for education, decided he should go to a boys' grammar school in the same town. There was no possibility of a scholarship for him, they expected to pay but would gladly bear the expense, his mother confided to Auntie. It was wonderful what a bit of education could do towards raising people up in the world and Charlie was likely to be a farmer in a big way after he took over from his father, come another twenty years or so.

'That is if nothing goes wrong,' she added, 'you never know what can happen these days, farming's in such a bad way.'

'She always gets that in,' said Uncle later, 'in case I put the rent up.'

'You and Charlie can cycle to Welham together,' Aunt said when time had passed and I had won a scholarship and was ready for Fulford, 'you'll be company for each other in the mornings and coming back at night.'

So fate dragged Charlie and me together again.

Fulford was a small town ten miles from Welham. Welham Station was four miles from our village so Charlie and I had a long bicycle ride, morning and evening, as well as a ten-mile train journey twice a day.

I was full of enthusiasm and pride at the thought of our new lives but Charlie was furious. He had been looking forward to leaving school like the other boys in

11

the village, now he was plunged into a dangerous future where education, like an unbridled horse, could run away with him.

'I can't leave until I'm sixteen,' he groaned. 'Sixteen at the earliest – they had to sign for it – and it could be worse if I don't look out, some fellows stay till they're eighteen and even then they've not had enough but go somewhere else to colleges and things.'

'You mean universities,' I said, 'like the ones at Oxford and Cambridge.'

'I don't care where they are or what they are,' he replied, 'as long as I don't go.'

I suddenly said I wouldn't be surprised if I went to a university some day.

'You would,' said Charlie, 'only a clever dick like you'd be daft enough to keep on going to school when you don't have to.'

Hatred of school and longings for the extinction of education were now his constant theme. He was angry with his parents for getting him into something behind his back when he wasn't looking.

'Books, bloody books.' He threw new textbooks all over the kitchen table. 'Bloody Latin, bloody French, bloody – God knows what this is.'

'It's algebra,' I read from the cover and although I was as baffled as he was by the symbols on the pages I added, 'it'll be easy once you've begun learning how to do it.'

'That's right,' nodded his mother, then said in the same tone of voice in which she urged him to take doses of medicine, 'it'll do you good.'

'I'll never see any sense in it,' groaned Charlie.

'You'll never see any sense in a lot of things,' said my aunt, who had dropped in at his house with me to check arrangements for the next day, the first of our new scholastic life, 'but you'll have to put up with 'em just the same, so you might as well get used to 'em.'

Charlie's mother was not pleased with my aunt's acerbic remarks and said in an ameliatory effort to dispel her son's despondent looks that he would be sure to understand everything if he put his mind to it, all the same he mustn't worry his head – which at the moment was plunged into his hands – for that wouldn't do a bit of good, then as if to reassure herself as much as Charlie she supposed all this education must be a good thing or so many folks wouldn't make such a fuss about it and wouldn't be ready to pay so much for getting it. Charlie's father wasn't taking on the extra expense just for the fun of it, farming being in such a poor way – at which Aunt cut her short, dislodged me from the end of the table where I was looking at the new books, advised Charlie to have a good night's sleep as she was going to make sure I would, and hustled me away.

I didn't have a good night's sleep. Charlie's bicycle bell rang outside our front gate at seven o'clock next morning and I wasn't ready. I had been restless in the night and was heavy with sleep when Aunt came to wake me at six o'clock. It was some time before I remembered why I had to be up so early and some more time before I struggled downstairs still undressed and rubbing my eyes.

'You must have a good breakfast,' insisted my aunt as I stared at my plate, 'even if it's only a little bit of toast.'

I was trying to eat the little bit of toast when Charlie knocked at the door and came in, accoutred for his new career in grey flannel shorts, a red and green blazer over a grey flannel shirt, and a red and green striped tie. His mother must have set about his rough hair for instead of looking like a half-worn brush it was lying almost flat and was wet. He had politely taken off his red and green striped cap. Aunt and I gaped at the metamorphosis. Before I could ask him if he had seen any rhubarb lately

– I was dazzled by all the red and green – Aunt complimented him upon his appearance and the new status conferred upon him by the privilege of wearing such distinctive uniform.

'Now everybody will know you're a grammar school boy,' she said, 'and you should be proud. It's a very old school and was founded by Edward the— well, a very early Edward, I've forgotten which one but I'm sure you'll soon find out.'

Not completely dressed, I was sitting at the table in a white winceyette blouse and navy blue knickers, admiring my long black woollen stockings, the longest I had ever worn. They came nearly to the top of my thighs and were held up by black elastic garters.

'Stop showing off,' said my aunt as she took a navy blue gym tunic from the fireguard and put it over my head. She smoothed the box pleats over the newly expanding curve of my chest, which under the tunic and blouse was firmly encased in a fleecy-lined liberty bodice, then put a navy blue girdle round my waist, the knot carefully in its regulated place on my left hip. With a navy blue blazer piped in red, and a navy blue felt hat trimmed with a band of the school colours, I was garbed for my future.

On the back of Charlie's bicycle was a new leather satchel bulging with the new books. Alas for me! instead of the usual school bag I had been given one of Aunt's unique leather cases which were specially made to carry her registration books. A large shallow unwieldy rectangle, there was plenty of room in it for my books, but it caused me embarrassment, even misery, for several years making me different from anybody else.

'But it's real leather,' protested my aunt in response to some lack of admiration on my part, 'and better than any you could buy in a shop. It was issued officially by the government to me because I'm a registrar.' Her voice implied it was an honour to own it and I didn't remind her I wasn't a registrar but was only a schoolgirl pained by the peculiar possession of it. I longed to look exactly like the other girls and it was the first thing to proclaim me different.

As time went on I realised more differences. My uniform was always in good order by Aunt's patient stitching and pressing, my stockings were always of good black wool, the best, expensive at six and eleven a pair, my black shoes polished by Uncle every morning while I was having breakfast, yet something, subtly, somehow, seemed to be wrong. There was always a discrepancy somewhere upon my person. Those long black stockings wrinkled while those of other girls, the good girls, the best girls who were always right, never failed to be smooth and tight. The regulation knot of my blue girdle continually slipped from its appointed place on my left hip-bone and appeared on my front like a navel or at the opposite side on the forbidden right hip, sometimes even behind so that the ends of the girdle hung like a tail. The brim of my navy blue hat wilfully turned itself down at the back instead of keeping itself up. Ink found its way from my pens to my fingers to my white blouse. Worse, and not to be remedied, my figure began to sprout under the firm fitting box pleats and pushed them out of shape.

On the first morning however, fresh from my aunt's hands, I left home as tidy a facsimile of academic girlhood as could have been seen in any English high school on any school morning. True, by the time Charlie and I arrived at Welham Station having left our bicycles by arrangement in the yard of the Railway Inn where Charlie's father was an esteemed customer, I was rather less tidy than Aunt had made me. My hat had moved round my head, the badge over one ear. I quickly realised this as my cousin – one of those mysterious

15

second or third cousins I owned so plentifully – came forward to greet me as she had been deputed to do, looked ashamed of me and said under her breath, 'Your hat's not straight,' then jerked it into place before introducing me to other girls.

Charlie had left me as soon as we arrived on the station and I walked forward alone to join the huddle of blue serge where the High School girls were concentrated. It was a crime for them to mix with the boys, though not for the boys to mix with them. From the girls, but not from the boys, the utmost decorum was demanded. In the press of travel if the sexes found themselves together the slightest relaxation of manner, let alone any suggestion of frivolity, on the female side was watched for by eagle-eyed High School prefects who roamed the train.

It had not always been so. Under a former head-mistress there had been a time when girls were free to acknowledge the existence of boys while travelling but this had led to hilarity and good times, even romps which, though necessarily short-lived in the fifteen-minute ride between Welham and Fulford, had caused "talk".

On the train I sat between two senior girls. My cousin sat opposite, watching. The girls were so kind I soon stopped feeling shy, defied the concentrated gaze of my cousin and chatted fluently about the village school and life at home. I told them about Charlie and me and our chequered past together and about the morning and evening bicycle rides we were to share. They raised their brows at this, but in general were so much amused and interested in what I said I was dazzled by a feeling of success. One girl teasing, drawing me out even further than I had gone, asked what I was good at. 'Everything,' I said, 'except maths.' The other wanted to know what I intended to be when I left school. I replied promptly

"Famous" then caught my cousin's look and for a moment was abashed, but the other girls' laughter was reassuring and I went on talking until we got out of the train at Fulford when the two big girls went off together without another look at me, leaving me to face the fury of my cousin who grabbed my arm and pulled me to her.

'That was the head girl you were jabbering to,' she said, 'and the vice-prefect. I didn't know where to put myself, I was so ashamed – and you'd better keep quiet about you and Charlie riding together or – ' she paused as if to find words sufficiently dire – 'or I wouldn't like to be you.' With an angry gesture she pushed me into a group of girls of my own age, then walked away.

Under the supervision of prefects the High School girls walked in a crocodile, the two imposing seniors, trying to look as if they had no connection with it, walked by themselves and the Grammar School boys drifted away as they pleased.

Soon I was entering the main doors of the Hockey School.

Chapter Three

I was at the Hockey School and soon I hated hockey which was never a game to me but an ordeal in which my legs were hit with sticks. I hated maths too, and science and art which to my surprise had little to do with colour and pictures but much with keeping a pencil sharp, closing one eye and squinting along my arm at a collection of cardboard cubes and pyramids. Science was hanging over a bunsen burner evaporating liquids to dryness, maths a bewildering tangle of symbols and shapes whose meaning for ever eluded me. I blundered from one of these subjects to the other with nervous and bewildered mind, a lost little alien from the warmer kinder world of Mr Pinder.

Aunt was surprised when I failed to shine.

'Not like hockey!' she exclaimed one night as I ruefully examined my bruised legs. 'After all that running about and romping with Charlie I should have thought you'd excel at it, and at everything else as well. You did here.'

But "here" wasn't like Fulford. "Here", for instance, I had never even heard of *esprit de corps*. At Fulford I was constantly being reproved for not having enough of it, that very day had been kept in after school to write a hundred times how much I deplored being deficient in it.

'But what is it?' asked my puzzled aunt, and when I told her spirit of the corps, meaning care for the others or the regiment she said, 'Rubbish, you're not in the army,' thus revealing a lack of it in herself.

'You're quite intelligent,' she said after a pause, 'and don't give any trouble, what exactly do they want you to do?'

Whatever it was I seemed not to do it. Although I wrote the words over and over again in the following years, *esprit de corps*, I never had enough of it, the magic ingredient which would have ensured my success at Fulford. As time went on I stopped feeling lost, found a place somewhere in the middle of the form at the end of every term and was easily top in English, too easily so I received little credit for it.

At Fulford there was no dancing, no drama, I heard no music except in a singing lesson once a week when surely, said Aunt, if at no other time I ought to shine a little.

'You've a very nice voice,' she said, 'and can sing alto very well, especially when you stand near me.'

But in singing lessons at school I didn't stand near Aunt. I stood at the back of the class because I was tall and nobody bothered to hear my alto; it wasn't required, and when I instinctively picked out the alto line in songs I was thought either to be singing out of tune or perversely singing my own way, once more completely out of line with the regiment.

Summer was coming. We played cricket at Fulford. Aunt brightened and said, 'You'll be good at cricket, it runs in the family.'

'It doesn't run in me,' I said. 'I never make runs.'

She ignored that and went on, 'Your father would have played for Notts, if he hadn't died. Even your uncle was good at cricket though you wouldn't think so to look at him now,' and she gave him a dispirited side look as he sat reading a newspaper and propping up the fireplace with his feet.

'Well, I'm not good at it,' I said, 'I hate it,' and tried to

19

describe my fear and loathing of that detestable pastime and the dread with which I saw the mounting arc of the cruel ball in the sky while waiting for the malevolent beeline it inevitably made for me as I hid myself in the deepest part of the deep field.

Aunt sighed. I felt sorry for her and apologised for not being good at so many things.

'I can't understand it,' she said, 'it was different with Mr Pinder, now you don't even want to talk about school.'

'I don't mind talking,' I said, 'I'm talking now.'

She was silent then said more cheerfully, 'Perhaps you'll be a monitor next term.'

'We don't say monitor, we say prefect,' I said, then gabbled, 'there's form prefects and house prefects and school prefects.'

'Then why aren't you one?' she asked, though by now she ought to have been getting a good idea why not.

'I couldn't be a house prefect or a school prefect' – I was glad at last to have a reasonable excuse – 'I'm not old enough.'

'Couldn't you be a form prefect?'

'*I* couldn't.' I emphasised the "I".

'Why not?'

'They wouldn't choose me,' I said, 'I don't know how to be chosen.'

I must have looked glum because she suddenly changed her rueful expression for a confident one and said, 'There's the school choir. You'll be chosen for that.'

'We're having tests next week,' I said, 'but I don't suppose I'll be in it.'

But Aunt was sure of her ground in this at least. 'Dr Peterson says your voice is quite good enough for the choral society,' she said, 'and if it's good enough for him it's good enough for the school choir.'

* * *

The village choral society had been flourishing into a local fame since Dr Peterson had taken it over. He was a distinguished musician, choirmaster and organist at a well-known church in the Dukeries, in Sherwood, and it was a feather in the society's cap to have him as conductor.

Once a week for several years Aunt and Charlie's mother had gone to the village hall to sing, Auntie her alto, Charlie's mother soprano, in *The Messiah, The Creation* and other oratorios. On one great occasion the society had been invited to the Cutlers Hall in Sheffield to sing excerpts from *The Messiah* before a distinguished audience. When Uncle, who wasn't musical, asked, 'Distinguished for what?' Aunt, who was, had snapped, 'For having enough good taste to listen to our choral society which is more than you do.'

When the two women went to sing Uncle and I used to drop in at Charlie's house to see Granny. Charlie and I were encouraged to play in her room, the myth being she delighted in our young company. This satisfactory arrangement lasted while Granny lasted.

I wasn't so very fond of Granny, neither was Charlie – she was in such a nebulous far-away state it was almost as if she were not there at all – but I took the chance to demonstrate she was mine, not his, though she lived in his house and he called her Granny. I took every opportunity for the first quarter hour of being possessive and attentive, but Charlie was soon bored and gave up bothering with her. It always made me furious when he lay claim to her as well as to the old cherry tree in the garden and Moco the pony and Moco's stable, all of which had been ours. His argument was that everything left in the house had been taken over by his dad and as Granny had been left in the house – well, Granny was theirs, Charlie's if he wanted her.

Every afternoon in one of the front windows Granny was to be seen neat and pleasant, a white cap on her white hair, like the granny in the song I had been taught to sing to her – 'Who's that sitting in the old armchair, white cap resting on the soft grey hair?' – thus earning myself the name of Warble-lip from Charlie. She was going to die and showed signs of her impending journey, even Charlie and I knew she was going soon. Her small grey elephant eyes, almost lost in a myriad wrinkles, sometimes twinkled at us but usually had no light in them under their papery lids.

Uncle was supposed to keep watch in a chair opposite hers by the fireplace while Charlie and I played, but as soon as Auntie and Charlie's mother were safely out of the way and he had paid some brief filial respects, he slipped thankfully from the dim sitting-room through unlighted passages and unused rooms, like a familiar spirit returning to its old haunts, to the cheerful regions at the far end of the house where, in the biggest kitchen, Charlie's father was sitting with stockinged feet on the side of the fireplace, a glass of whisky in his hand, the bottle waiting for Uncle. There they sipped and smoked in peace while from the other side of the fireplace in the second kitchen came the murmur of the living-in boy and the all-purpose maid. If they forgot themselves and made too much noise Charlie's father soon quietened them by a few imperious knocks with the poker at the back of the fire.

After her first vague smiles Granny took no notice of Charlie and me but went on nodding and incomprehensibly murmuring as we played ludo and snakes and ladders. We were quiet at first, affected by the subdued character of the occasion. The fire burned in a subdued way, the light from the hanging-lamp over the green-covered table was subdued, so we instinctively subdued our impetuous natures and played in whispers till potent life asserted itself in us and our games became as noisy as usual and our disputed-over granny kept herself company or was in the company of others in the mystery of her being.

One night, after a particularly triumphant swoop up a ladder, Charlie rattled the dice like a kettle-drum, then looked at Granny. From the table where we were playing we could see, over the back of her chair, the top of her white cap and one of her arms hanging at her side.

We were both quiet and stared at the arm.

'Go and put it back,' said Charlie with a tiny rattle of the dice, but I didn't move so after a moment he went. He came back to the table, shook the dice, threw them and moved his counters.

'Her hand is still there,' I said.

'I know it is,' said Charlie. Then I said, 'Shouldn't we put it back under her shawl? She gets cold.'

The temperature in the room dropped, the light falling on the green tablecloth dimmed, the room was different, incomparably still. My heart began to thump and Charlie said, 'I think she's dead like old Rover was this morning.'

We had been told to play quietly and not disturb the grown-ups in the kitchen till somebody came to fetch us for supper and though we were not always so obedient we stayed, perhaps because of the long dark passages and empty rooms on the other side of the door. The fire died. Neither of us liked to go near and mend it.

The room grew cold. We played till we were chilled and heavy with sleep. Charlie kept yawning and tears rolled down my cheeks. This exasperated him and in a voice which began loud and finished in a whisper he asked why I was crying.

'Because my granny's dead,' I replied, perhaps emphasising the "my".

Charlie retorted, 'She's my granny and I'm not crying.'

'She's not your granny.'

'Yes, she is. She belongs to the house and it's our house, so she's mine.'

'No she isn't,' I wept and, as if this proved it, 'you're not crying and I am.'

It must have been a particularly long choral practice that night or time changed in its relation to Charlie and me as we sat close together feeling more and more lost and cold and forgotten. At last we crawled where we couldn't see the chair by the fire and huddled under the table.

I woke in the kitchen. Set down in the rich warmth of the fire I was some time trying to think where I was. Charlie was saying he was hungry and his father calling for somebody to give the bairns something to eat. Uncle wasn't there and Charlie's father soon hurried away.

There was the sound of high voices in the front of the house which meant Charlie's mother and my aunt had come back, the men's deep voices answered, then all the voices mixed, high and low, on and on.

In the morning we were told Granny had died in the night. She had only been asleep when we were with her.

'She made a funny noise,' said Charlie.

'She was dreaming, love,' said his mother.

'Her hand was as cold as ice,' said Charlie, 'and she looked like Rover when he was dead.'

His mother was shocked. 'Granny couldn't look like Rover,' she said, 'he was a dog.'

'She fell asleep when you were there,' said Aunt, 'and was cold, that's all – so don't argue.'

It was as if they couldn't bear to admit Granny died in our presence. Perhaps they were trying to spare our feelings about having been alone with a dead person so we spared theirs and let them pretend Granny had only been asleep, but we knew differently. They felt guilty for letting us see what they thought we shouldn't have seen. We felt guilty for them because they had let us see it, and for knowing they were trying to deceive us, so we pretended to believe them to save their feelings and let them think they were saving ours. Anyway it was no use arguing about it with them, but we talked about it to each other.

We soon got over it. We had one reason fewer for quarrelling and stopped bickering about whose granny she was. We had plenty of other things to quarrel about.

Chapter Four

Aunt was wrong about my being chosen for the school choir though her confidence persuaded me to be hopeful and I looked forward to the special singing lesson during which the headmistress was to come into class and hear everybody sing separately and together.

She had an imperious bearing, powerfully shaped in the front like the prow of a galleon but slim below with silk stockings and elegant shoes. She sailed the school's breezy corridors, black gown flowing, creating about her an aura of majesty and omnipotence. Her name was Isa Ibald, I. I., the double eye, and we called her, with not much irreverence, the Great Orb.

We were singing when she glided in, her wings folded about her to keep her arms warm – it was a cold day.

There were coughs and hoarse throats in the room but my voice was undamaged. I could hear its clear warble and was pleased, my heart beat faster but in a pleasant excitement. The Great Orb walked slowly amongst the singers sometimes inclining her head in a thoughtful pause then continuing on her enigmatic way until she had heard every voice, after which she consulted the singing mistress and the senior girl at the piano. They turned pages of song books and had a conference, then the singing mistress told us Miss Ibald was pressed for time and unable to hear everyone individually, but that during the singing of the next song, *Nymphs and Shepherds* – my hope sank a little, my developing alto was unhappy with sequences of high notes – she would come amongst us and choose those voices she considered good enough for the next test. The singing mistress had already given her recommendations. I fancied she caught my eye at this though I was at the back of the class as usual and she could have been looking at somebody else. Nevertheless, I felt a throb of optimism.

The Great Orb's method of choosing was simple. She would walk amongst the singers and listen to each voice. The girls she touched on the arm were to sit. After the song she would tell us whether the sitters or those left standing were the chosen, though perhaps by then, she smiled, we would have guessed.

The accompanist played the opening bars, the singing mistress raised her baton and we began to sing. The Great Orb walked amongst us with inscrutable smile or forbodingly slight frown, listening intently, sometimes touching an arm and murmuring "sit", then moving on. She stayed longer when she stood by me, I was sure I had been recommended and, full of elation, trilled even the highest notes with truth. Then she moved on without remark or touch upon my shoulder. Some of the vivacity left my voice which gave an apprehensive wobble I was glad she didn't hear, but I went on singing and watching her as she progressed round the room. Soon my doubts changed to horrified certainty as I saw who the sitters were; they were the ones who were on the right side of everything. I was left standing amongst the groaners who never hit a right note in singing, in life, in anything.

The song ended. The standing girls looked at each other then at the confident sitters. I was in agony. I had been left out – I was both disbelieving and convinced – even in singing. Confused thoughts of Aunt and the choral society and Dr Peterson rushed through me. Even to the last second I prayed in an incoherent mental jumble to the obscure and incomprehensible god who usually spoilt my chances at school for it to be the sitters who were out and the standers in.

There was another murmured conference at the piano. The sitters were told to assemble in the hall after school for another test, then the Great Orb inclined her head in a gesture of farewell and arrived at the door a second before somebody sprang to open it. During this frowning second my hand went up. My fellow rejects had thankfully collapsed into their chairs but I was still on my feet. The door was open but she saw me and hesitated, a wisp of irritation showing in her look.

'Well?' She was half out of the door.

I heard my voice saying, 'Dr Peterson thinks I have a good voice.'

The displeasure in her expression deepened then her lip was touched with amusement as she looked from me to the singing mistress, then to the class, then to me and said, 'May I ask why I should be interested in your doctor's opinion of your voice?'

'Because he's a doctor of music,' I said with every consonant sounding, 'and he has chosen me to sing in our choral society at home.'

'Impertinent child!' Frowning, she swished herself and her draperies through the door, leaving me with every atom of my will determined not to cry.

'Not chosen for the choir!' My aunt was aghast. 'But you have a very good voice, anybody can hear that. Dr Peterson thinks so. What more do they want, for God's sake?'

'Maybe they're all budding prima donnas at Fulford,' said Uncle.

I assured him that was not so. Some of the chosen squawked on high notes and some had wobbles in their voices – anathema to Dr Peterson. I decided I had better confess what I had said to the Great Orb in case she sent a letter about it. I expected Aunt to tell me off but instead, with an expression of grim satisfaction, she said she was glad I had spoken.

'It wasn't me who spoke,' I said, 'my voice spoke. I heard it speaking but inside I was surprised.'

As I went upstairs I overheard her telling Uncle how much she would like to give that woman in Fulford a piece of her mind. 'As for knowing anything about music,' said Aunt, 'she can't know much if she hasn't even heard of Dr Peterson.' Then she called for me to hurry or we'd be late for choral practice. Later in the evening we took our hurt pride to be mollified under the baton of Dr Peterson and were both softened and elevated by our musical efforts.

After practice Frankie Slack asked Auntie if he could join us on our way home as he was going the same way on an errand. The path was too narrow for four people to walk together, especially when one was as wide as Charlie's mother, so she and Aunt went ahead, Frankie and I following. He was a pleasant boy with a tuneful tenor voice, reddish ears and an amiable disposition. He had left school two years ago and worked for his father on the family farm which was considered in the village to be so small as to be hardly worth the name. The Slacks were laughed at because they couldn't get up in the mornings and were called afternoon farmers and The Can't-get-ups. It wasn't a fair criticism of Frankie. He was different. Every morning he was early out of the decrepit cottage everybody called the Ark, because it was old and stood in the lowest part of the village between two streams which were often in flood and sent their waters through its doors.

I liked Frankie. When he took my hand and squeezed it I didn't snatch it away, but after a slight hesitation and with a mixture of sensations, let it stay in his though I hoped Aunt wouldn't turn round and see. I was glad nobody at school could see me letting down its tone by being so vulgar and rustic, and yet was pleased in an obscure way to be getting one up, especially on the Great Orb who would certainly have forbidden, and would have liked forbidding, what I was doing but hadn't the power. I faintly squeezed Frankie's hand. He was such a nice boy and had liked me for years even when he was at the leaving end of the Big School and I was at the beginning. He created new sensations in me, both pleasurable and confusing, when I was close to him – but he dropped his "h"s. When we reached our gate he gave my hand a goodbye squeeze, put his face near mine then quickly moved it away again, said good night softly to me and louder to Auntie and Charlie's mother when they turned round, and disappeared.

'What's he doing round here?' asked Charlie's mother as she watched him go. 'It's not on his way home. Perhaps he's got his eye on somebody.'

'He'd better not have,' retorted my aunt, 'he can't afford to have his eye on anybody with all the mess they're in at the Ark – besides he's only sixteen.' Then we said good night.

In the house Aunt said, 'He's a very nice boy is Frankie and quite nice looking. It's a pity he'll never amount to much. He's just like his father and all the Can't-get-ups, they're not called afternoon farmers for nothing.'

I was indignant and said Frankie got up at four each morning.

'It's a good thing somebody at the Ark can get up early,' said Aunt, 'and most unusual. None of the Can't-get-ups ever got anywhere,' she added.

'They're thinking of leaving the Ark,' I said, 'and finding another place. Frankie told me.'

Aunt laughed. 'They've been thinking that for years. Thinking's all they ever do about it, except talking. They'll always be stuck in the Ark.'

As I set the supper table she went on, 'Not that I dislike Frankie, he's a nice boy, the best one of the lot and he sings nicely. We'd miss his voice if he ever did leave, but he won't.' She hesitated, busied herself at the fire then added, 'I shouldn't be too interested in him if I were you.'

'Me?' I said. 'He drops his "h"s and he says "aint" sometimes for "isn't". The girls at school would think he's awful. They'll laugh when I tell them about him.'

Aunt looked at me then said no more about him.

Soon after this I saw Mr Pinder in the village.

'How's school?' he asked, turning to walk with me in the direction of the post office. I gave a reply shadowed by recent puzzling efforts to analyse the disappointing state of my affairs at Fulford and he gathered all was not well.

'Fulford's a highly academic institution,' he said. 'I knew that and I did wonder about you. Still, with just an ordinary bit of luck, you'll find your feet.' He patted my shoulder. 'Don't worry, you'll survive.' We walked in silence while I considered my chances of survival then he said, 'It's maths, I suppose. That'll be the bother.'

I admitted maths was the bother, one of the bothers. Others were science and Latin which I hated almost as much as I hated maths.

'What a pity. You liked Latin here,' he said.

'That was different,' I replied. 'Everything was different here.'

'Of course it was,' he said, 'but you couldn't stay here, it was good for a beginning, that's all. What about the other subjects? No need to tell me about English. It goes without saying that's all right. What about history, for instance?'

I told him the Great Orb taught history and, although on the whole I did well at it, I sometimes found in red ink at the bottom of my essays remarks like "Verbiage", "Mere fluff" and "Nothing but padding".

He said I must stick to facts, cultivate precision, cut out purple passages. 'Save those for your stories,' he said, 'which brings me to that little play of yours.'

'Which play?' I asked.

He pretended to be surprised. 'How many have you in stock? I mean the play you wrote just before you left for Fulford. What happened to it?'

I shrugged. I hadn't been thinking about it.

'Well, I have,' he said.

There was to be an entertainment in the village hall in aid of the Red Cross, there was so much trouble in the world, the Lord knew what was going to happen, but never mind that for the time being. Half the evening would be taken up with a concert. Local singers had already been roped in – they would cost nothing, glad to do it for the fame – and one or two well-known ones had promised to come from Sheffield for expenses only. Something was needed to fill the first half of the evening and my play would be just the thing. What did I think?

I was dubious. 'It's a bit childish,' I said, 'I was only eleven when I wrote it.' With a smile Mr Pinder said he realised I'd grown a lot older but he was sure it would do, then asked, 'How old are you now exactly?'

'Thirteen.'

'Ah, well. H'm. Anyway, I'd like to do it but I need the author's permission.'

I gave it readily and parted from him much encouraged.

Aunt and Uncle were pleased. Aunt had been brooding about Fulford and my news cheered her but Uncle gave me a warning not to say much about it at school.

'Why not?' Aunt reared her head. 'It's an honour for the school if she has a play acted even if only by children.'

'Which school?' he asked.

'Both schools,' she replied, but Uncle persisted it would be better not to talk about it at Fulford. He couldn't say why exactly, he just had a feeling. He looked at me and said again, 'I shouldn't mention it if I were you.' But I couldn't help mentioning it at Fulford, though only to my special friends who were impressed, and the English teacher who was interested.

The evening's entertainment was a success. I stayed away from school on the day of the performance and dashed between home and the village hall being Mr Pinder's right hand and giving authorial opinion when asked for it. I loved him more and more and wished he could be my headmaster for ever instead of my having the Great Orb for headmistress.

I hadn't seen much of Charlie for some time but he appeared at the concert purified with soap and water and smooth with Brylcream. He looked impressed when he opened a programme and saw my name on it, then quickly put me in what he considered my proper place by calling me Warble-lip and accusing me of still trying to be clever. I was much too elated to argue, then was called away to shake hands with somebody and had no time to speak to him again but I saw him looking at me and was glad. Frankie was in the audience on the benches at the back but I was too busy to speak to him.

The Hall and Rectory had sent hot-house flowers and

33

pots of trailing greenery and glossy-leaved bushes in tubs which were banked at the front and on each side of the stage. The air was filled with their scent, the audience rustled with expectation, the curtain went up and my Fulford problems vanished, only the intoxicating present remained. I breathed it in, then a strange thing happened. As I watched the scene on the stage it became smaller, went further away, became part of the larger scene of the hall and audience as if I were at a distance, like a photographer peering into a lens. I was watching myself watching, separated from everything, even myself.

There was applause, the curtain came down and went up and down and up again. I was back in the scene and in myself. Somebody called "Author" and I was presented with a large ribboned chocolate box given by one of the village's most imposing matrons. When I opened it at home I found inside, instead of chocolates, sheet upon sheet of paper and at the heart, the mean little heart, a tiny bottle of scent. 'Not even good scent,' Aunt sniffed. 'It's cheap.'

It was a slight disappointment – I had been looking forward to eating the chocolates – but I soon got over it.

The next day there was a notice in the *Welham Guardian* in which I was referred to as a promising young author.

'Talent,' murmured my aunt, 'imagination.' In her gratification the pince-nez nearly slipped off her nose as she looked at Uncle and me and said, 'I hope they see this at Fulford.'

'I hope they don't,' said Uncle.

The next day, Saturday, I met Mr Pinder for an aftermath of discussion and compliments and the anticlimax of dismantling the stage. When we had finished our work and all signs of the evening before had vanished it seemed to me I had put part of myself away

with the script and the props and only a part, a small
disconsolate part, was left for life at Fulford.

Half way through a French lesson on Monday morning I
was called to the Great Orb's study. I went through her
door expecting to be praised. I came out of it crushed by
a sense of shame and disbelief, amazed that I had been so
wrong. Everything I had ever done was wrong. Writing a
play was wrong, having it performed was wrong,
certainly being written about was wrong. I was too
confused to know why, there was something about the
dangers of being encouraged by foolish people to have
too big an opinion of myself, something about the
flimsiness of easy praise and the meritricious pleasures of
so-called success. 'Success of a kind,' she said, and
repeated the words to make sure I realised mine was of an
inferior kind. She touched on the egotism of accepting
vulgar applause. Whatever the words she poured over me
with delicate but devastating contempt, and all with a
smile, they struck down my hopes of pleasing her, of
doing well at school, of being somebody who counted
there. They made writing that silly play seem foolish and
vulgar, not in keeping with the high standards of the
school. I had somehow let the school down, exposed it to
the lurid gaze of common local papers which were full of
– she flicked at them with one of her favourite words –
verbiage.

To make the school proud of me, to be a worthwhile
member of it and bring it honour, couldn't I really try,
couldn't I really put my back into those subjects in which
I was so weak, like maths, for instance, which was
appalling, and science and Latin? Couldn't I stop being
so pusillanimous at hockey? When she could see me
making a noble effort at those then she, the school,

would be proud of me and would have no greater pleasure than in seeing me finish in a blaze of glory.

I crept away in a mood the very antipodes of a blaze of glory. It lasted a long time and the glory never came. All I ever did to appease Aunt's hungry hopes for me at school was to be editor, when I was older, of the school magazine, perhaps the appointed editor was ill or had died. Aunt was proud of me and must have put her copy away to treasure in secret for I found it years later in the family bible and threw it away.

Chapter Five

It was a relief when Christmas came and I had a month's holiday from Fulford.

'Lucky you're at home,' said Uncle who was mooning about the house with bronchitis and feeling the separation from his apple trees, 'it looks like snow.' He had come to a standstill at the window in one of the front rooms where we were hibernating with fires of logs and orchard prunings, the reason for his bronchitis Aunt said as she swept up the ash. It was all that messing about outside through the last week's bad weather which had nearly finished him off and she was the one to suffer.

'Why you?' Uncle was surprised. 'I'm the one who has the cough.'

'And I'm the one who has to listen to it,' she snapped. She was on edge these days, what with the weather and the cough and Christmas. 'Blithering nuisance,' she kept saying. 'blithering Christmas.'

I looked warily from her to Uncle. 'Watch out for the Haggard mountains,' he had warned me earlier, in private. This was his term for a particularly exhausting registration errand but he also used it to describe one of the inward journeys she sometimes made to a dark and baffling part of her nature we could never understand. When she went there we had to look out for ourselves and he was liable to have asthma so as not to be got at.

'Somebody's coming.' He made a diversion just as I was thinking he and Aunt were heading for a collision.

'It's not my hours,' she said, 'so whoever it is can go away again.'

Certain hours of my aunt's time belonged to the state. A board on the wall of our house outside the front door proclaimed that on Tuesdays and Thursdays between the hours of nine and eleven a.m. and six and eight p.m. she, the Registrar of Births and Deaths, would be available within the premises to the public. On other days, several times a month, she visited outlying villages where she sat for an hour or two in the back rooms of post offices with her books and special ink and official expression.

We were used to people knocking at the door at all hours of the day and evening, sometimes late at night if urgent over the registration of a death, 'as if I'm a doctor,' she said, but she never turned anybody away for coming out of hours. Whatever she was doing in the house her domestic personality was immediately put aside and her official one put on with the pince-nez for which her delicately acquiline nose and serious face seemed specially designed.

'You should take to wearing a wig,' said Uncle, 'then we'd all start calling you m'lud.' It was his pleasure to equip her pens with efficient nibs and to replenish two small bottles of ink from the large stone ones under the roll top desk which dominated the room we called the office while she was registering in it and the dining-room when she wasn't. Not everyone who registered a birth bought a "full" certificate, two and sixpence for the certificate, a penny for the stamp. The two and sixpence was Aunt's fee, the penny went to the government. She had a small salary as well but the best part of her remuneration – she loved the dignified word – was the money for the certificates and it was a disappointment felt through the house if some obstinate or impoverished parent insisted on having only the threepenny slip of paper which briefly recorded the date of the child's birth and its name.

'It's a boy,' said Uncle from his post at the window, 'it'll be a message,' and beat me to the side door where the letter box was being rattled up and down. 'What's wrong with the bell?' he asked.

The boy, who was out of breath and leaning against the doorpost, ignored the question. 'Special message,' he gasped, 'I've been runnin'.'

'Where from?' asked Uncle, 'Buckingham Palace?'

'Post office,' said the boy, 'they wrote it on a bit of paper, anyway it's for your missus, not you.'

'None of your cheek,' said Uncle, 'where is it?'

'Got it somewhere – ' the boy was going through his pockets – 'anyway it don't matter if it is lost I know what it is. Old chap at Old 'all is dead, died last night and they want it regist'rin' out there quick as possible so your missus'd better be sharp about it. It's not lost, I knew I'd got it,' and he produced a crumpled piece of paper upon which was the handwriting of the postmistress.

Uncle dismissed the boy and shut the door. Both Aunt and I had heard what was said so there was no need for it to be said again but he said it. It provided an interest in a long day and he was glad of it and immediately began putting ink and pens and the registration books into their leather case.

'They've telephoned the post office for the registrar's attendance,' he said as if we couldn't read for ourselves, 'you'd better be off before it snows. I'll see to your bike,' and forgetting his bronchitis he went to the outhouse.

'Today or tomorrow,' Aunt read, 'between three and four o'clock. Just like them, thinking everybody exists to do exactly what they want – and when. It should be me who decides what's convenient.'

'If it isn't convenient don't go,' I said.

'Ah, but it's a death you see,' said Aunt. 'Special consideration is due to a death.'

'But it's not your hours today – ' I didn't approve of the imperative tone of the message – 'you could make them wait till tomorrow. You could make them come to the office if you wanted to.'

Aunt considered then said, 'They can ask me to call on them, that's quite in order, and it's in order for me to charge a shilling for going and I shall. So get ready, it'll do you good to get out of that chair. You've done enough lolling about for one day.'

We had known for some time of the illness of Sir George St Orbin at Orbin Old Hall and had expected his death to be registered in our house. The office had been kept specially tidy and dusted and Aunt, determined not to be dropped on, primed for action during the last few days. She had also considered the likelihood of being called to the Old Hall and was prepared for that too so there was no need for Uncle to "see to" the bike. It had already been seen to.

'It'll be an experience for you,' Aunt said as we made ourselves ready, 'interesting and educational as well. The place is so old.'

I knew the place, had bicycled round there but not often, it was too far away.

'You've never been inside,' said Aunt, 'and neither have I. We'll have a good look round if we can. You'll be company for me. I don't fancy going through the woods by myself at this time of the year and your uncle can't go.'

At midday Uncle urged me to have a second helping of pudding to fortify me for the journey, saying it would be a long cold ride and God alone knew if we'd be offered anything before we came back, then Aunt and I put on clothes suitable for cycling and presentable enough for the Old Hall.

'Go in your school uniform,' Aunt insisted in spite of my agonised protests, 'at any rate in your school hat and coat, they look more – ' she searched for a word – 'well, they show you're not just anybody,' and when I protested the coat was too tight she said I shouldn't have eaten so much pudding and I needn't fasten the top buttons as nobody would see. It was no use my saying if nobody would see it didn't matter what I wore, school uniform or not, she shut me up and called to Uncle, 'What about my things? Make sure nothing's forgotten.'

'Everything's ready,' he assured her, 'you'll only be taking the black ink. I've filled the bottle.'

This black ink was of the most profound blackness. No other ink would do for the registration of Death. It was so special I was never allowed a dip in it even for my homework.

Uncle strapped the leather case on to the back of Aunt's bicycle, Aunt and I put on the last layer of our winter wrappings and set off on our journey.

'Take care,' called Uncle at the door, 'be back before it snows.'

The domain of Orbin Old Hall lay just inside our parish several miles on the other side of the far wood. We could have gone down the track between the two orchards beyond the stables and over the field, then taken a short cut through our wood but we would soon have been smothered in mud and would have had to lift the bicycles over fences and styles. It was better to go the long way round through the low-lying part of the village up the hill on the other side and into the lane leading through the far woods. Even that way the road was not only a bad road it was often no road at all, a mere track, not always a cart track, sometimes only a woodland path deer or gamekeepers had made. Wherever we went in those days, in our part of the world, we soon came to woods which had once been part of Sherwood, though the old trees were dying or being felled and the spaces filled with conifers. We didn't go far without finding small thickets and plantations amongst the fields. Copse, spinney, ash-holt, oak-hurst, fox cover and badger's brake, old names, old places were still there.

Aunt and I bicycled for three miles through true forest of beech and oak in direct descent from Sherwood, through ash and birch and the sombre shadows of yew which had been there since Agincourt, then several miles over fields on cart tracks and bridle paths.

'I'd as soon live on the moon.' Aunt breathed hard as we hoisted our bicycles out of the mud, for even on this so-called good way we had plenty of that. Orbin Old Hall was almost inaccessible from our village.

'No wonder we never see any Orbins,' said Aunt. 'I don't know why they think they're in our parish.'

We reached the hamlet of St Orbin, wobbled up its one unpaved street and into the woods which surrounded, almost obliterated, the Old Hall for they cast their shadows up to the windows. What with having made detours around impassable mud and dodged cows whose horns Auntie didn't like the look of and having jumped off and on our bicycles to open and shut intractable gates, our journey had taken more than an hour and light was fading when we saw the Hall.

It was a gloomy old house, the dusk of the woods touched it everywhere, the windows seemed as lightless as the stone walls which were the colour of rain on a dark day. Over the doors and windows and on the main chimneys crosses were engraved in the stone.

'That's because they're R.C.s here,' said Aunt, 'always have been since it was an abbey.' The abbey had long since gone though its ruins were supposed to be in the gardens. No church was to be seen. 'It's inside the house,' Aunt said. As we pedalled nearer she added, 'The old man will be buried out here somewhere, there's a graveyard in the wood.' A tremor shook me as I looked at the dark trees and she said, 'It's enough to give anyone the creeps, fancy being buried in a wood like a heathen.'

When I reminded her of Uncle's often repeated remark about wanting to be buried under his apple trees she laughed and said he *was* a heathen, wasn't he? I said it was a good idea, I couldn't see why he shouldn't be buried under them if he wished and she said he was turning me into a heathen like he was, anyway it wouldn't be allowed for us, only rich and important people could be buried in woods or under their apple trees.

Which shows how unfair it all is, I cried, following in my uncle's argumentative footsteps, even though death is supposed to make everything equal.

We had to stop the discussion – it must have been the wan twilight of the place which had led us into it – and get off our bicycles as we arrived at the front steps of the house. There were several imposing entrances and we held a short conference as to which of them we should approach. Aunt hesitated at the bottom of the steps then remembered who she was and the importance of her errand and lifted her chin accordingly.

'I'm certainly not going to the back door like a servant,' she said, 'I'm on His Majesty's business and though I'm his servant and proud of it I'm not theirs,' and I remembered how she always signed her letters to the Registrar General, 'I am your humble and obedient servant,' and how much I disliked her thus describing herself, and how strange it seemed for her to be regarded as anybody's servant.

As we propped our bicycles against the stone balustrade a footman appeared on the top step. He looked down at us and said in the supercilious tones which never failed to act on Aunt like a red rag to a bull, 'You'll be the registrar, I suppose.'

'There's no need for you to suppose,' said Aunt, 'I am the registrar,' and raised her chin higher. Her dignity was diminished however by his being at the top of the steps and she at the bottom.

'Hey, boy,' said the footman over his shoulder but without turning his head, 'take the bikes round the corner. Quick sharp!' and a boy immediately appeared, ran down the steps and grabbed each bicycle by the handlebars.

'Just a moment,' said my aunt whose hackles were now considerably raised, 'don't be in such a hustle,' and to make it clear nobody was going to hustle her she slowly unstrapped the leather case. Its weight and importance must have inspired her with new confidence for she went up the steps with a firm tread which declared she was an important person on official business and not to be put down by anybody.

The footman led us through a vast hall towards the foot of a great staircase. 'I suppose it won't be necessary for you to see a member of the family,' he said to Aunt over his shoulder, 'as I have all the necessary particulars of the death.'

'You do rather a lot of supposing, young man,' said Aunt, coming to a standstill to give more force to her reply, 'but your supposing is liable to be incorrect.'

The footman slowed down and Aunt caught up with him.

'Oh?' he said. They stood face to face weighing each

other up.

'Was a member of the family present at the death?' asked my aunt.

'I believe so,' he replied.

'And are members present in the house?'

'I believe so,' he said again, 'but the family is deeply grieved and would prefer not to be disturbed. I assure you I have the necessary authority – '

'And I assure you,' said my aunt, 'I have every intention of following the correct procedure and the authority of His Majesty's Government is invested in me to do so and I shall require the signature of whatever member of the family I deem suitable to give it.' She paused, aware of my admiring glance.

'In that case,' replied the footman who, Aunt said later, had been trying it on to annoy her, 'perhaps you'd better come this way.' Then he added sharply, as if pleased to have the chance of annoying somebody, even one as low as me, 'not the little girl. If you will wait a moment I will conduct her to the housekeeper's room.'

As if on cue a figure emerged from the shadows and he said, 'Oh there you are, Mrs Bunch – ' or what sounded like Bunch – 'will you kindly take charge of this young person until the registrar has finished her business in the library?'

The housekeeper asked Aunt if she would care to step aside for a moment and tidy herself but Aunt thanked her and said it wasn't in the least necessary and then, fortified by her registration books, her special pens and special ink, firmly ascended the staircase side by side with the footman while I gave myself to the rounded figure of the housekeeper and was led to more humble regions than those I could glimpse through half-closed doors in the hall.

The housekeeper's room was like her – round. In it

45

were a round table covered with a red cloth, a curved sofa in black horsehair and two matching chairs, one each side of the fire.

'You may sit and warm yourself,' said the housekeeper, 'but I shall have to leave you as I have various matters to attend to.' She picked up a red shawl and put it over her shoulders before she disappeared.

I wondered how long Aunt would be. It didn't take long to register a death. I could have made the time shorter by making copies of the death certificate if any were required. It would have been better than sitting alone doing nothing.

The room was on an unimportant side of the house and overlooked a dismal garden of empty flowerbeds. Near the window was another door under a red curtain so I went outside. It was much colder and I pulled up the collar of my coat, straining it to fasten the top buttons. Somebody was playing with a dog on the other side of a thick yew hedge and I hurried to the end of it.

On a stretch of grass more like a field than a lawn a middle-aged woman and a young man were playing with a small girl and a dog. I stayed in the shadow of the hedge, watching. The cadences of their voices, the charm of their style and manner, at once proclaimed theirs to be a different world from mine. It seemed to me as I watched in the twilight, the bitter fragrance of yew around me, a world from a fable with its mythical house where death was, and a graveyard waiting in the wood.

The scene jerked itself into reality. The ball came towards me, the dog saw me, planted his forefeet in the ground and barked. I was discovered. The young man ran to the dog, seized its collar and said smiling, 'He barks but he won't bite.' I was rooted in shyness as if I had fallen under a spell. He seemed surprised I didn't answer and looked at me curiously as if not used to finding strange girls hiding near the yew hedge on winter afternoons, then patted the dog and let it go. He was tall, very tall – perhaps that was the beginning of my predilection for tallness in men – and for one ineradicable moment smiled down at me. I filled with a passionate longing not to be ordinary, not to be a schoolgirl in a coat grown too tight with buttons bursting off. I wanted to say I was an orphan of mysterious origin, probably noble, and had no connection with that undistinguished person who was upstairs in the house with her leather bag and shabby hat. I felt a madness of contempt for my world and a longing to rush out of it.

The little girl was cold, the woman called impatiently, the young man gave a last smile and followed them to the house and I knew I had fallen in love. People were right. It *was* falling, down, down, overwhelmed. I wanted to curl into a ball and roll into some deep place where nobody would see me or speak, where I could cherish the last few moments again and engrave them on my inner self for ever. Something had happened in me. I wanted to guard it in secret like a treasure.

With a sudden pop the top buttons of my coat flew off and I was surprised to find myself in the same place by the hedge shivering with cold while a voice was asking, 'Who are you and what are you doing here?'

A portly man in hat and gloves and carrying a cane was coming towards me with peevish little steps across the grass, making exasperated sounds about getting his feet wet.

'Well, you're not a poacher whoever you are,' he said as he drew nearer, 'I suppose that's one good thing.' Then, inspecting me from top to toe, he added, 'I'm speaking to you, are you dreaming or are you deaf?'

'I'm with the registrar,' I said. My voice sounded so

heavy, so local after the voices I had just heard though it was as good as his.

'No use looking for her here, is it?' he replied. 'Whoever you're with you shouldn't be wandering about here. This is a private place,' and with an imperious movement of his stick he waved me back to where I had come from.

Chapter Six

I could feel him watching me till I turned round the hedge, then I ran without stopping until I reached the outer door of the housekeeper's room at the same time as she came in by the other. She looked astonished as I burst through the red curtain but recovered herself immediately and told me to stay on the mat until I had taken off my shoes.

'You'll tread mud over my carpet,' she said. 'I never allow anyone to use that door, it lets the cold in.'

As I stood holding my shoes she looked me up and down saying, 'Your hat's not straight and you've lost two buttons off your coat,' before allowing me to move from the mat to a chair by the fire.

'Sit still until your mother comes back,' she said.

'She's not my mother,' I replied, 'she's my aunt.'

An impatient sound escaped her and she gave the fire an exasperated poke. 'Well, she'll be here presently, whoever she is.' Then, as if I were a wearisome child, 'You may look at the photographs if you wish but don't touch.'

There were photographs all over the walls, I hardly knew where to begin looking. 'Those are of Master George,' she told me, as I looked at the ones on the chimney shelf. 'They're arranged in order year by year since he was a baby.' And there was my hero, as child, schoolboy, cricketer, oarsman, horseman, smiling at me again.

'Yes, he's good at everything in the Great Outdoors –' she was aware of my admiring gaze – 'I dare say he's riding in the woods at this very minute. He's down from Cambridge. He always comes for Christmas. Of course this year everything's different.' Her face grew doleful as if to reflect the solemnity upstairs then brightened as she picked up the most recent photograph. 'He's the new St Orbin you know, Sir George St Orbin. We're expecting big changes here now he's inherited.'

So all this magical ruined place was his.

We heard voices and footsteps in the corridor, the footman opened the door and Aunt appeared, flushed with the completion of her task above.

The footman had from the first reminded me of someone. Now I knew who it was, the Frog footman – no, the Fish footman; he was an unattractive mixture of both, froggy and fishy, and still apparently trying to annoy my aunt. With a supercilious look he began to bow himself away when she stopped him.

'Just a moment –' she was at her most patrician and compelling – 'you are forgetting the little matter of my fee which I understand you have been deputed to transact.'

'Oh lor', sorry,' and his expression described the matter as being too trivial for him to remember. With the tip of his fingers he gave her a small envelope, inclined himself in a sarcastic swoop and disappeared, leaving with us the effect of his aggravating smile.

The housekeeper once more asked if Aunt would care to step aside and make herself – the word used was "comfortable" this time, not "tidy" – and this time Aunt accepted, gathered me to her with a thankful look and we left the room for a few minutes. When we came back tea was on the table. Again the housekeeper had matters to attend to, begged Aunt's pardon and went. Aunt gleefully looked at the potted-meat sandwiches and scones and began to pour tea crying, 'Come along now, what's the matter with you? We've a long ride ahead of us so stop dreaming and tuck in.'

What was the matter with me? I couldn't tell her. I didn't want to speak. My thoughts were attached to a scene just past, a vision which was enclosing itself in me more deeply minute by minute, to be borne within like an imprint which I must grow around and guard as a sheath enfolds a seed.

I heard Aunt's voice again urging me to wake up. 'You're in a trance,' she said, 'aren't you hungry?' So I ate to please her and because there was such a good tea on the table and I was hungry even though I had just fallen in love. Then I suddenly lost my appetite and was ashamed of her. In spite of her patrician nose and positive manner she was such an ordinary person eating a second piece of cake, wiping her fingers on a handkerchief as cheerfully as if she had never written DEATH in black ink and had forgotten our impending ride home through winter woods and lanes. We were saved from it. A servant appeared to say there was a van going to the gamekeeper's lodge and we could have a lift. Aunt quickly finished her cup of tea and we left the table. 'It's our lucky day, you don't know how lucky,' she whispered in the courtyard at the back of the house where our bicycles had already been put in the van.

When we reached the cottage we were half way home and the worst of our journey was over. It was snowing. A powdery white lay on the earth. Our way was magical in the flickering light of our bicycle lamps sparkling on the snow. Riding behind the sheltering figure of my aunt I lost myself in dreamy consideration of the crisis of the heart which had befallen me.

'You're half asleep,' Aunt said over her shoulder. 'It

must be all this fresh air. I've spoken to you three times and you haven't answered, and you've bumped into my back wheel twice.'

I said I was sorry.

'What did you do with yourself while I was gone?' she asked presently.

'Nothing much –' I hugged my secret – 'just walked around. That's all.' I walked into another world and lost myself in it. I'm still in it. That's all.

We pedalled briskly over the snowy lanes. I was hard pressed to keep up with Aunt, she was so eager to be home with the story of the afternoon. After a time, when the road was wider, I drew up to her and cycled abreast.

'Did you see what that odious footman gave me when I mentioned my fee?' she asked.

'Only the envelope,' I replied.

'I won't tell you what's in it till we reach home,' she said. 'It'll be a surprise for you and your uncle, you can enjoy it together.'

Though I was aware of the suppressed jubilation in her voice I was indifferent to it, being occupied with important and fascinating thoughts.

Aunt flopped into a chair and stretched her feet to the blaze. 'What a day we've had! What a long way we've been,' she sighed. 'I feel as if we've been into another world.'

'So do I,' I said.

Later, when we were having supper by the fire, she showed Uncle the entry in the black registration book.

'H'm,' he said. 'So that's what he died of. They said he would.'

'What a name!' mused Aunt. 'George Aloysius Geraint St Orbin.'

'R.C.s,' said Uncle. 'They go in for fancy names.'

In a smiling mood Aunt opened her purse and took out the small envelope. 'Now let's see,' she began, 'there's two and sixpence for the certificate, a penny for the stamp and a shilling for making the call.'

'A shilling!' exclaimed Uncle. 'A shilling for going all that way and coming back in a snowstorm.'

'I don't mind,' replied Aunt, 'we had a good tea and I always wanted a look inside Orbin Old Hall. I'd have gone for nothing.'

There was a small comfortable silence. Then, 'So it wasn't a trip to the Haggard mountains,' murmured Uncle, 'thank the Lord.'

Aunt wasn't listening. She held out a closed hand then opened it. There was a half-sovereign in it. She was delighted by our reaction. 'Yes, it's better than a shilling,' she said, 'and I know what I'm going to do with it.'

As we drank our bedtime cocoa she said, 'Isn't it strange how people live in such different ways? Not that I'd like to live in their way. Ours is best – for us. Still, I've enjoyed the day.'

'You're lucky,' said Uncle, 'not many in this world manage to enjoy themselves and be paid for it.'

On Christmas morning I discovered what Aunt did with the half-sovereign, she bought a new schoolbag for me, a proper one with a shoulder strap like everybody else's. I was pleased though my joy was moderate compared with what it would have been, one, two Christmases ago.

'I used to pray for one like this –' I slung the strap over my shoulder – 'actually pray so that I needn't use the leather case.'

'Not use the leather case,' echoed Aunt in amazement, 'not use my leather case!'

'I told you so,' said Uncle.

'But it's real leather,' cried Aunt, 'better than this. This has only got leather round the edges.'

'I was the only one who had such a funny shaped schoolbag,' I said, 'and it made me feel peculiar.'

'Told you so,' said Uncle again.

Aunt looked so crestfallen I suddenly felt a rush of affection for her and was ashamed of being ashamed of her because she was ordinary, and of pretending to myself I was somebody else.

'I'm pleased you're my relations,' I cried. 'It doesn't matter a bit if you're not aristocrats like St Orbins.'

'I should think it doesn't,' said Aunt as I hugged her. 'St Orbins indeed. Goodness knows where they've come from.'

We knew where we came from. Here. From this village, hundreds of years of us. She caught sight of herself in the looking-glass over the fireplace. 'Heavens! What a mess,' she cried. 'Just look at my hair!'

'Like a last year's bird's nest,' said Uncle, 'with frost on it, you're going grey.'

'Thanks very much,' said Aunt, 'for one of your typical compliments.'

I changed the subject, or got back to it, and said it was a lovely schoolbag, then swung it about and danced round the room.

I caught a cold from the ride to Orbin Old Hall and was glad of the excuse it gave me for daydreaming and sitting about the house with my knees hunched, so absorbed in the scenes before my inner eye I had no interest in those of the world outside. I refused to go to parties, even to the musical soirée at the home of our most eminent music lover where we always enjoyed ourselves. St Orbin's image hung between me and everything which was supposed to be reality, intimate and remote, occupying my thoughts. When Aunt reminded me I was to sing a duet with Frankie Slack the sound of his name made me jump, I cringed with embarrassment at the thought of him, my cold grew worse, I had a temperature and Aunt went to the soirée without me.

Chapter Seven

Charlie had been making himself scarce. Since his birthday at New Year I had hardly seen him on the journeys to and from school and was beginning to wonder if he had left without telling me.

'More likely he's playing truant,' said my uncle, 'so you'd better say nothing to his parents.'

Aunt's reply was decided about that. 'If he's not going to school they ought to be told. They're paying a lot for his education,' and she gave me an approving look because we weren't paying anything for mine.

'It's none of our business,' Uncle said. 'He hates school and now he's fourteen he could leave if they weren't too pig-headed to listen to him.'

'They want to do what's best for him,' protested Aunt.

'Maybe he knows what's best for him – ' Uncle was now in one of his awkward moods – 'being at school when he hates the place won't do him any good.' But Aunt refused to give in and said school was good for everybody, especially Charlie. From what she'd heard of him lately he was turning into a rough boy and rough boys were anathema to her, although not as bad as rough girls.

I didn't know how much Aunt knew but I knew and had known for some time Charlie was not always the little gentleman he was expected to be. His behaviour depended on the company he was in. Even as early as our days in the Little School I realised there were different Charlies. There was one Charlie with some little girls, another Charlie with others. He never ran after my friends and me grabbing our frocks and shouting, 'Let's have a look at your knickers,' but he ran after others. Sometimes though, even with us, polite little girls from refined homes, the wrong Charlie showed through and gave us enjoyable feelings of surprise and disapproval before he quickly reverted to more polite behaviour. It was the same with his language, even with his accent. In the farmyard or fields with rougher children of the village there was no difference between his speech and theirs. At home he spoke as we spoke though liable to lapses quickly pounced on by his mother but tolerated by his father who, in a lesser degree, was guilty of the same verbal and social dichotomy and stuck up for Charlie, reproaching his wife for nagging and begging her to have more common sense than to expect a lad to talk la-di-da and have fancy manners in a farmyard.

'How he behaves out there is one thing,' she said, 'but how he behaves and speaks in the house and in company is another, and that applies to you too so you can both watch your manners and mind your tongues when I'm around.'

Her husband agreed with her on that, she told Auntie who told me, and said if he ever found Charlie misbehaving himself with nice girls either in speech or – er – um (and here Auntie underlined the words she didn't say to express a meaning I thought I understood), he would have a good hiding to remember all his life.

'So you'd better be careful,' Aunt said.

'Me?' I was surprised. 'What have I to do with it?'

'A lot depends on girls,' she said. 'A woman's behaviour sets the tone for the man's. Remember that!'

I was pleased at the implication I was a woman. It was

like being a new member of a club, one who was in, not out. I liked that, and assured Aunt my behaviour with Charlie was always as it should be, he was in no danger of deserving a hiding on my account; but I laughed. Charlie and me – and that!

Aunt was nettled. 'It's nothing to laugh at,' she said. 'He's a boy and knows a bit more about certain things than you do, and you're a girl, and you're growing up.'

Charlie, though often rude and arrogant, usually curbed the grosser side of his tongue and kept his conversation with me free from sexual innuendo and his hands to himself which was not always the case with other girls; with Ivy Holt, for instance, as I was soon to find out.

She was a rough girl, a shocking girl and lived in a gaunt house whose outside walls were painted black. Nobody but Holts knew the colour of its inside walls for nobody but Holts ever went inside. The house was apart from the village at the end of a long lane which led into bleak fields of perpetual turnips, where hedgerows were thorny stumps and never softened into leaves and flowers, no may bloom in spring, no berries in autumn. She and three taciturn brothers and a father with a wooden leg were supported by the struggles of a fierce mother who trudged, winter and summer, up and down the lane with bundles of washing, though how it became clean within those black walls was a wonder.

Out of that house every day Ivy Holt shot like a stone from a catapult, rushing down the lane, a streak of energy made visible, electric hair flying around her, bare legs in wretched boots making giant strides which nobody but her wild brothers could keep up with. She haunted the Little School like a demon. When I began there she had already been the reigning despot in the girls' playground for two years. Every playtime as soon as the teacher's back was turned Ivy made her subjects quiver. All in turn must suffer, go under or survive as well as they could under her heel. Even the boys who played apart were wary of her forages into their territory in search of more savage combat than she could find amongst the girls.

I had been no more than a day at school when I became aware of the terrifying shadow over playtime and quickly learned to shrink into insignificance once I was outside the classroom. No showing off for me with skipping rope or ball or hopscotch. With others like me I clung to the sanctuary of the wall under the window of the classroom a scream's distance from the teacher inside. Yet, as I saw the other newcomers put to torture one by one, sick with apprehension, I knew my turn would come. One playtime, about a week after my arrival at school, it did.

I had daringly, or forgetfully, left the safety of the wall and was in the middle of the playground humbly kicking a stone when, with a lurch of the heart, I received warning from a dark shadow on the ground before me. Sound seemed to stop. I looked up knowing at once my time had come. In front of me, at least a head above me, towered Ivy Holt, her hair in rat-tails, black eyebrows drawn together in a frown as black as night, the picture of menace.

I made no plan, I thought no thought, I stooped, my right hand tore the sandal from my right foot and slapped it across her face.

There was silence, then children around us yelled and laughed. When I realised what my hand had done I cringed into myself, my heart banging, waiting for punishment. Nothing happened. Ivy Holt stared at me,

59

at the jeering audience, at me again, puzzled as if uncertain of her next move, then walked away. I put on my sandal, went back to the wall and leaned against it.

Ivy left me alone after that, the other children became less frightened of her and I took no further notice of her. Poor Ivy, our paths were soon destined to diverge, hers into the grinding poverty of work on the land and mine to Fulford High School and academic opportunities she never even heard of. Occasionally my wanderings in paper-chase or hare-and-hounds took me to her part of the world. Stopping sometimes to get my breath and sitting on a fence at a safe distance from that peculiar house, I wondered at its strange inhabitants, the toiling mother, the morose father who couldn't work but haunted the place like a satyr and cursed his unruly brood and hit them with his wooden leg. Sometimes as I mused the door opened and a wild body rushed out, there were sounds of distant battle, of clash and fury within the black walls, then I ran to find my companions, curiosity dispelled in the urge for safety, and rapidly made a distance between myself and the Holts and their unholy existence.

As I grew older Ivy faded into the background of my life though I saw her sometimes in a sacking apron and her mother's worn out boots as she stumped from one potato field or turnip patch to another, from hoeing or pea-pulling or the cruel backbreak of picking stones from the unkind ground. She had nothing more to do with such as Charlie and me, or so I thought.

On those Sundays when there was roast beef for dinner it was left to me to fetch horseradish for the sauce, so after coming back from church and changing my best for my second best frock I used to go to the waste ground at the bottom of Charlie's orchard where there was a patch of horseradish near the old stable. One Sunday in spring just before my fourteenth birthday I had dug up as much horseradish as I needed and was pulling off the long dark leaves when I heard sounds in the loft above the stable.

Moco, the pony which used to be ours and which Charlie and I quarrelled over, pulled the milk cart every day and was still out. I stood at the open door and listened. There was laughter above, then silence and more laughter, then Charlie's voice and a girl's, whose rough accent was already striking a chord of memory within me. There was a ladder leading through a hole in the roof and I went up till my head poked into the loft where I saw Charlie and Ivy Holt rolling in the hay, arms and legs winding about each other, Ivy's skirt above her waist, her thighs bare, not a sign of knickers. As Charlie rolled on top of her he looked up and saw me – perhaps I had given an exclamation as I began to descend backwards. He swore – I vaguely thought, 'That's a new one –' then jumped to his feet, bits of hay sticking to him everywhere. I noticed he had some rag of a garment in his hands, Ivy's underwear I confusedly guessed as I stumbled down the ladder. His eyes had blazed with so much fury I was too frightened to think clearly of anything but flight, and ran home, not stopping for breath until I was within reach of my aunt. I pushed the horseradish at her and bolted upstairs.

Charlie, Ivy Holt. Ivy Holt, Charlie. The names went round and round my brain. Charlie, Ivy – and horseradish sauce.

Aunt made it that Sunday. It burned my throat and exploded behind my eyes till tears ran down my face.

Horseradish has a sharp and bitter taste.

                    *   *   *

I meant never to speak to Charlie again. I meant our
friendship to be over for ever. I could have got him into
trouble, I supposed, but I wouldn't. He wasn't worth the
act of tale-telling. I would never mention what I had
seen, never. Talking of it would contaminate me. Seeing
it had soiled me. I was as sullied as he was. I comforted
myself by a mental list of demeaning adjectives for him.
He was depraved, debased, degenerate, a dictionary of
disrepute, and also a hypocrite who, forgetting his
traditional behaviour with me, had once made degrading
jokes about Ivy, so degrading I had pretended not to
understand, and he had quickly taken the cue and
covered up and we both behaved as if his crude remarks
had never been said, but now I remembered them.

   The worst of my present distressing state was the way St
Orbin kept coming into it, somehow mixing himself with
the sordid jumble in my mind. I fought to put him back
in a dream worthy of his image, into an imagination
cleansed of thoughts arising from the memory of Charlie
and Ivy Holt romping in the hay.

A few days after the episode I was sitting in the yard
letting the sun's warmth dry my hair. For some time I
had been hearing without knowing I was hearing the
particular sound by which Charlie communicated with
me from a distance. It was supposed to be a private
signal but by now was no secret and Aunt soon put her
head out of the kitchen window saying she wished I would
go and see what Charlie was up to, that row of his was
setting her teeth on edge. If she knew we two were on bad
terms she hadn't mentioned it.

   In the orchard Charlie said, 'Hey! I'm up here.'

   He was at the top of the oldest damson tree amongst

the blossom. He swung himself to a lower branch and sat with his legs dangling, his face split by a grin which showed small white teeth with spaces between.

'You've been a long time,' he grumbled, 'I've been whistling for hours.'

I was silent while I tried to think of something to say which was cool but not so cutting as to make our quarrel worse. I wanted to be unpleasant without seeming to be.

He came further down the tree. 'I wanted to speak to you,' he began, then hesitated.

I gave him a steady look but said nothing.

'I wanted to say,' he went on in a rush, 'I mean I hope you haven't blabbed to anyone about – about that hayloft business on Sunday.'

Still I didn't speak.

'Not that there was anything to get excited about,' he said, 'it was nothing – but you're such a – you're so – '

'So what?' I asked.

'Oh good – ' he pretended to be relieved – 'I thought you'd gone dumb. You're so green.'

I turned away.

'Wait a minute,' he said, 'you don't want to get Ivy Holt into trouble, I suppose? I mean if Dad finds out about her and me, I know it's nothing but – well, she'd lose her job, he'd be sure to kick her out and they need her money up there in the Black House. They're practically starving. As a matter of fact – ' he had a brainwave – 'I was just giving her some turnips.'

'Turnips?' I said. 'I didn't know you kept turnips in the hayloft.'

'Oh you!' he said. 'That's the worst of you, you're always so clever, or think you are.'

Turnips! If I knew Ivy Holt, if anybody knew any of the Holts, she, they, all the Holts were capable of helping themselves to all the turnips they wanted from anybody, anywhere. I said I didn't care what he had been giving her in the hayloft, as far as I was concerned he could give her anything he liked. He stared at me, then laughed as if I'd made a good joke.

'P'raps you're not so green,' he said.

I began to walk away.

'Hey, wait a sec.' He swung on the branch upside down.

'You look funny from here,' he said.

'Not half as funny as you look from here.'

He pulled himself right way up. 'You're not going to say anything are you?'

'Wild horses wouldn't drag it out of me,' I told him, and hoped he would realise how contemptuous I felt about his sordid little secrets and Ivy Holt, then I went away.

Chapter Eight

One morning in early summer when Charlie was sitting under the ash tree opposite his house I sauntered over the road to join him. Our ash tree, as we called it, somehow escaping the hedge cutters, had grown out of the hedge and become a tree. It was old now with a gnarled and weather-beaten trunk but its curving branches still exploded into entrancing greenery every spring. Some of its roots stuck out of the sandy bank making seats for idlers like Charlie and me and exposing sandy hollows we had called caves when we were children pretending to be at the seaside, or "post offices" when leaving messages to each other. Sunlight glanced through the leaves and birds flew in and out.

Charlie's gaze was fixed on his home opposite where men were painting Granny's old rooms. When I spoke he jumped.

'Oh it's you.' His manner made me wonder if he were still holding the hayloft scene against me. I hoped he didn't think I had talked about it. I decided to be positive and warm and said I was glad to see him, I had thought he was dead or something. He made a non-committal sound and looked so vague I asked him if he had gone off his head or had forgotten how to speak.

'Nagging already,' he said fretfully, 'that's too much,' and made a move as if he were going away. I quickly apologised and sat beside him on a root.

'I've come out here for a breather,' he said, 'not to be

nagged at. I'm supposed to be helping with the painting.'
There was paint on his clothes and fingers.

He frowned. 'I wish your aunt hadn't said anything to
Ma about those people who want rooms. It'll be an awful
bore.'

I was relieved. So that was what he was sulking about.
Somebody Aunt had known years ago wanted to come to
the village for the summer and had written enquiring
about lodgings and Aunt had thought of Granny's rooms.

'I wish she hadn't,' moaned Charlie. I tried to cheer
him by saying it would be interesting to meet new people
but he was not convinced.

We dug the toes of our shoes into the sand beneath the
tree, pushing it into little heaps and patterns as we used
to when we were trying to find seashells in it. Sunlight fell
warmly upon us, soft air played around us, light and
shade danced across us, patterns of the leaves above
trembled over us and something of the delight of our
childhood came back to me. The old fondness for Charlie
stirred in my deep self, not like the feeling for the St
Orbin boy, which was poetic and longing, already tinged
with despondency at the unlikelihood of anything ever
coming of it; nevertheless to what I felt for Charlie as we
sat under the ash tree on that spring morning I could give
the name of love, a sort of love. It moved in me, whatever
its name, perhaps its waves spread out and touched him
for we both softened into a mood of repose and gentleness
as we watched the white-coated painters in the house.
Unfortunately they soon reminded him of what was
coming and he reverted into gloom saying with a groan
there would be two more women about the place.

'What does it matter?' I said. 'The house is so huge you
needn't even see them if you don't want to, but I think
they'll be nice, especially the young one.'

This should have cheered him up but, 'I expect she's

clever,' was his reply, 'and looks like a beanpole,' and he moved to a higher root so as to be able to look down on me. He wasn't growing as fast as I was. 'Besides,' he added, 'even the young one's old, at least eighteen or something. What's the good of that? Just about the worst age for a girl as far as I'm concerned.'

'You needn't be concerned,' I said.

We were silent again, then like an idiot I remarked, 'She's not much older than Ivy Holt,' and waited for him to explode. Perhaps he hadn't heard, perhaps he ignored what I had said to teach me to mind my own business. Whatever the reason I was thankful for escaping an outburst, then quickly, but tactlessly, introduced another poisoned subject and asked, 'How's school?'

'How's yours?' he replied.

'Mine?' I shrugged. 'Oh – well – '

He laughed. 'Oh well or Oh 'ell?' then without waiting for an answer said, 'Mine's hell. Bloody hell. I'm hopeless, but they keep thinking they can drive things in if they hit hard enough.'

I was horrified. 'Hit! Surely they don't hit you!'

He didn't answer but stared glumly at his house while I stared at him. Tufts of hair were growing at random over his face. He saw me looking at them, stroked them fondly and said more cheerfully, 'I'm practically shaving. If it grows any thicker I'll have to get a razor.'

I wondered if I ought to say "congratulations". What I said was, 'You'll look better when you do shave, it's a bit of a mess at the moment.'

'It's no use arguing with them – ' he jerked his head in the direction of the house – 'they won't admit I'm a man.'

'You're only fourteen,' I said, 'and I'm fourteen now. If you're a man I'm a woman. Everybody's saying how grown-up I look, especially when I don't wear school clothes.'

He laughed, 'You look like a sack tied up in the middle whatever you wear.'

This remark went home with a deep and painful throb but before I could think of a reply I saw somebody climb from the field over the hedge farther up from where we were sitting. 'That's Ivy Holt,' I said.

He gave one look, then like a startled rabbit into its hole, bolted across the road into his house to hide amongst the painters.

I couldn't help smiling at his speedy exit. Some vestige of the smile remained as Ivy Holt came up, a harden apron over her figure, dinner tin clanking against the side of a bucket she carried.

As she had no smile for me I wiped the remains of mine from my face and, looking serious in case she thought I had been laughing with Charlie about her, I said, 'Hullo, Ivy, it's a nice day.'

She answered my polite remark with rough questions. 'Was that 'im? Was that Charlie? Where's 'e gone?' Her dark brows frowned.

'Charlie?' I looked round in surprise.

'I know it was Charlie,' she said, 'so you needn't pretend 'e wasn't 'ere. I've got to speak to 'im.'

I hadn't seen her for a long time, except in the hayloft. Her dark hair was in its usual disorder as if it had exploded from her head, not grown from it, her angry eyebrows met over her nose in the same old way, her face was more brown than ever now she was working on the land. She was the same Ivy Holt, but bigger and older and she had a gap in her front teeth so that some words came out with a whistle. As she spoke she put her hand over her mouth.

'Me front teeth got knocked out,' she explained, 'with a pump in 'is dad's yard. Folks say I should get comp- ess- ation for it.' The word whistled out.

'Is that why you want to see Charlie?' I asked in relief.

'It is and it isn't, any'ow it's my business, not yourn.' She frowned more deeply. 'I've got to go now. You tell that Charlie I'll be in Black'us lane at six o'clock tonight, and tell 'm it's urgent.' With a final emphatic glare which managed to include both me and Charlie's house across the road, with her tin clanking in the bucket she went towards the village.

I stayed under the ash tree until she had gone some distance. I expected Charlie to reappear but he didn't so I went across the road and looked through the windows. He was not with the painters so I supposed he intended to lie low for a time.

The district nurse bicycled past and saw me. 'Looking for Charlie?' she asked flashing the smile I had disliked for so many years. Our antipathy was mutual and dated from her attendance on my childish ailments when she decided for ever I was spoilt and wilful. I didn't answer but made a face at her behind her back, then went home wondering how I was going to deliver the message to Charlie from Ivy Holt.

'That was Ivy Holt, wasn't it?' asked Aunt. 'What did she want with Charlie?'

I wondered how she knew Ivy wanted anything from Charlie. 'Charlie wasn't there,' I said. 'He'd gone before Ivy came, I don't know what she wanted, something to do with having her front teeth knocked out.'

'Surely Charlie didn't –' cried Aunt.

I explained about the pump handle in the farmyard. 'She wants compensation from Charlie's father.'

Aunt gave a short laugh and looked at Uncle who also laughed.

'I feel sorry for her,' I went on. 'It's a shame she's lost her teeth.'

'She'd have lost 'em soon enough, all the Holts lose teeth,' said Aunt.

'But she's only sixteen,' I protested, incensed at the injustice of Fate to the Holts, 'and it makes her look awful.'

'Her mother hadn't a tooth in her head by the time she was thirty,' said Aunt, 'through having too big a family and living from hand to mouth and never much in hand either.'

'It's a shame,' I cried, 'why do they have to be so poor?'

'They've always been poor.' Aunt was ready to turn from the subject, but I wasn't.

'That's not a proper reason.' I was becoming angry.

'They're poor because they're Holts,' said Uncle, 'and they're Holts because they're poor. One thing equals another and there's no way out of it unless – '

'Don't you start,' said Aunt, 'anyway she'll have two or three bairns before you can look around, if there's not one coming already.'

'Let's hope it's not Charlie's, then,' said Uncle.

My heart gave an alarmed thump. Aunt glared a warning at Uncle.

'It's all right,' I said, 'I'm not green. I know everything.'

'Oh?' said Aunt.

'Well, not everything – there's some things I'm not sure about.'

'Really?' said Aunt.

I briefly and privately reflected upon what I knew of Ivy Holt's habits in haylofts, then said again, 'Anyway I'm not green. I know more than anybody thinks I do.'

'I'm glad to hear it,' said Aunt.

She considered herself modern and in some ways she was. She dared say "sex" out loud though not often and only at home, having become familiar with the sound of it during the course of her registration duties when the official form required her to ask, 'Of what sex is the child?' As for Uncle, only recently he had remarked on the fuss the new generation was making about sex. When he was young it wasn't talked about, and certainly wasn't written about, so much, but people knew how to get on with it and enjoyed it. 'And still do now and again,' he added, 'especially on Sundays.'

'What?' snapped my aunt.

'In the newspapers,' said Uncle, 'they're full of it on Sundays.'

Sometimes I cycled home with Charlie. More often I didn't, not because I was keeping the school rules about associating with Grammar boys – I had long ago received special indulgence on that because of the long ride between home and station – but because Charlie was usually missing. One evening, however, he caught up with me in the yard of the Railway Inn and we began our journey home together. We soon passed a group of his contemporaries who were larking about on the pavement. They called after us with remarks and laughter which made me uncomfortable and Charlie get off his bicycle and pitch into the lot of them. He came back with a bloody nose and lip, refused my sympathy and was surly all the way home as if I were to blame. 'Bloody girls,' he kept saying. 'Bloody girls.'

When I remembered St Orbin – when! he was always in my mind, coming forward or receding as it occupied or emptied itself of other less interesting thoughts – I shrank from connecting him with the muddle of physical sensations which disturbed me, or the confusion of images based on inaccurate details I had picked up, which haunted my dreams both waking and sleeping.

Eroticism. I looked up the word, spent time staring at it. Even the sight of it was disturbing. Eroticism. So that was what I was experiencing, this groping amongst incomprehensible emotions, this mixture of excitement and shame, this feeling of longing and bewilderment. This was me, a unique and messy mixture I must keep secret from the world. Then I would drift into a different kind of daydream both ardent and exalting, about me and St Orbin, until I came back to earth again, looking amazedly at the ordinariness of people around me and marvelling because I was me.

I began to look at Charlie with different eyes. He had already dabbled in mysteries I could only imagine. He not only knew, he did. Yet I was as old as he was, looked just as grown-up when I was out of the body-mistreating gym tunic which disguised, and was meant to disguise, every hint of sexual attractiveness not only from the world but from myself. I began to look at him with curiosity and envy though he considered himself an uneviable person.

'You seem to be taking a leaf out of Charlie's book,' said my aunt one night as, groaning over homework, I tore a leaf out of my own.

'I can't do it,' I pushed the book away. 'I'm sick of it.'

'You used to do so well.' Aunt spoke sadly, as of a radiant past now slipping away.

'Well, I don't now.' I was brusque, not wanting any sentimental memories of my early days. 'I've fizzled out, lost ground, fallen behind, slipped downhill. That's what the Orb keeps telling me.'

Aunt picked up an algebra book, glanced into it and put it down again. Poor old Aunt. Poor old Uncle. They were miles behind in everything. Suddenly I shoved my books and papers into my satchel and said, 'To hell with being clever. Who cares?'

'I care,' said Aunt.

'People laugh if you're clever,' I said, 'especially boys. They call you cleverdick and brainybox and swot. I used to cry about it – when I *was* clever.'

'Cry about being clever?' Aunt was amazed.

'You'd cry if people thought you were a freak. That's what boys call you if you're clever – if you look it, that is, if they find out. A freak.'

'There are lots of clever girls at Fulford.'

'Yes, and the boys call 'em freaks. Well I'm not going to be laughed at and called a freak, anyway I'm not clever.'

I reminded her how, one night when I had helped Charlie with English homework, his mother had warned me not to sound so clever, Charlie didn't like it, and Aunt had protested that as he was so ready to profit from my cleverness he had better put up with it.

Charlie's mother had gone on, 'It won't do her any good in the long run, men don't like clever women, at least not the ones who aren't clever enough to hide it.'

Aunt stared at me as I reeled off the conversation as accurately as if I'd taken it down in shorthand. It had made a deep impression on me.

'Yes,' I went on, 'and she said I'd spoil my chances if I sounded so smart, and you said, "Chances? What chances?" as if you didn't know she wasn't thinking of universities and degrees. Then you were sarcastic and said you supposed she meant I wouldn't get a man.'

'She did mean that,' said Aunt.

'And you said well, you weren't exactly a fool but you'd got yours, and she said, "Oh – Ben!" and smiled just as if Uncle didn't count.'

'Perhaps she was right and I don't,' said Uncle, who

was in a placid mood with a new pipe.

Aunt put her hand on my shoulder. 'Don't stop being clever,' she said, 'not for any man. Any woman who does is a fool and deserves a fool to live with, any man who wants a fool of a woman is a fool and deserves what he gets.'

'Don't look at me,' said Uncle, puffing dreamy smoke towards the ceiling, 'you can all be as clever as you like as far as I'm concerned.'

But I was glad to lighten the conversation and asked what sort of woman he preferred, a stupid or a clever one, 'for living with, I mean.'

'How should I know?' he answered, 'I've never tried living with a stupid woman, the one I live with is as sharp as a rattlesnake.'

The next time Charlie made a sarcastic reference to my brains I told him I no longer had any.

'I don't care if you have or you haven't,' he said, 'your brains don't mean a thing to me.'

'Because the opinion at school is,' I went on, 'that I'm no good any more. They say I'm not fulfilling my promise.'

'What promise?' he wanted to know.

'My early promise,' I explained, 'when I first went to Fulford.'

'Idiot!' said Charlie. 'Just like you to be such a fool. You shouldn't have promised 'em anything.'

Chapter Nine

'They're here,' said my uncle coming in from cutting roses a few weeks later. 'I've just seen them get out of the taxi – they've gone inside already,' he added, 'it's no use going to look.' So Aunt and I had to contain our impatience until a more favourable moment.

I had been waiting for the arrival of our new neighbours since the morning of a few weeks ago at the beginning of May when Aunt opened a letter at breakfast and exclaimed. 'I can't believe it, it's from Lucy, of all people in the world.'

Uncle looked up. So did I.

'It's from Lucy,' Aunt repeated, rapidly turning the pages of a long letter, 'as cool as you please, writing just as if she left yesterday and has forgotten what happened.'

'Take her tip then,' said Uncle, 'and don't start remembering.'

'Remembering what?' I cried, 'what are you talking about?'

Aunt ignored me and went on. 'And look how she signs herself – ' turning the last page with an exasperated flick – 'Yours affectionately Lucy Denham-Lucie.'

'Denham's the fellow she married so Denham's her name,' said Uncle, 'if she hasn't married anybody else since.'

'But two Lucies,' said Aunt, more and more exasperated.

'Lucy's her name,' replied Uncle, 'she's a right to use it twice if she wants to.'

'One with an "ie",' muttered Aunt, 'and Denham-Lucie with a hyphen. I'm not having that. She'll be plain Lucy Denham to me.'

'She was never plain,' said Uncle.

'She was pretentious,' Aunt said, 'always putting it on. She's just the same.'

'It won't make any difference to us,' said Uncle, 'if she is or she isn't.'

I saw Aunt prepare for a triumphant stroke. 'Oh, but it will, she hasn't written merely to wish us good day and sign herself with two Lucies and a hyphen.' She returned our questioning looks over her pince-nez. 'She wants to live here.'

Uncle shot up from his chair. Aunt went on, 'She wants to know if I can find rooms for her and the child.'

'Child?' I cried.

'Child?' echoed Uncle. 'Good God, I hope she's not hinting about staying here.'

Aunt sounded calmer now she had disturbed Uncle. 'We've no room for one extra here, let alone two,' she said.

'What sex is the child?' I asked in a copy of her registrar's manner.

'Don't be silly,' Aunt said, 'a girl.'

I was disappointed – a boy would have been better – but I wanted to know name, age and description.

'I've never seen her,' said Aunt, 'all I know is her name – Zoë. Zoë Vardoe and I don't know how she got that. She must be, let's see she was born in May 1915, as far as I can make out.'

'Zoë Vardoe.' I was immediately charmed by the name and said it again, 'Zoë Vardoe – but why isn't she Zoë Denham-Lucie?'

76

'Denham wasn't her father, I suppose,' said Aunt, 'don't ask me about Lucy Denham's affairs.'

But that was what I intended to do. I could sense a story and could also sense Aunt was brimming over with it, but she said I was becoming too inquisitive, always wanting to know about everything, especially about things which were no concern of mine.

'Lucy's affairs are her own business,' she said, 'I've never said a single word about them to anybody who wasn't in the know.'

'Then don't say one now,' said Uncle.

I got up in a fury – a pretended fury that is, for I was calculating its effect – and accused them of tantalising me with snippets then drawing back and said I would make my own conclusions about Lucy Denham and her past. With a sudden spurt of inspiration I asked if she had murdered anybody, or perhaps she'd stolen things.

'I bet that's what you're hiding,' I said. 'I bet she was a thief.'

They were both horrified and Uncle said to Aunt with an accusing look, 'Now see what you've done.'

She was taken aback and I pressed my advantage by saying on second thoughts she needn't tell me anything. I would ask Charlie. 'He'll find out,' I said. 'He always does.'

'I forbid you to mention anything to Charlie,' cried Aunt as Uncle went out muttering about gossip and idle talk.

I bided my time and sure enough little by little, encouraged by several judiciously timed questions from me, Aunt dredged into history and told me about Lucy Denham.

It was in Aunt's first year as a teacher in the village school that Lucy had arrived fresh from a college in London. She already had her teacher's certificate but Aunt was still studying for hers at home, you could do that in those days. Lucy lived in our house, with Aunt and her mother and my father.

'Your mother and Ben were living at the farmhouse,' said Aunt, 'and soon we were all friends.' She paused, and suddenly I caught a glimpse of a golden age of friendship and youth.

'Yes, we had good times together,' Aunt continued. 'It was before the war, everything was different then. We were so young, your mother and me, and Ben and your father – and Lucy.'

'One out,' I said. 'Nobody for Lucy.'

Aunt laughed. 'Nobody for Lucy. Everybody was for Lucy – except your father. He was already attached to your mother. We always knew they'd be married some day.'

I was glad about that.

'Everybody loved Lucy at first,' Aunt continued, 'but it wore off. She could charm everybody, but she lost everybody.'

Some people were very impressed with Lucy. She talked about books and art and went to Sheffield to music recitals and the theatre. She played the piano well, not just thumping out hymns at school. She wore striking clothes, 'Too striking, some thought,' said Aunt, and everybody, including Lucy, thought she was the last word in fashion.

'I never found out how she did it,' Aunt said, 'a teacher's salary wasn't much, and even in those days it didn't go far, not as far as Lucy's seemed to go.' Again she paused, perhaps to gaze at a picture she had conjured up in her memory. I too saw a picture and it was fascinating.

They rode bicycles and had lovely times at weekends and holidays, cycling to distant villages and into Sherwood. 'You know that picture in the old album,' said Aunt, 'we're all in it – in Sherwood.'

I remembered the photograph, brown and faded, the girls in weird clothes.

With picnics, bicycles, socials, singing and music in each other's houses and dancing in the big barn at the farm, life was a feast. I sighed with longing to think of it and compared it with the dullness of the present – my present.

'We got up concerts and pantomimes and melodramas,' said Aunt, 'and did them in the Big Room at school or at the rectory. We hadn't a village hall then. We never had such good times before Lucy came.'

We were busy all this time and never had I been so helpful as I followed Aunt about the house.

'The funny thing about Lucy,' Aunt obliged me by continuing, 'was her remarkable talent for having adventures, at least that's what she called them. Whenever she stepped out alone, if she only went to buy a reel of thread, she'd come back sparkling and laughing, saying she'd had an adventure. Adventure! That was Lucy's word for a meeting.'

'Meeting?' I said. 'What sort of a meeting?'

'I thought you said you weren't green,' said Aunt with a smile.

It was always somebody special whom Lucy met, somebody who couldn't wait to see her again, ask her out, buy her flowers, gloves, and take her to the theatre in Sheffield, even London was spoken of, though she never went as far as that. 'She only laughed at us when we told her to be careful,' said Aunt.

There was a pause in the story-telling over the registration of a birth and I gritted my teeth with impatience, but Aunt gave me the half-crown she earned because I had gone on with some housework. This put us both in a good mood and she continued the story.

It was in the summer of 1914, just after war broke out; Lucy never went away in the holidays, perhaps she had nowhere to go, Aunt never found out. There was a strange feeling in the air of unrest and excitement, a disturbance of lives and ideas, which seemed to affect everybody. Towards the end of the August holiday Lucy made her great plan of a trip into Sherwood, not by day, this time, by night. Moonlight in Sherwood. The other girls were pleasurably shocked, rather scared, hesitant but tempted, but the men were busy on the farm – my father was on the point of joining up – and were not interested so the plan went on without them. 'Lucy was so set on it, we found ourselves agreeing with it,' said Aunt.

I was full of admiration for my feminine predecessors, but they backed out. The scheme fell through. I ached with disappointment. 'Cowards,' I said.

The school managers wouldn't have liked it. There would have been serious disapproval. Women teachers riding around Sherwood at night!

'It certainly would have been an adventure,' said Aunt, 'and I was sorry later, I'm sorry now, but I didn't go. None of us went except Lucy.'

I praised Lucy lavishly.

The other girls watched her go. She set off alone about ten o'clock one night when there was a full moon.

'Of course she might have turned back, not gone at all,' said Aunt, 'but she didn't appear at our house till next morning. She was very quiet, wouldn't say much, and she had a strange air about her, a little smile. I can remember that smile even now. I could have kicked myself for not going.'

I let my mind dwell on its own picture of Sherwood at

night, mysterious in moonlight, the branching colonnades of trees. 'It was an adventure,' I cried, 'a real adventure.'

It was, and Zoë was the result of it.

I quietly awaited the rest of the story, awed by its climax. At first Lucy had said little about her night out, then had begun to hint at a secret of great importance. After a time she gave Aunt the idea she had met someone so elevated his name could not be mentioned, at least for the present, and hinted at a secret which must be kept hidden because of large antipathies. Sherwood was the home of ducal families, she reminded her friends, then smiling, would say no more until the next hint of mysteries and rhapsodies.

'We were all thrilled and envious,' said Aunt, 'and sorry we'd stayed at home, but as time went on – ' she paused and was so long searching for the right phrase I grew impatient and supplied it.

'I suppose it was Zoë,' I said.

The engagement to the important person was off – if it had ever been on. Lucy disappeared several times afterwards, it was understood, for significant rendezvous. There was no marriage. She lost some of her high spirits and didn't talk so much of adventures.

By now I was feeling a strong response to Lucy's plight of so many years ago, I knew much about the longings of unrequited love.

'Then she left,' said Aunt. 'Without telling us, she had given a month's notice to the managers, and went away just before Christmas. Of course, it was all war and talk of war by then, but news of a baby seeped through. It arrived some time in the spring.'

I smiled to myself at the way Aunt used the word "arrived" instead of born, unconsciously trying, I supposed, not to create disturbing images for me of painful bodily experiences and laborious mysteries she considered to be beyond my understanding.

As the war went on Lucy had written to tell of her marriage to a soldier, a Major Denham, and 'there you are,' said Aunt, 'there's your Lucy Denham. But Zoë is Zoë Vardoe, don't ask me why.'

Chapter Ten

I was fascinated by the story but Aunt seemed guilty at having told it and when the characters arrived in their flesh and blood she reminded me urgently of my promise not to discuss what I knew about them to anybody, especially not to Uncle who despised gossip. I promised again.

Already I had a strong sympathy for the newcomers as victims of an ill-fated love affair – a sure way at that time into my esteem – although with a temporary unfaithfulness to St Orbin I admitted feeling disappointed it was to be a girl, not a boy, next door. Aunt said sourly we had enough boys about the place with one, Charlie, who was growing so much more rough and wild every day she had come to the opinion that the money spent on the Grammar School was wasted.

By habit I put in the ritual remark about farming being in a bad way, and added, 'They're supposed to be quite hard up.'

'If they are,' said Aunt, 'it's not because of the miserable bit of rent they pay us.'

Uncle appeared at the door. 'Nothing's ever right for farmers,' he said. 'Don't break your heart for them. They made enough money in the last war to tide 'em over till the next.' Aunt begged him not to talk about war, it wasn't the fashion, everybody was talking peace.

'They can talk peace as much as they like,' he replied, 'it won't make any difference in the long run. There's trouble brewing at this very minute in Germany but fools want to shut their eyes to it. Has anybody seen my pruning knife?' And he hunted in drawers for several disturbing moments before he went out again to the rose trees in the garden.

I wanted more talk about the newcomers. Aunt was puzzled.

'I should have thought Lucy Denham-Lucie – ' she put ironical emphasis on the name – 'would care for more elegant society than she'll find here.'

After a time Uncle called out to tell us Lucy had appeared outside Charlie's house and if we were quick we could catch her before she went in again. 'I've told her you're coming out,' his voice boomed, 'so look sharp.'

Aunt had meant to be properly dressed and renovated before showing herself for inspection by her old friend, but realised the encounter was to be now, there was no time for changing a dress, only time for a quick scrape of a comb and the assumption of a welcoming manner. She gave me a quick look to see if I would "do", then said, 'Come on, let's get it over,' and led the way outside where we found Mrs Denham-Lucie talking to Uncle.

'So here you are again,' said Aunt, her manner slightly tinged with the acerbity which was her discouragement of effusiveness rather than the outward sign of a sharp heart. If Mrs Denham-Lucie had intended being effusive she took the cue and said simply, though with a sigh, yes, here she was again.

'Just the same,' said Uncle, then spoilt his gallantry by saying, 'only different.'

'We're all the same and we're all different – ' Aunt's tone was decided – 'except Kate – ' she introduced me –

'who wasn't born when you were here before. She's only fourteen.'

'Dear Kate!' Mrs Denham-Lucie gave me her hand, then inevitably, 'How tall she is! What a blessing she must have been to both of you after you lost your two poor darlings, one so soon after the other. I grieve for you, they were such dears,' and she gave me an up-and-down glance as if swiftly computing my worth as a substitute.

A strange and delicate fragrance was about her, a scent of violets mingled with something heavier, something woodland and mossy, something to evoke a medley of fancies. Utterly charmed I was drawn into it. Uncle, who had left us for a few minutes, returned with a bunch of rosebuds and, presenting them, leaned towards her as if he too were in danger of being beguiled. I stared at him, then saw Aunt was as surprised as I was. A sudden chill touched me, only a wisp, quickly gone, and some words of Aunt echoed in my head. 'I hope she's not going to stir things up,' she had said of Lucy's coming and I had said to myself, 'I hope she is.' Now those words sounded in my mind like a challenge to the fates.

Mrs Denham-Lucie buried her nose in the flowers and said how exquisite they were, she adored tea-roses, especially *Gloire de Dijons* – with the right accent – and I could feel Aunt thinking, 'She's still putting it on.'

'But where's your beautiful daughter?' asked Uncle after a pause during which Aunt said nothing and Mrs Denham-Lucie kept putting her face in the roses.

'Ah! my darling Zoë,' murmured Mrs Denham-Lucie, 'she's resting at the moment.'

'Resting?' Aunt was astonished. Even Uncle who would have appreciated being allowed to stay in bed till nine o'clock in winter on wet days – even he looked surprised.

'Resting,' repeated Aunt, 'on a day like this?'

Her voice was so full of disapproval I was embarrassed

but Mrs Denham-Lucie only laughed.

'Still the same old puritan,' she said. 'We've had a long journey you know, and one thing and another. As a matter of fact the darling hasn't been quite herself lately. She's not too robust at the moment.'

There was an air of hesitation about the reply which implied something was being hidden or at least not spoken of, yet.

Aunt looked thoughtful. I met my Uncle's eyes which said, 'She's in her bloodhound mood, we'd better be going,' and he began side-stepping away murmuring remarks about seeing more of each other before long.

Aunt cut through him, turned to Mrs Denham-Lucie and said as if determined to have everything made clear, 'I thought from your letter it was you who had been ill and needed to recuperate here for the summer.'

'That's true,' cried Lucy, 'quite true, I assure you. We've both been unwell.'

She was flushed and I could see her quailing before my aunt's truth-discovering gaze. 'I've been very ill, quite a wreck, but I won't go into that now, it's such a sweet morning.'

Uncle was moving away with definite steps but I was hovering, loath to go. She said to Aunt in a low voice, 'We must talk some time, soon perhaps,' but it was no good, Aunt was in full cry now Uncle had disappeared into our garden and I was trying to look as if I were going away. She said, 'I hope it's nothing serious with either of you, especially Zoë, she's so young.'

Mrs Denham-Lucie thought for a moment, looked at me as I took another token step backwards, then said as if drawing inspiration from the sight, 'Oh no, it's her age, that's all, the malaise of her years you know.'

Aunt was astonished again. 'Her age,' she cried. 'Surely she's over that. She's nineteen, isn't she?'

Mrs Denham-Lucie looked at Aunt as if conjecturing how much she had discovered about the past, then gave a sigh which hinted at much experience. 'Yes,' she agreed, 'it's true, she's nineteen,' and made it sound as if she had voluntarily offered a confession, 'just nineteen this month of May.'

I was bowled over by the thought of the girl I had not seen, the being composed of moonlight and forest and engendered in an August night amongst the trees of Sherwood, and who had made her appearance in the world in the loveliest of months, like a goddess.

This powerful image put an end to my slight powers of social participation, and soon Mrs Denham-Lucie put an end to the meeting. Murmuring an invitation for us to visit her some day soon when Zoë would be "up", she glided into Charlie's house and Aunt and I, silent but full of thoughts, went home.

Later in the day Aunt decided I was growing out of my clothes. Nobody knew that better than I did. I couldn't help it and was sick of being told about it, and was sulky when she began letting down the hems of my last year's cotton frocks saying she didn't want me to look a mess now Lucy Denham was on the scene. 'I bet Zoë has plenty of frocks,' I said, 'and I bet she doesn't have to wear last year's with the hems let down.'

'It's beginning,' said Aunt. 'They're affecting us already with their airs and graces. Damn Lucy Denham, Denham-Lucie whatever she calls herself, she's going to be a nuisance.'

The next days were cool and cloudy and there was no sign from the occupants of the front rooms next door. We saw several vans stop outside and delivery boys getting out of them with burdens, and getting in again without them and Aunt picked up the idea that Lucy Denham was too busy settling in to be disturbed so we kept away, but we talked continually about her.

'I shall have to listen to her tales all over again,' grumbled Aunt.

'She'll have plenty of new ones by now,' said Uncle who sometimes stayed to listen and sometimes said he was sick of the subject and disappeared, 'you'd better make up your mind to enjoy them as if they're in a book.'

'But she's always the one who's living the story,' said my aunt, 'and I'm always the one who's reading it, and she knows it and I'm fed up with it before it's begun.'

I sympathised with her. I knew how she felt but the story I had heard already was so fascinating, and more of it so likely to be, I could hardly wait to hear and see its continuing chapters lived before my eyes.

'Especially as I don't believe half she says,' my aunt continued without bothering to notice my remarks. 'There's nobody like Lucy for making things up.'

'What does that matter?' said Uncle. 'You don't expect everything in books to be true.'

I was on the defensive for Lucy and refused to believe she had made everything up.

'Of course she hasn't,' said Uncle, 'or there wouldn't be Zoë.'

The next day was wet. Mild rain made the world intoxicating with fragrance, not the sort of rain to keep anyone indoors, certainly not Uncle who prowled incessantly amongst his blossoming fruit trees, not me. I went for the next-door dog.

As I passed Charlie's house I caught neither glimpse nor sound of the two visitors hidden within but I saw Charlie looking glum on Moco the milk pony, our old Moco, as they trundled together over the field. Even when I went round the house to the back door for the dog I didn't see the mysterious lodgers. Perhaps they were still "resting". Restless myself, I took the dog for a rain-bespeckled walk. Swallows dipped across the meadows. The cuckoo's vibrant voice called from the wood. I looked for birds' nests, gathered flowers, my face wet with rain, May rain for beauty, that's what people said.

After my walk I delivered the dog into the back kitchen of Charlie's house where one of the farm boys was cleaning mud from his boots, and left a bunch of meadow flowers with my best wishes for the front room tenants. There was still no sight of them even though I passed the glass-panelled side door of their sitting-room, then the bay windows at the front. Trying to look as if I were not looking, I looked and lingered, but they could not, or would not, be seen. If they were determined to keep to themselves I hoped it was not to be for ever.

Aunt counselled patience saying we should have the royal summons before long, waiting for it always enhanced the value of an invitation as Lucy Denham knew very well even if I didn't. Even as the words were spoken the same boy I had seen cleaning his boots came dashing through the rain with a sack over his shoulders to deliver a note.

'It's from Mrs 'er that's come to live in front,' he said, 'an' she told me to wait for an answer.' He leaned on the side of the doorway as Aunt read the note.

'Does it require a formal reply?' she enquired as I leaned over her shoulder, and in her voice again there was the sarcastic note which was becoming more and more usual in her references to the Denham-Lucie establishment. The boy looked blank, and she told him to go back and say thank you to Mrs Er in the front rooms; we would send a note. And he scuttled away in the rain.

'One thing's sure,' Aunt said as we went into the sitting-room, 'your uncle won't go.'

'Won't go where?' he asked from the window through which he was looking into the orchard and enjoying the rain as if he were one of his fruit trees.

'Lucy Denham's asked us to supper, tomorrow.' Aunt showed him the note. 'I'm surprised she didn't call it Late Dinner, it's not till eight o'clock, but of course you won't go, you never go visiting,' and she sat at the table with pen and paper.

'Wait a minute,' said Uncle, 'this is different.'

Not to go calling was a precept he had established in the past before my time, and though he sometimes allowed himself to break the rule he considered a rare exception only served to prove the strength of it.

'I'll go,' he said after a moment's reflection and Aunt, whatever she was thinking, wrote accordingly.

Chapter Eleven

I could hardly believe I was in Granny's old quarters. Their greeny dimness was now dispelled by rose-coloured lamps, the old furniture had been moved around and disguised with bright covers and cushions, the table was no longer in the middle of the room under the hanging lamp but against the wall, the hanging lamp replaced by a basket of greenery. The bay window which looked on to the damp May twilight was hung with rose-coloured curtains which caught the gleam of the lamps. There were rose-coloured candles in silver sticks and vases of flowers everywhere, though I didn't see my wild flowers. A baby grand piano had come from somewhere. It was open and there was music on it as if waiting to be played. There were photographs in silver frames, new pictures on freshly painted walls, elegant rugs over Granny's faded carpet. Even Aunt was confounded as we stood at the door and she cried before she could stop herself, 'Good gracious, it's like the transformation scene in a pantomime.'

As for me, I felt as if I had wandered into an Aladdin's cave of splendour. When I saw the assortment of dishes on the table I had to stifle gasps of wonder at enticing confections such as I had never seen but had imagined as existing only in fabled banquets.

Uncle had stayed at home. Hay fever, so often a means of escape from tiresome social congress, had struck him down in earnest after a day in the orchard. As Aunt and I stood at the door Mrs Denham-Lucie's glance over our shoulders was followed by a shade of disappointment when she saw he wasn't with us, but she commiserated charmingly over his affliction and led us into the room, when we had put our wraps away, saying she hoped we agreed with her it was nicer to have a little light supper, buffet style, than to sit at table. I would have agreed with anything she said at that moment.

Though it was nearly June the weather was cool and it was pleasant to see the fire of apple logs. I sat beside it with such a deep breath of pleasure the seams of my out-grown frock protested and I looked at Aunt wondering if she had heard the ominous sound, but she was exchanging light remarks with Mrs Denham-Lucie – or rather Mrs Denham-Lucie was making them and Aunt was considering them seriously before giving her answers – so I was able to absorb the scene at my leisure. How it had been brought about was for the moment a mystery which Aunt and I solved later with the help of Charlie's mother. Some of the furniture had been hired from the best shop in Welham – that explained the piano – and baskets of luxuries had arrived in vans from Welham and even Sheffield. As for the rest, Mrs Denham-Lucie confessed she always kept by her a little store of pots and bottles from Harrods and Fortnums, in case – she gave the impression – the rare delicacies, upon which she sustained herself and her daughter were unobtainable in a desert like our village. Most surprising of all, she had made a lot of the stuff herself.

'I borrowed the kitchen,' she cried, 'for two whole days! You remember how I always adored cooking.' This was to Aunt who looked as if she remembered nothing of the kind and asked, 'What's this pastry thing?'

'Oh the quiche! Do try it!' And Aunt, though suspicious, was persuaded to experiment and admitted it was good but not something she would care to eat every day.

Mrs Denham-Lucie was a gracious hostess as she moved poetically about the room in an elegant gown. I felt sorry for Aunt in her wintry grey though she had put a lace collar on it.

Mrs Denham-Lucie poured wine into tall glasses and was ever on the alert for our comfort saying we must try this and try that, pressing us to have a little more of this, another one of those. Those, to my downfall, were little patties whose shells exploded into melting fragments in the mouth and whose filling was more delicious than anything I had ever tasted.

'Lobster patties,' said Mrs Denham-Lucie amused by my transports and by the fact of my never having eaten lobster, 'do have another.' Unable to resist the exquisite temptation I did have another, though I was aware of Aunt's disapproving look.

The evening passed pleasantly yet fell short of perfection. Though Mrs Denham-Lucie did everything to please us I sensed a faint touch of discontent about her sparkling performance as if Aunt and I were not completely satisfying as an audience and I knew she would have sparkled even more brightly if Uncle had been with us.

Zoë did not make an appearance and it was some time before I could forbear restless glances towards the door. Aunt too retained a look of enquiry until at last she could contain her curiosity no longer and asked what was the matter with her. Mrs Denham-Lucie let the question be asked twice before she said she was sorry her darling wasn't with us, unfortunately she had been persuaded to go to Welham in the afternoon with Charlie and his father for a little motor ride.

'Isn't she home yet?' Aunt, in surprise, glanced at the clock, 'I thought I saw the car in the yard as we came in.'

'Oh, they've come back but I'm afraid the expedition was a little too much for the poor dear, she came home quite knocked up so I persuaded her to stay in her room and lie down.'

Aunt murmured some flabbergasted sympathy and I said nothing, not being able to understand how anybody could need to lie down as often as Zoë seemed to.

'But we mustn't be too serious,' cried Mrs Denham-Lucie pouring wine into the silence, 'it's nothing time and your country air can't heal. She's not quite up to meeting new people at present and didn't want to spoil my evening, the pet – such an important evening too, with my friends – by not appearing at her best; but you're not eating,' and she encouraged Aunt and me to pay attention to our wineglasses and the seductive concoctions on the table.

After a time I walked about the room, eating and chatting, looking at pictures and photographs and answering Mrs Denham-Lucie's silvery questions with style – I thought – and she said I was a sweet girl and would blossom, it would take a little time but I would eventually blossom, and my hair, now rather distressingly flaxen, would ripen into corn colour when I was thirty, perhaps.

'But she must lose that accent, my dear,' she told Aunt as they sat on the sofa, 'you must be adamant about that.'

'Accent!' repeated Aunt with a bemused look at me as I was taking another lobster patty. 'But she speaks very nicely. I've always been most particular about that.'

'I'm sure you have, I'm sure she does,' Mrs Denham-Lucie soothed, 'but there's a trace, more than a trace, of the Midland "a" and "u", and in the cadences, perhaps, more than the accent. It's the cadences of the voice which give the game away.'

To me the cadences of her voice were delightful and I

wished I could improve mine but Aunt showed disapproval of her remarks.

'Kate speaks as I do,' she said, 'and I'm most particular,' and she glared at me as if I had shown her up by inventing peculiar cadences of my own.

'Never mind.' Mrs Denham-Lucie sensed Aunt's annoyance. 'All will come right if she tries. Just watch the "a"s and the "u"s, and remember the cadences,' she added especially for me which made me dumb for some time afterwards.

Fortunately at this stage Charlie came to pay his respects. He looked a different Charlie, trouser creases in their proper places, shoes polished, an air of civility about him, the effect of being in contact with superior society during the last few days. He declined an invitation to help himself from the table saying he had just eaten in the kitchen thus sounding a coarse note in the general euphony. Mrs Denham-Lucie patted his hair then couldn't help looking at her hand which was wet and said he was being a sweet darling boy to poor homeless strangers. For a second I wondered who these were then was astonished twice over, first at the thought of Mrs Denham-Lucie and Zoë Vardoe being either poor or homeless, and second at the thought of Charlie being sweet. I caught his eye and he stared me out as if daring me to laugh.

His mother appeared at the door looking like a bit of real life which had strayed into a fairy tale. She had popped in to say she had taken a bite of supper to the upstairs room – I noticed she didn't say bedroom – and to ask Charlie to carry more logs up to the fire. A fire in the bedroom! What was happening? An exclamation burst from Aunt before she could stop it.

'It's more of a bed-sitting-room,' explained Mrs Denham-Lucie as Charlie and his mother went away, 'a sort of boudoir, a very modest little boudoir,' she smiled, 'if you know what I mean.'

Aunt said she did know what was meant by "boudoir". What she didn't know was that there was one in Charlie's house, but any further remarks she might have expressed about boudoirs were nipped on her tongue as Mrs Denham-Lucie struck a chord on the piano and asked our opinion about its tone and Aunt was charmed and softened as ever when there was music.

Mrs Denham-Lucie nodded approvingly when she heard my voice and said, 'Quite a little songster,' which elated me, but I spoiled myself by saying, 'That's why Charlie calls me Warble-lip,' and she gave me a little lecture about acknowledging compliments gracefully.

For the rest of the evening Mrs Denham-Lucie played and we sang. There was a moment when I stepped back to watch and listen, when everything in the room and in the world beyond seemed to be in harmony, a moment unimportant in itself but which I was sure I would remember for ever.

'Come again soon,' murmured Mrs Denham-Lucie as we said our goodbyes and thanks, 'and meet my poor little invalid. She does so want to know you and be friends. It's such a blessing to have friends,' and she pressed our hands and gave me a special look, I thought, as if to tell me I had been singled out and placed amongst the blessed.

'I wouldn't have missed it for anything,' said Aunt as we went home. 'I don't know where she learned it all.' Then, a little later, 'Cadences!' she exploded, but I was still under the spell of Mrs Denham-Lucie's soft voice and manner, remembering her movements in the flowing folds of her dress, and wishing . . . and wishing . . .

'To think of her getting herself up like that, just for us,' Aunt's voice broke into my dreamy state.

'She thought Uncle was going,' I said.

He wanted to know all about the party.

'There was a rose in the blancmange,' I told him, 'a rose stuck in it. A real rose.'

Aunt was pulling off her shoes, taking no notice of us. 'It was an instruction to me,' she muttered, 'that's what it was. She was showing me how far she's got up in the world.'

'She seems to have come down again,' said Uncle, 'however far up she's been, for here she is back in the same place.'

I was sick in the night and next morning was covered with spots. Uncle had seen Nurse gossiping in the street and my alarmed aunt sent him to fetch her. She came in smiling, then looked serious and asked if Charlie and I had been playing romps in a nettlebed. I hated her and shrank from her cold touch on my hot skin, and refused to answer when she asked me what I had been eating.

'Oh, sulks as well as spots, is it?' she said.

Aunt mentioned the party of the night before. Of course Nurse knew about that. She knew about everything in the village as soon as it happened, before usually.

'Tell me everything there was on the table,' she demanded – her way of gratifying her curiosity – so I told her I couldn't remember. 'Just the usual things,' I said.

'Just the usual!' echoed Aunt. 'There was nothing usual about all those lobster patties you couldn't stop eating.'

'Lobster!' cried Nurse. 'There you are then. You've got a lobster rash. You're the one who has the strawberry rash every summer, aren't you?' She looked as if she was enjoying my misery. 'We've been rather greedy, haven't we? So perhaps we're getting what we deserve. Nothing to eat today,' she said to Aunt, 'and plenty of water to drink. She'll get over it.' Looking at me she added, 'The wages of too much feasting is fasting. A hungry day or two will do you good,' then went away gloating.

'I hate her!' I cried while Aunt was dabbing my spots with calamine lotion, 'I hope she falls off her bike,' and I promised I'd knock her off it myself if ever I got the chance.

Of course Aunt called at Charlie's house during the day to let it be known I had a rash from eating lobster patties at the party. Mrs Denham-Lucie was most upset, they had been freshly made and sent by special delivery in a van from a high-class shop in Sheffield.

'Well, she's got spots,' said my aunt, 'however high-class it is.'

After this I sometimes thought Mrs Denham-Lucie didn't like me as much as she had seemed to for she often gave me a wary look especially when offering me something to eat, as if she expected me to burst into spots.

Chapter Twelve

We called it Zoë's summer, Charlie and I. Long after it was over certain cream-coloured roses, the mingled scents from meadow and hedgerow, the sound of cuckoos stammering from the woods, all revived the memory of its halcyon days. Halcyon. I said the word aloud, its sound was so pleasing to me, the images it evoked so magical. I wrote it, I looked it up. Halcyon, the kingfisher, once believed to have made its nest on the sea which remained calm during hatching time. I cherished the fancy of a nest floating on the waters, our kingfisher's nest of pleasure and pain skimming perilous seas which still to us seemed calm in that summer of 1934. Zoë, of course, was the rare and beautiful creature whose exotic visitation lifted it to the realms of fantasy.

Several days passed before she revealed herself. Uncle was at his usual Sunday morning recreation of tidying the rose trees in the front garden where he stationed himself, according to my exasperated aunt, to see and be seen by the church- and chapel-goers who walked past our house, one lot one way, the other lot the other.

This traffic gave him much entertainment, moral and social. 'Hypocrites,' he muttered as he snipped dead roses, 'fakes and shammers,' then called to me to look at the charade. 'It's better than usual this morning,' he said, 'it's the fine weather, they've all got their best clothes on.'

I was doing homework at the dining-room table while Aunt flitted about with a duster in the background, grumbling because he showed her up every Sunday by behaving like an infidel. 'And you're as bad,' she darted a sudden attack at me, 'you never think of going to church.'

In a conciliatory gesture I indicated the books on the table but before I could say anything Uncle put his head at the open window. 'You'll never believe this,' he said, 'I reckon Charlie's going to church.'

Waiting in the dappled shade of the ash tree was Charlie in a grey flannel suit and looking like the risen cream of all Sundays. Mrs Denham-Lucie was hovering in front of the bay windows, then out at last came Zoë.

Zoë Vardoe. Here at last she was, the elusive girl who was made from a fantasy, who owed her being to an enchantment in a forest at midnight and who, springing at least in part from a source unknown but of high degree, thus became the embodiment of my own favourite daydream with which I had comforted many childish longings. Not having known the flesh of my parents I had often pretended I was of a rarer lineage than theirs, a recurrent fantasy unwittingly reinforced by Aunt's insistence on my having been found under a gooseberry bush. Now this dream of mine was over. Somewhere in the back of my mind I said goodbye to it, and relinquished it to Zoë. It was her reality.

We shook hands and smiled, we exchanged polite regrets for not having seen each other before and assurances of seeing each other again soon and often. Uncle found a half-opened rose of a deep and thrilling ivory which she took from him with the careless grace of

100

one who was used to accepting tribute. 'A rose to a rose,' he said. Thereupon Mrs Denham-Lucie, with a co-quettish look, requested one for herself so he gave her a full-bloom which she deftly arranged on the slope of her bosom – bosom was the right word to describe it for it was moulded in such a way as to seem one not two.

For an exquisite moment we were gathered together in an idyll then Aunt broke into it by saying the last bell was sounding, they would be late for church if they stayed longer and it would be a pity for Charlie to spoil his first appearance there for years by being late, so they plucked him from the roots of the ash tree where he had been fidgeting in resigned impatience and moved in the direction of the bells.

Uncle's gaze as it followed the three was tinged with sadness. He looked at some dead roses and said what a pity it was, they were hardly in full bloom before they began to die. I knew he was thinking of Zoë.

'Roses must die as well as weeds,' said my aunt, 'that's one bit of comfort for those who aren't born roses.'

I returned to the books on the dining-table, almost wishing I had gone to church. 'I could get there even now if I hurried,' I said. To my amazement Aunt banged down an ornament she was dusting. I was surprised to see how flushed she was. Her hair, as always when she was disturbed, seemed to be flying in all directions from her head, but I still didn't appreciate the danger signs and murmured, 'I wonder if they'll sit in our pew,' my mind busy with the elegant disposal in church of Zoë and Mrs Denham-Lucie, and Charlie kneeling on our faded ancestral hassocks.

'Our pew!' The words exploded from Aunt. 'They may as well sit there, none of us is ever in it.' She paused then rushed on, 'Ever since I was a child that pew was like a second home to me – till your uncle got at me.'

His face appeared at the window. 'What's that about me?' he asked.

'I was saying,' my aunt continued more calmly, 'how much I used to enjoy going to church, but you've been so successful at making a mock of everything I believed in, it can fall down now, for all I care.'

Uncle looked shocked, and made a move away from the window, but she called him back.

'I clung as long as I could to a bit of faith,' she said, 'it lingered for a time in some little corner of my brain –'each hectic cheekbone was now a warning to us – 'but it's all gone now, all wiped clean, thanks to you,' and she rushed from one piece of furniture to another dusting madly, while I had the notion of her clinging to the last frail strands of some tattered stuff called faith, like a spider in the remnants of its web. Uncle and I had smashed the web and were now confronted by the distracted spider as it darted amongst the wreckage, duster in hand, clattering ornaments. I quickly tried to erase this picture and was full of compunction for regarding Aunt, even in metaphor, as a spider.

Uncle and I were used to being collaborators. We liked sticking together and looking down from the elevation of what we considered an intellectual freedom on the outmoded beliefs of people like Aunt who, in clinging to their superstitions, made our disbelief more potent and daring so that we enjoyed it more. Now it seemed she was moving over to us we were discomfited and began to close ranks. Uncle lost no time in discouraging her from sharing our cynicism. Far from trying to discourage her faith, he wished she had more of it. Far from interfering with her church-going he wished she would go more often. Trying to inject some humour into the situation, he added it gave him a bit of peace when she'd gone.

Aunt refused to smile, turned a deaf ear to his placatory remarks, flounced into the kitchen and began banging things about.

'It'll be the Haggard mountains for the rest of the day,' he said with a downcast look. Then, 'Where did it all start?'

'With the Denham-Lucies going to church,' I told him, 'and you giving them roses.'

'So it did.' He looked thoughtful. 'So it did.'

Later in the week when Mrs Denham-Lucie had an important appointment at the bank and wanted to see a solicitor, Charlie's father drove her into Welham. What with one thing and another it was late when they returned home.

They found consternation and confusion. As Mrs Denham-Lucie and her dozen little packages, followed by Charlie's father carrying larger ones, went through the front door they met Aunt coming out. She made me her excuse for rushing home and left explanations to Charlie's mother.

I had found an empty house and was making myself something to eat when Aunt came in. From her air of intense interest overlaid with concern and a tinge of guilt, I knew something was going on.

'Zoë was taken ill,' she answered before I could put the question. 'Charlie's mother fetched me, she was scared, she's not used to dealing with girls, you know. I took one look and sent for Nurse. I hope I did right.'

As far as I was concerned it was never right to send for Nurse and I said so. Poor Aunt. She had not done right and when she returned to Charlie's house, her hands full of homely remedies for the invalid, she found Mrs Denham-Lucie raging from one side of the room to the other. I was there, of course, and was upset to hear the attack on Auntie.

'The village nurse!' cried Mrs Denham-Lucie, 'Of all people the very worst, the most indiscreet, the last person in the world I would have chosen to see – ' she broke off, then brushing aside the beginning of Aunt's reply, said angrily, 'What gave you the right to interfere and call in strangers?'

'But, Lucy,' cried my nonplussed Aunt, 'the girl was ill. Neither of us,' she indicated Charlie's mother hovering in the background, 'neither of us knew how serious it was. Help was needed and we could only think of Nurse.' Aunt stressed the "we" making it obvious she had no intention of shouldering all responsibility.

'You should have waited.' Mrs Denham-Lucie's look was bitter both to Aunt and Charlie's mother. 'I wasn't away for a week.'

'But you could have been hours,' protested my aunt, 'you know what you're like when you're shopping, we couldn't wait, the girl could have died, losing all that – strength,' she quickly substituted the word as she caught my eye, and Charlie's mother caught my eye, and Mrs Denham-Lucie caught their eyes. Eye messages flashed round as the three women looked at me, at each other, and away again. Charlie's mother murmured something nobody heard then vanished thankfully to her part of the house. I decided I, too, had better go. Regretfully, because I was so interested in the collision of the two friends as well as in the mysteriously afflicted Zoë behind the scene, I went home and before I reached our gate Aunt caught up with me, grumbling about the thanklessness of trying to help people, *some* people. It had been Charlie's mother just as much as Aunt who had decided to fetch Nurse. 'But she's keeping quiet and letting me take the blame,' said Auntie.

I would have preferred to die rather than have anyone fetch that nurse to me, so I only said, 'What happened to Zoë? Was it an accident?'

'Call it that if you like,' said Aunt.

Nurse was a gossip. She went on her rounds every day in her navy blue coat and pudding-basin hat, carrying as well as the black bag on the back of her bicycle, a head full of other people's business all of which ceased being private once she had heard of it.

'You should have called the doctor from Welham.' Mrs Denham-Lucie was still aggrieved an hour or two later. She put her hands to her head, saying her brain was throbbing and, though Aunt had hardly managed to say a word, begged to be allowed a little peace and quiet for a time without any fuss or argument. Zoë would be perfectly well in a day or two, there was nothing to worry about. 'Girls do have troubles like this,' she said.

'Not all girls – ' and Aunt, who was smarting about that 'fuss and argument', looked at me in such a manner as to make me decide never to have any such troubles as Zoë's, once I had found out what they were.

When the atmosphere had calmed Mrs Denham-Lucie resumed some of her charm and said to Aunt, 'You don't know what it's like to be the victim of idle tongues. I don't suppose you ever will,' and she made being such a victim seem much more interesting than being like Auntie who was undeniably one upon whom idle tongues would never waste a single word.

I offered to play Ludo with Zoë or to sit with her quietly and Mrs Denham-Lucie for the first time seemed aware of me. She looked flustered as if trying to remember what she had said, then refused my offer but touched my arm pleasantly and smiled. I said good night and went into the back part of the house looking for Charlie but he had disappeared so I went home.

The doctor came next day and Zoë was soon better.

After this, to our surprise, Mrs Denham-Lucie struck up a nervous friendship with the nurse, entertaining her to tea once or twice a week and showing her what seemed to Aunt excessive affability.

'Lucy is always affable,' said Uncle.

'Till she's crossed,' replied Aunt. 'She wasn't affable to me when I did wrong and called in Nurse she's now so friendly with.'

'Perhaps she wants to keep on the right side of her,' said Uncle, in the dark yet hitting the nail on the head.

I was surprised such a person as Mrs Denham-Lucie bothered with any side of Nurse, the right or the wrong, both sides were equally repellent to me. Once, long ago, I had run after her to ask where babies came from, associating their disposal with her black bag and thinking if anyone knew their origin she did, and she spurned me, telling me to get away from her and calling me a horrid child.

Everything was peaceful again but, 'I shan't forget how Lucy Denham flew at me,' Aunt said to Uncle and me, 'when she wasn't there in an emergency as she should have been.'

'A storm in a tea-cup,' said Uncle. 'Let it blow away.'

And so it did.

Occasionally I saw Aunt and Charlie's mother deep in conversation which they had a habit of breaking off as I approached.

The summer grew hotter, soft airs coming over the meadows were intoxicating with scents of flowers and ripe grasses.

I never saw Charlie on the road to Welham. 'He's busy in the hayfields,' said Aunt.

Chapter Thirteen

There was to be a picnic in Long Meadow before the mowers moved in. Charlie, Zoë and I went together laden with baskets, flasks and bottles; or rather Charlie and I were laden, Zoë kept herself free of burdens and strolled between us as light as air.

The grass was knee high, full of moonpennies, plantains and top-heavy grasses bursting with seed, botany specimens I was supposed to be studying for matric. I should have been sketching and classifying them in boring notebooks. Instead, I gathered them for Zoë's hat.

We knew better than to trample in the long grass and dutifully walked along the hedgerows to the stream at the bottom of the field where we threw down our bundles and made a cradle for ourselves in a patch of deep grass, which Charlie said, the mowers could spare from their cutters in honour of Zoë.

When he came back from the water where he had gone to dip his hands and cool bottles of lemonade he said we were completely hidden and had better keep a look out for the two mothers and my aunt who were to join us for tea. He had been working from dawn to midday with the men in the Far Field but had wangled a free afternoon to be with us at the picnic. He said he was worn out, people seemed to like the idea of killing him with work, and he flung himself in the grass with a vast sigh and looked up at Zoë.

Sunlight filtered upon her through the mesh of her straw hat in quivering patterns of light and shade. He watched her as if he were in a trance, not speaking till she took a stem of long grass to count freckles on his face, touching each one with the end of the stalk, jumping from ten to ten thousand, then flinging the grass away saying it was impossible to count so many. He recovered something of his usual self after that and tried to be amusing, at my expense of course, I was so usefully at hand and he had a lifetime's practice at it. I didn't mind, there was such an air of ease and indulgence about the afternoon nothing seemed to matter, discord was far away.

We laughed as if we had newly discovered laughter, pleasure in each other, in the summer day, and in the sensation of laughing mixed together. Zoë was not particularly witty but her being there made Charlie and me more amusing, more daring in our humour, our mutual insults rose to a high pitch of metaphor and outrageous hyperbole until she was helpless with laughter and Charlie and I rolling about with it, then the last few bubbles of it gave way to smiles until we flung ourselves backwards into the grass and lay still, softened and purified by mirth.

When Zoë and I sat up again, to my surprise, Charlie's head was on her lap and he was looking up at her like a worshipper. I was forgotten and apart, though sitting so close in the nest of wavering grass, a kingfisher's nest with the sea of the meadow around it. Tomorrow it would be gone and the grass mown. Words came into my head, part of a rhyme Uncle had said to me years ago,

'Let me a partaker, not a watcher be.'

I had often seen that watcher bee. It was fat and stupid, drowsy and fumbling like bees at summer's end. Now with a pang, I thought, 'It's me.' I was apart and watching, often. I was apart and watching now, fumbling in my head for words to describe what I was feeling about the other two so close together in the magical kingfisher's nest. I was there and not there. I couldn't bear it, wrenched myself from my separateness and forced a way back into the scene by throwing grass at Charlie and trying to make him romp with me.

'Get off, you idiot!' He pushed me away, pulling bits of grass from his hair, then told me it was time I grew up and stopped being an ass.

I was restored to decorum less by his words than by my frock splitting at one side. Seeing me cast down Zoë asked why I was making such a fuss, it could be mended, if it had to be, but it would still be too tight, I was growing and it wasn't, so it would be more sensible to have a new one. Not this year I told her, my frocks had to last all summer. She looked surprised at this and asked if we were poor, then laughed and said of course we weren't, that was obvious, so why be so upset about an old cotton frock?

She didn't understand about Charlie and me and money. We were living in "quite decent" houses, our people owned "fields and things", we weren't starving surely. She looked at me and smiled at the word "starving". We tried to explain. We had lots of good things and of course weren't poor – the word had connotations of disgrace – but there wasn't much money to spend. Here Charlie made the usual remark about farmers being hard up. Zoë hadn't known about that and was surprised, not having noticed any signs of deprivation about him or his household.

'I'm always broke,' he said, 'and so is she.'

I nodded, then went on to explain our situation at home.

What we were wasn't called "poor" it was called

"careful" and was regarded as a virtue. Though money was protectively looked at before it went there had never been a time when we halved an egg or ate half buns to think ourselves frugal. Neither Aunt nor Uncle was mean. They couldn't throw cold porridge away without wishing there was somebody to give it to, so many were hungry and would be glad of it but were never on the spot when we had too much of it. We were comfortable ourselves but aware of the hard times we lived in and paid tribute to them by making thrift a virtue.

'Not me,' said Charlie, 'just watch me when I get any cash.'

Zoë, who had been only half-listening to me, now showed more interest and assured us she knew about the bore of not having enough money but it never stopped her having things she wanted, especially dresses, and when I said mine were mostly ones which had been handed down from my legions of cousins, this dress for instance, which I had considered very smart until it was too tight, she said I was a poor dear, and could have some of hers when summer ended, then laughed as she looked from me to herself, and shrugged gracefully at the hopelessness of her idea. As for her, she went on, she meant of all things to be rich, and cut me short when I began moral reflections about money and happiness and told me not to talk bosh.

Delight diminished now and I was relieved to hear voices. Aunt and Charlie's mother were coming with baskets and flasks of hot tea, Mrs Denham-Lucie with a large bright cushion. In a pale dress and curving straw hat she looked like a more portly version of the china shepherdess on our dresser at home. Her face was soft and powdery and she kept it out of the sun.

Aunt and Charlie's mother were in old cotton dresses. Charlie's mother had a face as red as a poppy and she

110

wiped it with a handkerchief. Aunt screwed up her eyes, making little fans of wrinkles. Neither she nor Charlie's mother seemed to be aware of how they looked, but crawled in the grass from basket to basket, not elegant, not caring about elegance, but Mrs Denham-Lucie arranged herself with careful grace on the cushion and took all the time the others were setting out the picnic to put herself exactly right in relation to the sun and the draught – her name for the dulcet airs wafting around us. She looked charming and graceful, but she was too . . . I groped for the word . . . too fancy for a hayfield, too young-looking, too fancy to be believed in as a mother. Somebody had said something like that to her, she had told us about it several times already. She had taken it as a compliment, thinking it amusing and delightful when she and Zoë were taken for sisters.

Charlie's mother wasn't old. Her face was plump and smooth as well as red. She wasn't young and she certainly wasn't fancy. She was more like a comfortable brown tea pot than a china shepherdess. And Aunt – nobody could call her fancy, but Mrs Denham-Lucie – I rarely called her Zoë's mother even to myself – she was fancy, and I wondered how it would be to have a mother like her, elegant and pleasant, full of gracious airs, a walking volume of the rules of etiquette. She knew the ways of the world, that other world beyond the one I lived in, and would by its standards always know what to do, and would never be caught at a loss or looking a mess. If she were my mother I would never wear dresses whose hems were let down, whose split sides had to be mended. She would teach me her airs and graces and lead me into fascinating society, the kind of society St Orbin lived in. My thoughts drifted till they came to the young lovers who had been my parents, whom I knew only from faded photographs and family stories and I remembered again that often in imagination I had transmuted myself from their modest rank to more impressive ancestry, had pretended I was of different flesh and blood from that of my busy bothered aunt and was a changeling from a rarer sphere.

My thoughts came to Zoë. Dreamily I considered her. She had a mother whose mysterious union with a high-born stranger had bestowed on her the qualities of my daydream. It was as if she had taken it from me, pinched it. What I imagined, she possessed in fact. Here a jolt shook my reverie, my heart jumped and I thought of St Orbin again. If Zoë were living my daydream, he, being part of it, would surely meet her. Fate must arrange it if only for the sake of dramatic tidiness. They would fall in love, they matched in looks, ways, voices – each had the proper cadences – each had a background touched with fable.

Panic shot through me and I cried, 'No, no,' and stammered, 'no thank you,' as I came back from my inner wanderings and saw Charlie's mother offering me a piece of cake.

Everybody looked surprised at the forceful way I refused it then Mrs Denham-Lucie said I was quite right, I'd eaten two pieces already, I must learn to say no thank you at table more often than yes please, or I would go on bursting dresses. Charlie's mother said boys always preferred plump girls, which I could see by looking at Charlie and Zoë was manifestly untrue, midges began to bother us, Mrs Denham-Lucie declared the grass to be damp and we went home.

For some time afterwards, instead of pretending St Orbin was around every corner in the woods, I dreaded seeing him and prayed his long-imagined appearance should be delayed until Zoë departed. I enquired as to her outings, anxious that she should keep away from the

St Orbin woods. I needn't have worried. They were too far away for her walks and she couldn't ride a bicycle. After a time I became resigned and left everything to Fate.

The next week I was at school but rushed to the hayfields in the evenings. Charlie was there already – it was all right, apparently, for him to miss school for haymaking – and so were Zoë and Mrs Denham-Lucie who took tea there every afternoon. Zoë's ivory skin caught a touch of the sun and everybody said how much stronger she was looking. She laughed and bloomed, ate as much cake as she liked, drank creamy milk and still looked like a sylph, but I, with Mrs Denham-Lucie's words burning in my memory, said no thank you at meals so often that Aunt grew angry and wished Mrs Denham-Lucie had stayed wherever she had been before she honoured us with her company. 'And I still don't know where that was, now I come to think of it,' Aunt mused, 'it's strange how much she talks and how little she tells.'

Between us, from bits I gathered from Zoë and scraps Aunt picked up from Lucy Denham, we got together a little of their *petite histoire* which it was called when too much of it seemed in danger of coming out. 'But I mustn't bore you with my *petite histoire*,' cried Lucy and was adroit in changing the subject.

There had been money from somewhere. Lucy Denham could never have earned from teaching the means to supply the advantages Zoë had obviously been given. She had not been to a high school like Fulford but to a prestigious boarding school in the south, though she was too delicate to be a full-time boarder and had gone home

113

on Fridays. Yes, home, for Mrs Denham-Lucie had taken a small house nearby for a year or too. 'Such an expense!' she cried. 'You can imagine!' She paused, making sure Aunt had time to imagine it, then continued, 'But the right school is so important, don't you agree?' Of course Aunt agreed. That was why she and Uncle were doing everything possible to keep me at the High School which, although I had won a scholarship, demanded expenses.

Mrs Denham-Lucie cut her short saying, 'Oh yes, the High School, not quite the same thing but I'm sure it's excellent in its way.'

'In its way!' repeated Aunt. 'All the staff have degrees, some from Somerville and Girton.'

'I don't doubt it,' said Mrs Denham-Lucie.

'And the academic results are outstanding.' Aunt looked at me for support. Yes, I said, they were, with the exception of mine, but not wishing to exasperate Aunt who was already looking heated I kept the last part of my remark to myself.

Mrs Denham-Lucie was not impressed. 'Oh academic!' She gave a slight smile. 'There are more important advantages about schools than academic ones.'

'Such as?' snapped my aunt.

Mrs Denham-Lucie hesitated. 'To be socially edifying – ' she was choosing words – 'to lift a girl . . . to . . . to elevate her in mind and manners. My darling Zoë could go anywhere.'

'Where does she want to go?' asked Aunt.

Mrs Denham-Lucie remained silent, but retained the slight smile which was infuriating Aunt.

'Where can she go that, for instance, Kate can't?' Aunt demanded.

Mrs Denham-Lucie gave a slight shrug.

Sensing the unamiable drift of the conversation I put in a few words to the effect that wherever Aunt hoped I was going I must matriculate next year.

'You'd better remember that a bit more often,' she snapped, 'and get on with your homework, never mind romping about the hayfields every night.'

So for a few evenings afterwards I was fastened to the books spread on the dining-table, fastened like a kite which strains in the wind, for as the muted sounds from the hayfields came to me and their scent drifted into my intellect, though my body was fixed, my head was full of Charlie and Zoë and of schools, elevating and mundane, and of confused speculations as to where I was going and when.

Chapter Fourteen

The old cherry tree which should have been ours, as I annually reminded Charlie, excelled itself that summer and he took daily tribute from it, pouring cherries like a libation before the goddess Zoë. I had scarcely a handful but she and her mother feasted daily. I was always too late to share the feast.

Charlie picked the ripest and brightest for Zoë. She hung bunches over her ears and laughed at him, she threaded their stalks to make cherry chains for her hair, her hat, her neck and planted cherry stones all over the place, saying there would be a cherry orchard some day in memory of her, and Charlie watched her every movement with adoration.

I don't know how much time he spent with her during the day. He spent none with me. I went to school. He didn't. Even when haymaking was over I never saw him on the Welham road or on the station. In the evenings sometimes I saw him with Zoë, taking the dog for a walk in the mown fields, and coming back with the moon already bright, then watched them go into Charlie's house. I began to feel excluded from their friendship. There were signs between them, frequent glances, references to things told or done without me, jokes I didn't know how to share. They had drawn a charmed circle around themselves, I was outside it. This feeling was intensified every night when I wandered about our house and orchard or cycled up and down the road and heard through the open window of Zoë's boudoir the music from her wind-up gramophone.

One evening when Aunt and I were strolling past the house for something to do Mrs Denham-Lucie saw us from her sitting-room window, called us in, then told me to go upstairs while she talked to Auntie. When I knocked at the door of the boudoir – how easily I had slipped into using the word! – my heart was beating faster as if I were nervous, not knowing what I would find. There was a divan heaped with cushions. Zoë in its depths was listening with her eyes closed to the gramophone. Charlie had his back to me. He was choosing records and didn't speak, but his back looked annoyed.

The room was not dark but filled with a pale gleam and moths fluttered in it, searching for a stronger light in which to destroy themselves.

Below, Mrs Denham-Lucie talked on and on. I could hear her every time a record stopped. Zoë hardly seemed aware of me and I knew Charlie wished I wasn't there, so I soon made an excuse which neither noticed and went downstairs. Aunt was ready to leave and we said good night.

Outside the front door we met Nurse who showed her false teeth in a false smile.

'Hullo!' she said, 'how's things?' Then, without waiting for a reply, told us she was going to pop upstairs for a peep at the invalid.

'She's listening to music with Charlie,' I said.

'Oh is she?' said Nurse. Aunt gave me a jab with her elbow and I said quickly I had only just come down.

'Oh really?' Nurse smiled.

Music began again upstairs and Mrs Denham-Lucie

appeared at the door of the sitting-room. She stared at Nurse who once more announced her intention of seeing the invalid and brandished her black bag as if it were a weapon. Mrs Denham-Lucie quailed before it and Nurse ascended the stairs.

'Silly woman,' Aunt said as we went home. Which woman did she mean? I took it for granted she meant Nurse.

'Zoë will be furious,' I said.

Aunt replied, 'I've a soft spot for that girl,' and sounded as if she were apologising for it. Knowing there was a "but" hanging unspoken I said, 'Everybody has and it doesn't matter.'

'What doesn't matter?' Aunt was surprised.

'What you were going to say about her and Charlie.'

Aunt hesitated, then said, 'She flirts with him as if he's grown up.'

'She flirts with everybody,' I replied, 'even Uncle,' and we both laughed at the joke.

Inside the house Aunt went on, 'I know Charlie's only a boy but he has feelings and she shouldn't encourage him so much.'

'She can't help being encouraging,' said Uncle. 'It's encouraging just to look at her,' and Aunt looked at him. After a time she said, 'Lucy's desperate to get Zoë married.'

'Married!' I cried.

'Yes, married,' said Aunt, 'and I can understand why.'

'Why?' I asked.

'So that somebody else will be responsible for her.'

'Why can't she be responsible for herself?'

'Why indeed,' said Aunt, then thanked God I was like I was and not like Zoë. I said I wished I was like Zoë.

'Don't say that,' she cried, 'you won't be any trouble, at least not in the same way.'

118

I was pleased with her approval. I hadn't been much approved of lately, but I was sorry too. I would have enjoyed being like Zoë except for all that lying down and not being well. Then Aunt suddenly snapped at me and said I didn't know what I was talking about. But I was sure I did know.

As I was going to school next morning an aeroplane appeared over the woods, circled overhead with its engine shut off then hedge-hopped over the fields till it was out of sight. I nearly fell off my bike with surprise and considered turning back to see what had happened to it, then had second thoughts and went on my way to catch the 9.13 to Fulford.

One winter, after some eye trouble caused by cycling in cold winds, I had been given permission by the Great Orb to take a later train at 9.13, the supposition being the world would warm itself for me during the extra hour. I regarded this permission as never having been withdrawn. Other Welham girls caught the 8.3. I continued to travel on the 9.13 which gave me just enough time to reach my form-room before the first lesson began. So far my movements had given no rise to any more serious investigation than a question now and then, to which I always had ready the brief but truthful answer, "Special Permission", and quickly changed the subject. I dared not risk my discreetly guarded custom by lingering on the road with temptation from strange aeroplanes so I went to the station.

There was nobody I knew on the platform. I wondered again why I never saw St Orbin waiting for a train. Surely he caught one sometimes to go somewhere, London, Sheffield, Cambridge. Welham station served the villages for miles around. But he was never there, I had looked and longed in vain. Now however, I almost, but not quite, preferred not to see him. Let fate postpone our precious meeting until Zoë was gone, If once they saw each other all would be over for me with him, or rather it would never begin. I looked at myself in my gym tunic and I mentally looked at her and was sure of that.

My head was occupied by such random thoughts when the train came in and I spun them round as the wheels spun round . . . love . . . St Orbin . . . Zoë . . . then saw by the station clock at Fulford that the train was late. I bolted to school and managed to reach the form-room door as the last girl went in. I fell into my seat, saved by the skin of my teeth.

Exams loomed, practice exams, rehearsal for matriculation next year. Laden with books and papers for revision we drifted outside and lay in the grass and talked of ourselves and our future and love, especially love, and longed to be free of blue serge and black wool and the bell which summoned us too soon from the brief respite of the field.

I had an extra maths lesson after school, a private lesson for which the fee was five shillings. The maths mistress was sorry for me, trying to help me to scrape at least a pass in matric. It was no good. Her earnest gaze bored into my brain, my eyes blinked with the strain of trying to look as if I knew what she was talking about. I was hungry. It would be seven o'clock before I had anything to eat. I fidgeted with desperate impatience. Perhaps because the maths question was about travel and speed I suddenly remembered the aeroplane I had seen on the way to school. It was painted in bright colours like something out of a fairground.

The teacher sighed and closed the books. Her voice sounded tired as she gave me some extra homework.

I had no money to buy even a bun and there was nobody to borrow from. On the station some Grammar School boys were putting pennies into slot machines and devouring chocolate. I pulled the girdle of my gym slip tighter. I was thinner and pleased about that. At last I was on my bicycle, making for home.

Something was going on in Long Meadow. Cows were there now it was mown, but people weren't interested in them. They were only interested in a brightly painted aeroplane. Of course Charlie was there. He was wearing a flying cap and looked excited. The propeller was whirring, the pilot ready to take off.

I spoke to Charlie but he yelled, 'Can't hear you, just going up,' then waved and called, 'Come on, hurry!'

I thought he meant me but he was looking over my shoulder. Zoë was coming towards us in a white coat, a white scarf round her head. Charlie ran past me to meet her, then helped her to climb into the machine. The pilot gave her a flying cap. She put it on instead of the scarf and it suited her, then she waved to the watchers.

Frankie Slack appeared at my side.

'It came down in the wrong place,' he said, 'had a bit of engine trouble, but it's all right now. Charlie's getting a free ride because it's been in his dad's field all day.'

I was thinking, why couldn't I go? Why didn't Charlie ask me? It was really our field, Uncle's field, more mine than Charlie's.

'Anybody can go up for five shillings,' said Frankie as if reading my thoughts.

'Why don't you go?' I asked. He said he hadn't five shillings.

'Neither have I,' I said. He laughed. 'You! Your uncle's got all this land.' I was tired of trying to explain about

121

money, how even if you had some land and a house or two, it didn't necessarily mean you had anything to spend, not actual cash.

'If I had my own land,' said Frankie, 'I'd work it myself. You wouldn't catch me letting other folks have it, rent or not.'

'Look! It's going!' I cried and we ran forward.

The aeroplane was slowly moving, gathering speed over the mown field. Mind the cows . . . mind the hedges . . . it lifted as I watched, soaring up and away, with Charlie and Zoë flying together out of sight into the sky, leaving me on earth amongst the lumpy cows.

O Watcher Bee!

Chapter Fifteen

One Saturday afternoon Aunt came to Uncle and me in the orchard and threw a bombshell at us.

'Lucy Denham's got a beau,' she said, then cut through our surprise and informed us he was very rich, lived in Sheffield and had just arrived next door in a large posh car.

It certainly was large and posh and looked as if it belonged to somebody rich. We had plenty of time later to make up our minds about that for we often saw it outside the bay windows waiting on Lucy Denham's pleasure. To me it became a symbol of power and wealth like those chained panthers and cheetahs which sit by the thrones of potentates and I looked in the owner for some of its qualities of controlled opulence and arrogance, but his quiet manner, black suit and thin figure, and the glassy gleam of his spectacles, disappointed me.

'He's ordinary,' I said.

'Nobody as rich as he's supposed to be is ordinary,' said Uncle. 'Doing ordinary things doesn't make anybody rich.'

I failed to be impressed. A woman like Mrs Denham-Lucie should have found a man equally charming.

'His money will do the charming,' said Uncle, 'that'll be enough for Lucy.'

At first Aunt behaved as if she had been bamboozled.

Lucy Denham had seemed to be so set on one thing, Zoë's marriage, now here she was with a lover of her own. I balked at the word lover and Aunt said I could call him what I liked, follower, admirer, hanger-on or beau, it didn't make any difference to one sure thing, Lucy knew what she was doing. She wouldn't have to worry so much about money. So much! I hadn't noticed she had worried about it at all.

Aunt knew better. 'Lucy's crock of gold whatever it is – ' here she paused to give us time to appreciate its probable capriciousness – 'wherever it is – ' another pause – 'can run dry. I don't think she's any firm grip on it. She spends a lot of time in scheming.' There had been unpaid bills, some by post and some – here was another pause as if to underline the next words – some delivered at the door. It was obvious who had supplied the information and Uncle suggested Charlie's mother should mind her own business.

'It is her business,' Aunt said, 'when people come knocking at her door.' Then, with a self-congratulating air, thanked God she wasn't obsessed by the desire for money and possessions and was able to realise riches don't mean happiness.

'Riches don't mean happiness!' scoffed Uncle. 'That's exactly what the rich want us to think, so that we'll keep quiet and let them get on with being rich.' They were both talking as if they were poor.

'We may not be poor,' said Aunt, 'and we're certainly not rich but as long as we pay our bills we can hold our heads up.'

I said I hadn't noticed the Denham-Lucie heads not being held up.

'Oh Lucy!' said Aunt. 'Lucy Denham would stick her nose in the air if she were begging for a piece of bread – not that she'd let it look like begging. If she wangled five pounds from you she'd make you feel she'd done you a favour.'

'Has she had five pounds from you?' Uncle was suddenly interested.

'Don't be ridiculous. Where can I get five pounds?' said Aunt.

'Can't you get it from the bank?' I asked.

'The bank! We'd soon be in trouble if we kept getting money from the bank.' She shot a side-look at Uncle. I couldn't decide if it was ironical or not. There was nothing ironical about the way he looked.

It was true, though aware of its importance, we were not obsessed by money, we hardly mentioned it. I had heard the word far more often since the Denham-Lucies came next door. The word "rich" occurred frequently in their conversation. Their first question about new acquaintances was, straight out from Zoë, 'Are they rich?' and from her mother a more delicate probing but always the same question in different words.

The Beau was rich, at least he had every symptom of riches, well-made clothes, the car . . . and the gifts. Such boxes of sweets and chocolates as I had never seen in Welham shops, such baskets of fruit and arrangements of flowers – ridiculous, said Aunt, and all the gardens full – such scent and gloves and scarves. Largesse was left behind him every time his black car slid away from the house.

There were signs of subtler gifts, an aura of increased comfort about the place, a lack of strain, an effulgence about its inhabitants, a look of peaceful plenty only money can bestow. Both Mrs Denham-Lucie and Zoë appeared in new dresses, one after the other, until it was said in the village and reported by Nurse, their church-going was nothing but a mannequin parade.

*　　*　　*

The Beau came every Saturday and we became used to the sight of him.

'Trust Lucy to fall on her feet – ' in spite of her theory about riches and happiness Aunt's voice was tinged with envy – 'she's just like a cat, I don't know how she does it. It wouldn't happen to me.'

'No it wouldn't,' said Uncle.

The affair between Lucy and her admirer progressed until it was open enough for them to stroll together through the village on Saturday afternoons, Lucy nodding to her acquaintances but never introducing him, not even to Aunt who declared as she watched them from a window, 'She's still not sure of him but she means to have him.' But when Lucy appeared at church, Beau by her side, Zoë a pace behind, and firmly stepped into the front pew, that was it for Auntie. 'She's got him,' she cried. 'He means it, and she means everybody to know it.'

We had no idea how Zoë was taking it. She was keeping in the background, was hardly seen except on the visits to church when she trailed slightly behind the other two as if not quite sharing their company, but it was remarked how kind the Beau was to her, how thoughtfully he waited to allow her to catch up with them and tried to draw her into conversation and was ever ready to pay her due attention.

I was busy with exams but was always avid when I came home for Aunt's daily bulletin as to the progress of the love affair, though it was weird to hear of "love" in connection with middle age.

'Love!' scoffed my aunt. 'That's nothing to do with love. It's an arrangement, and it'll be a highly satisfactory one for Lucy. She won't make any other kind, this time. Once bitten, twice shy.'

'She doesn't seem shy to me,' I said, 'she walks arm-in-arm with him now.'

'That's to hold herself up on her high heels,' replied Aunt whose heels, like her chest and her accent, were always obdurately flat.

She waited until Uncle was out of the way then produced some verses about Lucy which, after some encouragement from me, she began to read,

> 'Lucy Denham's got a beau,
> Do we know him? Oh dear no!
> Will he stay or will he go?
> That's what we are dying to know.'

She paused and frowned over the bit of scribble.
'It depends on the money in the bank,' I said.
'That's it,' she cried, and went on,

> 'He's got money in the bank,
> Big posh car and lots of swank,
> Lucy D. is fond of spending,
> Likes supply of cash unending,
> If he's plenty she won't wait,
> Soon will fix the wedding date.'

We said the last line together and burst out laughing. Aunt was still looking pleased and fulfilled with her creation when Uncle came in and asked what was the matter with her.

'She's just written a poem,' I explained, but Aunt modestly decried it as being only doggerel.

'If it's only doggerel,' said Uncle, 'you can read it to the next-door dog, he's scratching the door down, I'm surprised you haven't heard him.'

The dog made such a fuss I decided to take him for a walk and went next door for the leash with him frisking and barking around me.

'He's a looney.' Charlie appeared from the back of the

house. 'I don't know what he's got to be so pleased about.'

Charlie didn't look pleased. When I asked him what was the matter his reply was a shrug and a gloomy kick at a stone which only just missed the dog's leg.

'Come on,' I said to the dog, 'let's go where nobody is bad tempered.'

Charlie said he didn't know where that was, everybody he knew was in a rotten mood, then decided without any show of enthusiasm to go with us as nobody else wanted his company.

We went into the part of the wood where we had played as children. He was silent, throwing pieces of stick for the dog to fetch but it soon found better things to do, bolted amongst the trees and didn't come back.

Presently I mentioned the Beau, explaining that was what Aunt and I called him.

'I don't care what you call him,' said Charlie, 'I know what I call him,' and exploded into derogatory adjectives until he could think of no more. 'Coming here, spoiling everything,' he said at last, chopping the heads off a lot of nettles. Zoë was never free, had no time to share gramophone sessions or private conversations or walks. 'Her mother watches her every minute,' he said, then asked if I thought anybody had been saying things.

I immediately felt guilty about the saying of things between Aunt and me, but it was Nurse he accused. She was the gossip, the bag of poison. That was true so I didn't deny it.

After a time his latest grievance emerged. Mrs Denham-Lucie was taking Zoë to Sheffield of all places to stay for a week with the Beau.

To his disappointment I took that calmly. It was reasonable, if the Beau and Mrs Denham-Lucie were going to marry, for them to get to know each other better and spend as much time as they could in each other's company. That was all very well, he agreed about that, but why should Zoë be dragged with them?

'She's bored to death with him already,' he said, then, 'a whole week in Sheffield with him.' But added as if justice demanded it, 'Still, he did give me five shillings.'

I was surprised and impressed and curious.

'What did you do?' I asked, half expecting to hear he had refused it.

'Put it in my pocket of course,' he said. 'I don't get five bob very often.'

His mood had softened. We were now in our own most special part of the wood and I reminded him of the times we had played together there before we were at the quarrelling stage, and how we were lost and found like the babes in the wood, except that they were dead and we were not.

'It saved 'em a lot of trouble, being dead,' he said in a heavy voice, then came back to Zoë, saying what a rotten time she had to look forward to with the Beau as her stepfather and life in Sheffield amongst all those trams. 'I wish to God I was older,' he said. 'I'm no use now. Not a bit of use.'

I didn't know in what way he meant he was no use, but to comfort him I assured him how much Zoë liked him, everybody could see that, and he gave me a side-long glance as if to weigh what I meant. I only meant what I said and he seemed to realise it.

Suddenly he asked how old people had to be before they could be married, expecting me to know because of Auntie being a registrar. I reminded him she didn't perform marriages. She had a chance once to be a superintendent registrar and might have been the first woman to officiate at marriages but she would have had to live in Welham and Uncle didn't want to leave the orchard, and I cried.

'All right, all right,' he said, 'I've heard that a hundred times. Do you know how old, or don't you?'

I didn't know but guessed sixteen or perhaps eighteen, and Zoë was old enough. She was nineteen. I urged him not to worry about her. She would soon meet somebody she liked and would be married and escape from her mother and the Beau, then she wouldn't have to live in Sheffield, she would fly far from there, would Zoë. There would be no studying for university or a degree, no bothering about a career for her. He wasn't listening.

'How about Gretna Green?' he asked.

I laughed. That was for eloping – then I understood. Oh Lord! Oh Charlie!

He went on, 'Is it true they'll marry you quick, if nobody catches you?'

'You're too young!' I cried. 'She's too old. You're not fifteen till New Year.'

He was annoyed. 'I'm old for my years,' he said, 'and I'm not green like you. I've had experience, lots of experience you don't know about.'

Oh didn't I! I supposed he meant Ivy Holt. That sort of experience wouldn't be of much use with Zoë. He didn't look very old or sound very old and he wasn't as tall as she was.

'Even at Gretna Green you'd have to be more than fifteen,' I told him, 'and it's a long way. It's in Scotland.'

He nodded gloomily. 'And I haven't any money, only that five bob.' He gave a sigh. 'We'll just have to wait, that's all.'

I was amazed he could imagine Zoë would consider marrying him. He saw my amazement and assured me she didn't think he was a kid and didn't treat him like

130

one. She treated him like a man. He looked older even as he spoke and stroked his jaws as if to reassure himself that manliness sprouted there, and I remembered the light in the boudoir late in the summer nights. Sometimes there had been no light, only sound, laughter, music heard from the road, then silence after the music stopped. Uncle had said Zoë couldn't help being encouraging, it was encouraging just to look at her. Perhaps she didn't know when she was encouraging, or perhaps she had encouraged Charlie merely to pass the time because it was so boring to be stuck in our village after the whirl of life elsewhere.

'They're forcing her to go to Sheffield,' said Charlie, 'her mother won't leave her behind.'

I could understand that now. Changing the subject, or half changing it, I wondered how the Beau had become so rich. Aunt thought he must be a cutler.

'A what?'

I was vague – it was something to do with knives and forks. There were a lot of cutlers in Sheffield where they were regarded as important people with a great hall of their own, the Cutler's Hall.

'Cutlers,' said Charlie, 'I thought they were mutton chops,' and I laughed, then he laughed. It was a relief to be laughing.

'That black car looks like a funeral car,' he said, 'I call him the Undertaker. He looks like one.'

I rushed to agree. He did, he did, with his black suits and his look of not having grown like a natural man from a natural boy but of being cut out of black paper with a white paper face and –

'Oh you!' he said, gloomy again. 'You always go on and on, still the same old Warble-lip.'

This put me down but not for long and for the rest of the walk we were in a lighter mood, laughing at Lucy

131

Denham's beau, calling him the Undertaker and Mutton Chop, enjoying the insults in the same way people like sticking pins in effigies of their enemies.

At the edge of the wood we had to wait for the dog. I whistled and called but Charlie took no notice. He was in a dreamy state, his gaze far away.

'It's not just her looks,' he said as if he'd been talking to himself, 'it's everything about her.' He looked at me. 'Anybody can have fair hair and blue eyes, but dark hair and blue eyes, my God! That's different.'

'She's got IT,' I said, being generous in my mind to Zoë, generous and fair. She had IT. I feared I had none and didn't think Charlie had any.

'Oh, the IT girl.' Charlie dismissed her. 'Zoë's a thousand times better than she is.'

We both knew about IT from seeing film stars at the pictures. We had heard about IT, talked about IT, seen IT in action on the screen, and longed to have IT, the vibrant message of one sex to another.

'Zoë's got lots of IT,' said Charlie, 'she's so beautiful.'

I explained that you need not be beautiful, you could be plain, even ugly, and still have IT.

'Even Ivy Holt's got a bit of IT,' I said.

He turned an angry face towards me. 'You must be mad to speak of her now,' he said, 'don't ever mention that name to me again,' and he strode away, leaving me to wait for the dog.

Chapter Sixteen

Mrs Denham-Lucie and Zoë were soon swallowed by the black car and borne away, escaping Nurse by a hair's breadth as she cycled up the road. Balked of her prey she came to us instead, frowning when she thought nobody was looking, but putting on a pleasant expression when Uncle appeared. She propped her bicycle against the fence and opened the conversation by wondering why there had been such a hasty departure from next door – as if she didn't know. She looked as if she meant to stay so I went out at the back as she came in at the front.

Charlie was on the waste ground near the old stable, cleaning his father's car, a weekly task he enjoyed. He had opened the bonnet and was busy underneath, his fingers so deft they could have been specially designed for twiddling things. The usual farm boy was scything weeds nearby and their rank odour underlay the brighter scents of the morning.

I sat on the big gate which opened to the low street of the village and said the Denham-Lucies had gone. I thought he was not going to reply, then he said without looking up, he was there to be out of the way because he didn't want to see them go. He was still resenting Zoë's departure for Sheffield, but when I reminded him they had only gone for a week he pretended he didn't care. He was busy making plans and needed time to think.

'Not about Gretna Green,' I began.

'Shut up!' He looked at the boy then frowned at me,

saying things got around quickly enough without my blabbing.

I said if he were going to be insulting I would go, I had come out only because Nurse was in the house.

He flew into a rage at the word "Nurse". I understood that and said she still thought I was indecent because I had once asked her where babies came from. He was so startled at the word "babies" I realised I had touched a delicate nerve.

'Do you know what that old cat's been saying?' he asked.

I shrugged. She was always saying something, she said things about everybody, she couldn't help it.

'But they're not true,' he cried.

'They don't have to be true.' We both knew we were thinking about Mrs Denham-Lucie and Zoë Vardoe.

'And that's another thing,' he said, 'it's nobody's business who Vardoe was, except Zoë's.'

'And her mother's,' I added.

He slammed down the lid of the bonnet and said, 'Bitch!' meaning Nurse I supposed. I was dying to know which of the several rumours she had been spreading he had now discovered but he began to polish the fittings of the car and said nothing.

'I suppose she doesn't like the Undertaker,' I went on after a pause, 'she seems to have been pushed out since he came.'

He shook his head and said, 'It's not about him. It's about Zoë.'

I was quiet.

'Lies, all lies,' he said.

I still said nothing. He looked at me. 'The old cat has spread it around – ' he looked away – 'she says that Zoë, before she came here – I can't tell you, you're so green.'

134

'If you mean she nearly had, or was supposed to have nearly had a baby – '

He stopped me. 'It's a lie!' he shouted, and gave me an accusing look as if I believed it.

'I mean, I've heard rumours, that's all,' I said. 'She was supposed to be having – anyway she took some stuff and it went away, just before they came here. That's why she was ill, supposed to be why.' I looked away from him.

With a mixture of surprise and annoyance he said he didn't realise I knew about things like that.

'Don't be daft,' I said. He wasn't the only one who wasn't a child any more, was he?

He looked severely at me and said listening to lies was as bad as telling them. Though I had been put in the wrong I had no wish to quarrel with him, besides I wanted to hear more, so looked suitably repentant.

'Lies! All lies!' he said again. Now it seemed he wanted to talk. He was the one person who truly knew Zoë, the real Zoë. She had told him, during those midnight sessions in the boudoir I supposed, about her thoughts and feelings as well as about her childhood and life at boarding school. He knew about that, how other girls who were supposed to be so prim and proper had egged her on to go out at night with them for meetings.

Meetings? The word struck a memory.

'With fellows, you fool.'

'That's how she got the baby then,' I said. 'I mean how she would have got it, if she'd had it.'

'Of course she didn't – hadn't. Don't you start – ' he glared at me. 'But she was the one who was caught. There's always one who is caught and pays for the rest. Poor kid.'

I made sounds of sympathy. Mollified, he continued. 'She had a nervous breakdown over it, that's what her illness was, all because of the way they treated her at that rotten school. Her mother took her away and brought her here to get better.'

'She'd have left anyway,' I said, 'she was old enough.' Then, because he was touchy about Zoë's age, I tried to hide the remark by following it quickly with another, unfortunately equally delicate.

'I wonder why Mrs Denham-Lucie chose to come here,' I said, 'especially after what happened when she lived here before – ' then tried to bury that one too. I had never mentioned her past to anybody but Charlie wasn't for the moment bothered about Mrs Denham-Lucie's past.

'They were a bit hard up,' he said, 'and that's no disgrace these days. She thought it wouldn't cost much to live in a place like this, and she liked it before, when she was young,' a dangerous point but he went on as if unaware of it, 'and she wanted to be near Sheffield for concerts and things. She seems to like Sheffield.'

'Perhaps she knew the Undertaker already,' I said, 'and wanted to be near him.'

He looked indifferent. 'Then your aunt told her about Granny's rooms, and that was it.'

That was the "it" which had brought the unique acquaintance into our lives, unique and likely to be brief. I warned Charlie that from the first Mrs Denham-Lucie had intended to stay only till the end of summer when she seemed to be expecting a legacy or something, or perhaps marriage to the Undertaker had already been thought of.

'Yes, I bet she'd got it all planned,' he agreed.

We had worked out Mrs Denham-Lucie's schemes and his task on the car was finished. 'Get in,' he said, 'I'll give you a ride.'

I hesitated. He hadn't a licence.

'I know that, idiot.' He got in the car and started the

136

engine. 'I'll drive round here, get in or not, please yourself.'

I got in.

The farm boy reappeared, scythe over shoulders and said, 'Ee, thi dad won't 'alf be mad if he finds out.'

Charlie glared at him. 'He'd better not find out, then. Shift out o' the way,' and he drove forward and backwards and round the waste ground as if it were the ring at a circus, making the boy hop out of the way so many times he was furious and yelled, 'I'll tell thi dad on thee, see if I don't.'

The car stopped. 'Now don't say I can't drive.' Charlie was restored to good humour, but I told him he'd better not drive like that anywhere else, not with me in the car.

'Oh you!' he said, 'Warble, warble, old Warble-lip.'

As I went away I heard him arguing with the boy.

After Mrs Denham-Lucie and Zoë had gone life pitched to a lower key. Although I had seen far less of them than Charlie had I had been aware of their presence. The four bay windows were so often wide open, sometimes with Mrs Denham-Lucie in full view as she took the fresh air, music came out of them, so did the sound of voices and laughter, deck-chairs were often placed in front of them, pots of plants were on their sills, signs to keep us interested in a more exotic existence than our own.

Charlie must have been put to hard work on the farm. He was up so early and off to outlying fields, and returned so weary and so late he had no time for me even when I did see him.

I was on holiday. The sun was hot, full summer had arrived, enjoyment seeped through me, I stopped bothering about him and Mrs Denham-Lucie and Zoë and went to the tennis courts morning, noon and night.

When I was not on the courts I banged a ball against a back wall of the house.

Cousins of varying ages between twenty and thirty-five appeared from other places to play tennis at our village club. They dominated it by their numbers and proficiency, and arranged tennis hops, and tennis teas on long trestle tables set on lawns around the courts. I had a week of pure enjoyment, the throb of the outside world and its troubles forgotten, until I saw Mrs Denham-Lucie at her window one night after the week was over.

It was still light, though late, and she greeted me as I strolled past the house with two racquets under my arm.

'Well, Kate,' she said. 'How are the cakes and puddings?'

When I told her I hardly ever ate any she nodded approvingly and came to the gate. I waited for her to say I was thinner but her gaze went over my head as if I were not yet important enough to be fully looked at.

I asked if Zoë were at home. She nodded, glancing at the boudoir window which was wide open. I was alarmed, thinking that Zoë was ill again after the arduous journey from Sheffield. Mrs Denham-Lucie hesitated. 'No, she's not ill,' she said, then added on a note of inspiration, 'she's feeling the heat.'

I said it must have been hot in Sheffield, but was quickly put in my place about that. They had been outside Sheffield in the hills, just the right place – here she lost herself in her thoughts. I was not sure whether to go away or wait till she found herself, but with a little shake of her head and shoulders as if she were throwing something off she said in a firm voice, 'It's just the right thing for somebody like Zoë.'

I said I was glad then, my social duties fulfilled, said good night and went home.

*   *   *

Uncle had been clipping roses and their scent was mixed with that of their own cut stems and of grass he had been mowing and of sweet williams and pinks he had been watering. He was filling a watering-can and greeted me as a stranger because he had seen so little of me that week and Aunt said she was surprised I remembered the way home.

Presently I ate supper in the orchard while they pottered about. It was too perfect an evening to be spent indoors. The thought of bed was hideous. People were in their gardens or strolling in the fields or talking in open doorways. Further down the street the postmistress was cleaning the post office windows. Children were still playing outside.

The moon which had been for some time only a faint disc now shone like a silver coin and reminded me of the half-crown Aunt had given me, her fee for a birth certificate. I felt rich, not rich like the Denham-Lucies were not but wanted to be, but for the moment rich enough for me.

I heard Aunt's voice further down the orchard. She had found somebody to talk to so I went to see who it was. Charlie's mother was at her wall, taking a well-earned breath of air. She had been busy all day, was wiping from her face the dew of her labours. She complained about the heat then the conversation drifted to the Denham-Lucies.

Aunt put her arm round my shoulders and we stood in the dusk close to each other, so close Charlie's mother seemed to forget we were two, not one, and that one, perhaps, should have been somewhere else. She lowered her voice and leaned over the wall. We did the same over our wall.

'They've had words,' Charlie's mother nodded in the direction of the house. She tried to lean closer, 'and hard words, in fact.' She sounded shocked, 'I was quite upset.'

I was tempted to ask where she was when she had heard the words as I wasn't sure if she had been part of the scene or behind it, but, 'I was moving about in the next room,' she went on, 'doing little jobs for them that they never seem to think of doing for themselves. I was making quite a bit of noise but I couldn't help hearing.'

Having thus exonerated herself she delivered her information. Mrs Denham-Lucie had been complaining of lack of appreciation. Nobody knew how much she'd done, how much she'd put up with, how much and how long she'd planned and schemed, and all for Zoë.

'Go on,' urged Aunt as Charlie's mother paused to take a gulp of air.

'I didn't hear the next bit,' she admitted. 'I couldn't stick my ear at the keyhole, could I? I'm not an eavesdropper. The girl went on about nobody caring for her or her feelings but said she was going to do as she liked, and nobody was going to stop her.'

'That's how they all talk,' said Aunt with a prod at me.

'And then,' Charlie's mother took up the thread, 'she burst out she shouldn't have been born, she was a mistake, it wasn't her fault she was alive, she should have died when she took all that stuff and was ill, and her mother cried. It gave me quite a shock to hear her crying.'

Here Charlie's mother remembered I was there and stopped abruptly. Aunt hadn't forgotten me but she knew I knew more than I was supposed to, and I was sure we'd talk about what we had just heard when we were alone.

'It'll soon blow over,' she said, and Charlie's mother said she supposed it would but there was an atmosphere. She had better go in now and see if Madam wanted anything before she went to bed. It would be a good thing all round when Madam was married. It would give the girl a chance to get away from her mother's eye.

'It doesn't do to hold the reins too tight,' she said, and it was my turn to give Aunt a prod.

'That's what I say to his father about Charlie,' said his mother, 'don't hold the reins too tight,' and we drifted away as the church clock boomed midnight.

As I went to bed my thoughts were of the Denham-Lucies and words kept repeating themselves in my head, it doesn't do to hold the reins too tight, the reins too tight.

But who was holding the reins and who was being held in them?

Chapter Seventeen

On such a night it was impossible to sleep. The moon, compelling and brilliant, sent down its rays. Their effect on me was sudden and strong. I obeyed their call, dressed quickly, and went out.

It was cool now, velvety cool, and thrilling to be alone in the secret life of the night.

But I was not alone. The window of Zoë's room was wide open and she leaned on the sill gazing at the moon. I startled her when I spoke. When she recovered she told me her head had ached from the heat, but was better now. I said I was going to roam about till the moon went down. Something extraordinary might happen, I could feel it in my bones, moonlight makes people mad, and I laughed. She warned me to be quiet. Her mother had taken a sleeping draught, her nerves had been troublesome, but she might not be asleep yet and I was standing outside her open window on the ground floor. I quickly moved away from it and was quiet for a time and so was Zoë.

She was Juliet, her cheek upon her hand, and Romeo in tennis shoes came round a corner of the house.

'Hullo, Charlie,' I said, but his eyes were on Zoë.

'Couldn't sleep,' he said, then, 'I've been trying to see you all day,' but she only smiled in answer.

'Shall I see you tomorrow?' he asked, looking miserable.

'You mean today,' I said, but he took no notice of me.

Zoë smiled again. She didn't know when she would see him. Her mother had things for her to do.

'Everything's changing,' he said in a mournful voice, then became aware of me and asked why I was hanging about at that time of night. I said I was going for a walk, and made bold by the exuberant moonlight, suggested they both come with me.

'Good idea,' he said, but Zoë put her head on her arms. She had done enough walking in Sheffield.

An owl hooted from the woods and in Low Street some cats squawked.

'Let's go for a drive then,' said Charlie.

Zoë lifted her head.

'What in?' I asked. 'A wheelbarrow?'

'You're smart tonight, Warble-lip. In Dad's car of course. Come on.'

Zoë hesitated, but was tempted. I too hesitated. I knew Charlie's driving but the night was touching me with a delicate frenzy. 'Oh come on!' I cried. 'The car's at the bottom of the orchard,' said Charlie, 'we can go the Low Street way. Nobody will know.'

My heart began to thump. This extraordinary night. It was beginning, had begun. Zoë was agreeing, was coming down. Soon she was with us, a white coat over her white dress. Charlie took her hand and we ran down to the waste ground where the car was ready and waiting, inviting us to madness.

A voice in my head said, 'He can't drive,' but I stifled it and opened the big gate. Charlie helped Zoë into the car then started the engine. After a lot of noise and some backward and forward jerks and leaps he drove into the street. As I shut the gate I thought they might go without me but he called to me to hop in quick, saying while I was messing about somebody would catch us. Immediately a picture of flight and pursuit shot into my brain, of Charlie and Zoë, her mother and the Undertaker pell-mell on the road to Gretna Green, but the car was moving, I fell into the back seat. 'We've done it,' cried Charlie. 'Nobody can stop us now.'

Whatever his restraints and tensions had been they were dispersed by the flowing air of the night and the bright rays of the moon. Zoë too was influenced, her usual dreamy indifference blown away. She tore off the scarf she had just put on and laughed as if she had never had a headache in her life. We sang and joked, and screamed when Charlie drove from side to side of the road and bumped the grass verges, though the voice inside my head still tried to make itself heard. Was it really so funny to be so dangerous? But I laughed as loudly as they did. The white road enticed us on, rabbits scurried to and fro, their eyes gleaming in the headlights.

As we rushed through a village, to my amazement Zoë leaped from her seat, flung back her head screaming for speed, more speed, she must have speed, shrieking to sleeping people to wake and come out, they were missing everything. She laughed as if she too were touched by the moon, and urged Charlie to make the car fly like an aeroplane, like the aeroplane they flew in before, and never let it come down, then she flopped in a heap while I looked behind to see if lights came on in the village.

'We're going to Sherwood,' yelled Charlie, and Zoë, at the sound of the name, came to life again as if the vital forces of the night were sparkling in her blood, and I thought of that other moonlight night, that other mad-cap expedition to Sherwood and wondered if her mother had ever told her about it.

*　　*　　*

There is something about forests, particularly at night, which subdues frivolity and we were quiet as Charlie drove the car off the road and stopped amongst the trees.

'This is it,' he said to Zoë. 'This is Sherwood.'

She got out of the car and looked around. This was her element, surely. Aware of its importance in her history I waited to see its effect on her. She yawned, said it looked eerie, then got in the car again, ready to go home, but Charlie insisted on a walk and we set off.

So many oaks were dead, their weird limbs flung in wild attitudes to the moon, they looked like ghosts. Soon we were deep in bracken. Scent from fern and root and the dark soil under the root flowed around us. My shoe came off. When at last I found it I was alone. I called once but was too startled by the sound of my voice to call again, I began to run, stumbling and falling, looking over my shoulder half expecting to see strange shapes amongst the shadows. As well as any other qualities Lucy Denham must have had courage.

Anger saved me from panic and I rehearsed insulting remarks as I stumbled in the bracken, then the path widened and I saw Charlie and Zoë so absorbed in themselves they hadn't even noticed I had vanished.

I stayed behind them, my anger gone, and wondered at the mysterious spell which had called Zoë back to the scene of her beginning that night all those summers ago. I checked. Nine months from her birthday at the beginning of May led back to just such an August night as this. This could be the anniversary of the night which had charmed her into being, and she in her white dress a wraith returned to commemorate it.

She and Charlie leaned together as they walked, his arm around her waist. She was taller than he was as well as older. I felt sorry for him. He was a fool not to see she was only a figure in a daydream and would fade away. I remembered St Orbin. What about him and me? She was to Charlie as St Orbin was to me, except that she was present and St Orbin was not, but it wouldn't make any difference in the end. Both would go their different ways, not Charlie's way, not mine. I didn't like my thoughts, they were confused and despondent, I had touched on a truth and wished I hadn't. I was left out again, on my own, watching like the Watcher Bee. I ran forward to the lovers and jumped on them from behind. They were annoyed.

We had come close to the road which wound through the forest, and saw a light ahead of us.

'Hell!' said Charlie, 'Police!' and suddenly became worried about driving without a licence, so we drew back amongst the trees and ghosted through them to the place where we had hidden the car.

It wouldn't start at first and he became more and more irritated. At last the engine caught and the car leaped backwards into a tree.

He was angry and it didn't improve his mood when I pointed out that if you drive a car amongst trees in the dark you are likely to hit something hard. At last we got away, without lights, until we were at a safe distance from the police further up the road.

We were not hilarious on the way home. A pall had fallen on us. Charlie was depressed about the dent on the back of the car, Zoë thought she had caught a cold. We were separate from each other, in body as well as spirit, and sat with as much space as possible between us.

The moon had gone, one of the headlights failed, but Charlie drove without incident until he killed a rabbit. We made him stop and look for it.

'Tomorrow's dinner,' he said, showing its corpse. Zoë screamed and turned faint and made him leave it at the side of the road.

146

At last we were home and Charlie put the car away. There was nothing to be done about the dent except to wait for retribution in the morning.

There was greyness everywhere. Morning had come and we hadn't been to sleep. There was a light in Mrs Denham-Lucie's bedroom. Lights in our house too.

'I suppose there'll be a row,' said Charlie, but Zoë didn't care. She said she would be in Scarborough tomorrow, she and her mother were going there till the end of September, her mother's friend had taken a suite in a hotel.

'The Undertaker!' cried Charlie, not bothering to lower his voice. 'You're not going to stay with him again!' and went on and on about it not being fair, 'After all you said, after all you promised.' His voice was loud and angry, and Zoë's was peevish.

I went away unnoticed.

Aunt was downstairs, looking haggard. When she began to speak I cut her short, saying we'd been for a drive in Sherwood, I was sorry if she'd been worried, we were back safe, then I rushed upstairs, flung my clothes about the room, got into bed and didn't sleep.

Next day the black car, driven by a chauffeur, took Zoë and Mrs Denham-Lucie away.

Chapter Eighteen

Summer drifted into autumn. The sun was hot but cast its shadows longer, the orchard enchanted with glittering webs and strands of mist. Aunt sang as she flung open the windows. It was her own weather, her birthday weather, she exulted in every turning leaf and burnished fruit. The profusion of the month accomplished something for the asperity of her nature and she became eager, sunny, blithe, queen of the falling rose and radiant aster.

I, too, was full of the gladness of life and gloried in the warmth of each new day like a ripe fruit stretching its skin under the sun. Uncle responded in his own way by softly wheezing as the golden pollen flew. The best time of the year, when all his precious fruit was yielded to him and he had asthma, one more example of the contrariness of Fate.

The Denham-Lucies were still in Scarborough. Picture postcards had come to both houses, but not from Zoë.

Charlie was exiled to harvest fields in outlying places. Either he had been formally banished as a punishment for the car-ride, or he had banished himself out of pique following a row over it. There had been some engine trouble as well as the dent and his father had demanded reparation in the form of hard work without pay. Why not without food as well, Charlie had asked, shrugging off his mother's sympathy, he might as well be starved as well as worked to death.

His mother told us this one afternoon as Aunt and I helped to dust and tidy Granny's old rooms which were looking more like Granny's now the Denham-Lucies had gone. Some of their embellishments had also gone. Different vans had stopped outside the house, different drivers had knocked at the door and requested the return of rugs, hangings and furniture whose time was up. The piano had gone, only the photographs in silver frames and a vase or two were left to remind us of the rooms' brief elegance.

Charlie's mother was mortified. Never had so many vans stopped at her door even to deliver things, let alone take them away. She felt shown-up and hoped nobody would think she couldn't pay for things. Not that money had been mentioned, everything had been hired not bought, the bill must have been paid, but people wouldn't know that. It must be a new-fangled way of going on and she didn't think much of it.

'It's the way of the world,' said Aunt as if the world were somewhere far away from our village, and Charlie's mother was partly mollified. If it were a way of that world out there it was probably right, as long as it stopped there, but, she sighed, it was the way of the world for a lot of things to be done as we in our world wouldn't do them; take Charlie – and she stopped, and I wondered if she knew about him and Zoë.

The denuded rooms now looked as if they were not expecting their tenants to return and Aunt asked a question shrouded in so much tact, unusual for her, that neither Charlie's mother nor I knew what she meant so she had to come right out with it. Were they ever coming back? Without waiting for an answer she added another question. Had they paid the rent?

'They're supposed to be coming back,' said Charlie's

mother, 'and they've paid up till the end of the month.'

'Thank the Lord,' said Aunt, 'that you're not out of pocket over 'em.'

'I wouldn't say that.' Charlie's mother looked dubious. 'I'm not exactly out of pocket, as far as I can reckon.' With a sigh she owned she wasn't good at reckoning and it had been a bit of a muddle, what with the chickens and the cream and all those eggs. 'I don't count the garden stuff and the apples, they're there anyhow, but the chickens and eggs are me living.'

'Disgraceful!' cried Aunt, a flush rising in each cheek.

'For two such delicate eaters,' said Charlie's mother, 'and one of 'em an invalid, it's surprising how many chickens and eggs they got through.'

Aunt said, 'Disgraceful!' again.

'Then there was the extra work,' went on Charlie's mother, 'not that I minded the cooking, while I'm making one thing I can make another, and I like to see people eat. It was the running about, up and down, from front to back and back to front, and the girl laid up and not a bit of help – ' for the all-purpose maid had put herself out of action by scalding her foot – 'I don't know how I kept on me poor legs, I don't think they could've stood it much longer.'

Aunt was shocked.

'But Charlie saw to the fires, when they were wanted, and they were wanted most days, I never saw such chilly folks, and the daughter was very good to him, always ready to help him with French and such-like, even late at night.'

French and such-like! Some hopes of Charlie doing extra French.

His mother went on, 'I won't be sorry when we're on our own again, there's nothing like having your house to yourself, but I'm not blaming you.'

150

'Me?' Aunt was astounded. Charlie's mother nodded, 'It was your idea about letting the rooms. I'm sure I'd never 'a thought of it myself. Still, they were standing empty and the money came in useful. These are lean times.'

Aunt agreed, yes, these were lean times, so it was a good thing lean was fashionable. She stroked her lean hips, looked at Charlie's mother's fat ones and smiled at me as she scored her small point.

Gardens flared into brilliance, field and orchard gave their bounty, the harvest was gathered in and Charlie's father once more performed the yearly rite of entertaining his harvesters, not in the manner of former times with beef and pork and pudding, but as befitted lean years with beer and buns and rabbit pies set on trestle tables on the waste ground near the horseradish patch. It was a modified feast but glorified by a man playing an accordion. Uncle said a bit of extra money would have been more appreciated by the men, they would have preferred the price of a few pints or a night at the pictures to this meaningless nod at the past, but Aunt was enthusiastic about the ritual and didn't want to see it go. It was a bit of old England.

'A bit of old fiddlesticks,' said Uncle.

The moon hung low like an enormous orange just over the hedge. Stars glittered, lamps winked on the tables and when Charlie's father turned the headlights of his car towards the scene we saw gold dust dancing in their beams. The scent from trampled grass grew strong and the rank underscent of cut-down weeds was like a message in the midst of light and revelry from the darkness under the earth.

Aunt said the place reeked of the old stables, the meal should have been set on the side lawn near the house. Uncle didn't care where it was. He drank a glass of beer and waited for the first wheeze which would be his excuse for going home.

It was the right of the all-purpose maid, though fully recovered, to sit and be waited on with the other workers, so Charlie's parents and Aunt and I were helping at table. Mr Pinder looked in for half an hour. He helped too. Frankie Slack came. Not sure whether his proper place was sitting at the table or serving at it, he fixed himself by my side, passed plates of buns and rabbit pie, and annoyed me with silly remarks whenever he thought nobody but I could hear. I soon grew exasperated and told him to look after Ivy Holt who was sitting with two smaller Holts at the end of the table furthest from the light.

Charlie appeared when supper was half over. He had been in the far fields shooting rabbits and carried a gun. I was glad when he put it down for he looked vague and incomplete and hung about in such a disconnected way his father called, 'Wake up, lad, or we'll all think you're as daft as you look.' Uncle was kinder and quietly told me to keep an eye on the boy and cheer him up a bit.

But the boy avoided me and it was some time before I had a chance to speak to him. When at last I pinned him down he said, looking past me towards the house, 'They're coming back. They've sent a telegram, they could be here already.' No need to say who "they" were.

"They" had been away for a month, now here they were, or rather here were Mrs Denham-Lucie stately in soft draperies and the dark form of the Undertaker a shadow between her and the moonlight. They had just arrived – the familiar cadences rippled through the air – had been in the house only long enough to wash and change but had rushed out, positively rushed, to see the charming and old-fashioned scene. 'That's us,' muttered Auntie in my ear.

What a pity such scenes were becoming so rare, Lucy's voice was going on and on.

'Oh shut up,' said Aunt by my shoulder.

Yes, Mrs Denham-Lucie would accept a glass, no, a tankard, how delightful! of good old English ale, such a refreshing change – 'From champagne, I suppose,' muttered Aunt – and so would her friend. So the Undertaker also drank ale which went down his long throat at full tilt. It had been thirsty work driving from Scarborough.

But where was Zoë? No need to tell us, lying down of course, tired from the drive, but she had promised to appear in half an hour.

The accordion player began another tune. The evening was so softly enchanted with the fullness of the harvest the harsh notes were mellowed in the golden haze.

I saw Charlie running through the orchard to the house.

A few couples began to dance on the lumpy grass. Frankie Slack pestered me to hop round but I was too busy, and I had Charlie on my mind. The scent of grass and rank weeds became more potent, the supply of ale thinned. 'When the beer's gone, they'll all go,' said Uncle, coming to rescue me from Frankie.

Aunt made us clear the tables, the maid having disappeared into the field with the stable boy. People were gathering their children together, thanks were given to Charlie's parents for the supper, somebody called for the harvest hymn. Mr Pinder gave the note and I had that inward jolt which marks a moment as never to be forgotten.

After the singing when people began moving away Mrs Denham-Lucie and the Undertaker were talking earnestly to Charlie's parents who looked more and more astounded. Whatever they were hearing Aunt decided to hear too and went to join them. Soon she looked astonished, but before I could go to find out what was surprising them Zoë came through the trees looking as insubstantial as the light and shade she walked in. She went to her mother's side and the Undertaker took her arm.

Charlie's father rapped on the table to stay the departing guests. Some of them had gone too far to be brought back but a few remained, the pickers-up of crumbs and snappers-up of left-over buns, Ivy Holt, for one, lurking in the shadows by the stable door. I wondered if she meant to go up to the loft. If she were looking for Charlie it was in the wrong place.

'Friends,' said Charlie's father unable to suppress the amazement in his voice, 'friends,' he pleaded to the disappearing figures, 'friends, before you go I've got something to tell you, an announcement, a bit of good news you can all share.'

That did it, that stopped the homeward drift. Everybody was interested. A few seconds of confusion went by during which parents hushed their children and dragged them back to the scene. There was an air of expectancy now.

'They think he's going to raise their wages,' muttered Frankie. 'Some hopes.'

I was sure the marriage of Mrs Denham-Lucie and the Undertaker was about to be announced but couldn't understand why my aunt and Charlie's parents were so dumbfounded. Surely they had expected it.

'Before you go,' said Charlie's father, 'I reckon you'll like to hear some news my missus and me have only just heard ourselves, and share in our congratulations to the lucky, to the happy –' he stopped as if he couldn't say the words and all we heard in the pause was a baby crying. He went on, 'I'm sure you'll wish joy on the occasion of their um – er – and join us in wishing 'em well, and giving a hearty clap,' and he began to clap, making as much noise as he could. People looked puzzled and Mr Pinder whispered to him.

'We'll clap, all right,' said the cowman, 'we'll clap all night if thee'll pay us for it – ' laughter – 'but tell us who it is we're clappin' for.' Everybody laughed again. Charlie's father laughed too, thankful to have something to laugh at. 'Why to be sure,' he said, 'our congratulations and best wishes,' he looked astonished at what he was going to say, 'best wishes to Miss Zoë –' words failed him at last and he took hold of the Undertaker and pushed him towards her. There was a gasp, then some embarrassed clapping, that silly Frankie Slack called for three cheers and some feeble hip-hip-hurrays were given, then people moved quickly, making sure they would get away this time.

I dodged Frankie, and hid behind the stable door till he had gone. Zoë, Mrs Denham-Lucie and the Undertaker went slowly towards the house. The Undertaker moved to Zoë's side and took her arm.

Charlie's parents, Aunt and Uncle and I set to work clearing the tables. Mr Pinder stayed to help as he wanted Charlie's father to go to the club for a game of snooker. They set off through the trees carrying a hamper between them and Charlie's mother followed with baskets of pots.

Only Aunt, Uncle and I were left amongst the ruins of the feast. We stared at each other, then – 'Lucy Denham!' said Aunt. 'Lucy Denham!'

'She's fooled you again,' said Uncle, 'I never thought she would, but she's done it. She's fooled you again.'

Chapter Nineteen

Aunt didn't intend to miss anything and bolted towards the house, leaving Uncle and me to carry the last heavy hamper.

We had struggled as far as the boothole and were having a rest when we heard a muffled sound. Somebody was crying and I knew who it was. So did Uncle. Suddenly the boothole door burst open and Charlie rushed out. There was just enough light for us to see the gun under his arm. Startled, we put the hamper down again and Charlie fell over it. Uncle grabbed his arm and there was a scuffle.

I was worried about the gun, expecting it to go off in story style and was already seeing headlines in print about the death of, or the murder by, the broken-hearted boy. Would it be manslaughter or murder if he shot Uncle, or if Uncle shot him? It was impossible to see whose hands were on the gun, or supposing – my heart gave a leap – Charlie intended to shoot the Undertaker or Mrs Denham-Lucie, or even Zoë? There were a number of candidates for the bullets, pellets rather as it was a rabbiting gun. Whatever happened I must say it was an accident – it seemed likely I would be a witness – but the gun clattered to the ground and was kicked aside. With presence of mind I didn't fail to note I put it behind a bush.

When I returned to the struggle it was over. Another struggle was going on however. Uncle was gasping and wheezing while Charlie made ineffectual pats on his back. I was familiar with Uncle's asthma and knew he would soon recover when the excitement was over but Charlie was agitated and told me to do something, not stand around looking useless, so I went for a glass of water.

They were sitting side by side on the boothole steps when I came back with it. Uncle was breathing more easily and Charlie was unburdening himself. Nobody understood him, at school or anywhere else, everybody was against him and trying to prevent him from being happy. Suddenly he burst out, 'It's me she wants, it's me she cares about, not that old dodderer, but she lets her mother tell her what to do. She's sorry for the old lady because she's had a bad time.'

Old Lady! Mrs Denham-Lucie! How would she look if she heard that? But Charlie was going on about Zoë. 'She promised to wait till I'm old enough,' he said, 'at least, she didn't say she wouldn't. Old enough! I'm old now. I've forgotten what it's like to feel young.'

Uncle was full of sympathy and, to my surprise, understood about broken love affairs. Everybody had them, or should have them, they were part of growing up. Charlie would feel different about all this when he was older, Uncle would bet his last ha'penny on it.

But Charlie was unconvinced and refused to be consoled. 'It won't make any difference if I'm older,' he said, 'I'll feel the same. I'll always feel the same about Zoë. What does age matter? When you're young, that is,' he added quickly. 'Of course it matters when you're old like him.'

Uncle sipped the water and murmured some interesting reflections, but Charlie didn't listen.

'It's because of the nurse,' he cried, 'spreading poison about Zoë and what she's supposed to have done. That's what brought it to a head. Now her mother wants to make sure –' He paused then burst out, 'It's Zoë I care about. I don't care what she did. I don't care if she ran away with that chap whoever he was, or if she didn't, and I don't care if she did nearly have a –' but here Uncle interrupted him and told him to be quiet, and not repeat gossip.

'Me repeat gossip!' Charlie was indignant. 'I like that! Me! All I'm trying to say is I don't mind what she's done, ever, if it's true or not, as long as it's me she wants now, and it is me, or she wouldn't have . . . we wouldn't have been together all summer, every night, well nearly every night. She couldn't have been pretending.'

'I should be quiet about that if I were you,' said Uncle.

'She don't care tuppence about that old man,' Charlie went on in spite of Uncle's attempt to stop him, 'we spent hours together laughing at him. It's her mother who's pushing and persuading. But he won't want her when he knows what she's done, or supposed to have done, and he won't like it when he finds out about me, and he's going to find out,' he cried, determined to have his say, 'because I'm going to tell him.'

'I wouldn't do that,' said Uncle.

'Why not?' said Charlie. 'It's the truth and he won't like it. He's a hypocrite. Where's the gun?' He began to look around.

'Gun?' repeated Uncle, a note of alarm in his voice. 'I should forget about the gun. You might have an accident and shoot somebody.'

'I wouldn't mind shooting him,' said Charlie. 'It'd serve him right if I filled him full of holes but I can't, it isn't loaded. I used all the pellets this afternoon.'

The atmosphere changed. Uncle's wheezing was over.

'It's Dad's rabbiting gun,' said Charlie, 'there'll be an

awful row if I don't find it.'

I wondered whether to disclose its whereabouts but decided to keep quiet for the time being. 'Come back and look for it later,' said Uncle, 'we need a bit of help with this hamper now. It's too heavy for Kate and me.'

I was caught in a beam of light as I passed the open side door and Mrs Denham-Lucie called me into the sitting-room. Aunt was already there, looking flushed and holding a full glass in her hand.

'You must drink their health, dear Kate,' cried Mrs Denham-Lucie, 'in champagne. You mustn't say no. It's unlucky to say no to champagne.'

Zoë was standing by the open window. She held an empty glass and came to the Undertaker for it to be filled. Smiling, he poured champagne for her then filled a glass for me.

This was the first time I tasted champagne. It was a pity it had to be for drinking their health. They didn't deserve my good wishes but I had drunk before I had qualms.

'Good heavens!' exclaimed Mrs Denham-Lucie. 'She takes to it like a Kate to cream,' and was delighted at her joke, then reading something in my face which was troubled or disapproving, she said, 'Oh you children, Kate, Charlie,' lightly and affectionately as if we were part of her fun.

'You're so serious,' she said, 'so adorably serious, but you must learn what is worth being serious about and what is *pour passer le temps*, a pastime, delightful but only a game.' She looked into my eyes. 'You must play the fool sometimes, you young people.' She smiled, 'It's part of the charm of youth, but you must realise when others are playing it, that's a rule of the game, dear Kate.'

I wanted to say Charlie hadn't been fooling. Zoë's way of passing the time hadn't been a game to him, but I couldn't find the words. Before I knew it I was drinking more champagne and so was Auntie, and words I didn't intend to say, pleasant words, silly words, were bubbling off my tongue.

At home I watched Aunt perform her usual nightly safety rituals with locks and bolts and listened to her going on about Lucy Denham and her devious ways, how money mad, clothes mad, comfort mad, she had always meant to be rich. In that case why didn't she marry the Undertaker? Wouldn't that have done just as well, instead of Zoë being pushed on to him?

'He prefers Zoë and he's rich enough to get what he wants,' said Uncle. I looked at him with new interest and respect, remembering his recent words about broken love affairs. I hadn't realised he knew anything about love affairs, broken or not.

'As long as one of 'em has him the arrangement will suit Lucy,' said Aunt, who was feeling less piqued, but I continued to be horrified by the union of youth and age and said the Undertaker, as well as being old and ugly, was dull, boring and not a bit exciting.

'It doesn't matter to them what he is, and what he isn't,' said Uncle, 'as long as he's rich.'

Aunt nodded and said money did its own wooing, which made me laugh, "wooing" had such a funny sound. Woo-woo! A froggie would a-wooing go. A frog, an Undertaker, or a mutton chop.

'I wouldn't marry him for anything,' I said.

'You're not Lucy Denham's daughter,' said Aunt.

'Zoë's been brought up to look for money and knows what she's doing. Don't worry about her. It's the man I'm sorry for. He won't get much pleasure out of it.'

Uncle, who had gone into the next room, came back in time to hear the last words and wanted to know whose pleasure she was talking about.

'Not ours.' There was the half concealed bite in Aunt's voice I was noticing more and more often. 'Nobody's bothering about ours,' at which Uncle said he was going to bed, and went.

'Early to bed and late to get out of it,' said Aunt, 'that's his way now. He's asleep when I go to bed and asleep when I get up. I could be out all night living a double life and he'd neither know nor care.'

'Oh yes I would,' Uncle's voice came from behind the door, 'at least I would in winter, I depend on you for keeping my back warm.'

The champagne had given me a headache. I leaned through the bedroom window and a cool breeze from the orchard reminded me of summer's ending. The halcyon time was over, the halcyon ready to fly away with a raven in a dark suit and a black car. I thought of the mythical Halcyon who, mourning for her lost love, was changed, as he was, into a kingfisher and with him built a nest on a sea calmed by the gods, and left for such as me her name to describe a never-forgotten summer.

My head burned. A confusion of memories rushed through it, images, scenes, sounds, the polished cadences of the Denham-Lucies, the hoarse misery of Charlie, the growing acrimony of Aunt and Uncle. All characters in turn had been the centre of some particular force, while I remained outside their spinning spheres, caught in their motion, sometimes whirled nearer as I breathed the essence of their dangerous energy, touched by their closeness but always separate. I had watched and listened and tried to understand, the watcher bee circling the kingfisher's nest but never inside it. Puzzled and mournful, muddled in myth and metaphor I got into bed.

Chapter Twenty

I slept late and woke to sounds of activity outside. The Denham-Lucies were going, the black car was humming. As I got out of bed my head spun and I had to sit still until it cleared, then I heard Aunt and Uncle at the front of the house and went to look out of their bedroom window. Goodbyes were being said but I didn't want to join in them. The Denham-Lucies, suave with success, were at our gate. Uncle, with a sideways look at Aunt, picked a last cool rose for Mrs Denham-Lucie who accepted it with her usual grace, but vaguely, as if her eyes were on richer tributes not far away.

Then, for Zoë, he sought amongst the leaves and found a bud, almost closed, but showing an ivory tip, which she twirled in her fingers while her mother sparkled to Uncle and the lean form of the Undertaker hovered nearby. Aunt apologised for my absence saying I wasn't very well, perhaps it was the champagne, and Mrs Denham-Lucie said it wasn't the lobster patties this time, was it? and anyway it was nonsense, a few glasses of champagne never upset anybody, you could give it to babies.

'Is that how you reared Zoë?' asked my aunt and Mrs Denham-Lucie said, 'Certainly, can't you see that just by looking at her?' then everybody shook hands and moved to the car. The Denham-Lucies were soon enshrined in it, the Undertaker drove them away and Aunt and Uncle came slowly back to our house.

Life gave a definite downward tilt. With a feeling of unutterable dullness I went downstairs where I huddled over a small fire saying I was cold and didn't want to do anything at all, but wanted to be left alone and not be bothered by anybody. Aunt immediately declared her intention of bothering me with a number of tasks which had been left undone because of the Denham-Lucies. Now they had gone, thank the Lord! we could get back into our old – she said ways but I said rut. I was bored already. Aunt repeated the word though she had heard me say it innumerable times before and wanted to know what I meant by it. What was this boredom everybody so readily talked about? It must be a plague of the times. She had never been bored. She had always been too busy, and could find me plenty to do at that very minute, there was no time for idle moping. I could begin getting my things ready for school in two days' time.

'Put all this Lucy Denham stuff out of your head,' she urged, 'both you and Charlie. They haven't done either of you, or any of us, any good, and get down to some hard work at school next term, it's matriculation year, remember.'

For the rest of the day she kept me so busy I hardly put my head out of the house but I escaped after tea. Hearing the next-door dog I thought he sounded as bored and dispirited as I was so I took him for a walk into the razed harvest fields where he rushed over the stubble, yapping and bounding and waving his tail in such fervent thanksgiving for being outside and free I felt better too.

I saw Charlie in the distance, coming from the far fields at a mournful jog on the debilitated milk pony, poor old Moco, whose days would soon be over. Already he wasn't worth quarrelling over.

164

I waved and yelled, 'Charlie!' but he only gave a glum nod. When the dog rushed towards him and yapped good naturedly around the pony's hooves he was called a daft thing and a bloody nuisance and told to clear off.

Not long afterwards I met Ivy Holt who was picking blackberries into her dinner pan as she went home from work, and I wondered.

A few weeks later a letter from Mrs Denham-Lucie came for Aunt. For me there was a small white box decorated with silver scrolls and bells. Inside was a morsel of wedding cake which I offered to share with Aunt. She accepted a crumb just to taste and supposed, knowing Lucy, the cake had been made by Fortnums or Harrods or some fancy shop in London.

I stopped the cake on the way to my mouth and said perhaps I ought to share it with Charlie. Aunt gaped. The crumb stuck in her throat. When she had finished choking I said, 'But I suppose they've sent him some for himself.'

'Sometimes I wash my hands of you,' said my aunt, 'you're so inept. How can you think Charlie wants a piece of her wedding cake?'

'Put it under your pillow and sleep on it,' said Uncle, 'it means something, I forget what.'

'It means you'll dream of your bridegroom,' said Aunt, 'and a fat lot of good that'll do you. You'd much better concentrate on school and getting a good matric,' and she threw the letter and the box on the fire.

Charlie's mother had opened the windows of Granny's devastated rooms to let air in and scent out and was busy inside, so Aunt and I went to tell her about the letter and wedding cake. She also had received a small white box and a mouthful of cake but no letter. 'Not that it matters,' she said, 'they've nothing to write to me about.' Of course, some people might have written a few words of appreciation, but it was the way of the world for others, like her, to do things without being thanked. She examined a broken vase which she could swear hadn't been broken before, then expressed the hope that they'd all be happy, mother, daughter and him.

'I don't know about him,' said Aunt, 'but the other two will have a rare old time with the cash.'

'Perhaps he won't be so ready with it as they've been expecting,' said Charlie's mother, 'he had a close look about him sometimes.'

'They'll manage him,' Aunt said. 'Lucy D. knows how to get blood out of a stone. As long as money's in the bank she'll get it out, and the daughter will do the same.'

Charlie's mother was shocked and said, 'There's better things to do with money than take it out of banks.'

Aunt sat in one of the old shabby chairs, pleased to see the place plain and tidy once more, the fancy trimmings gone. I had liked the fancy trimmings. The rooms had an air of sadness now Granny's old stuff was dumped in them again because nobody wanted it. The nest was desolate but the two women were oblivious of its pathos and were deep in conversation about its departed occupants.

'We've been thinking one thing,' Charlie's mother was saying, 'and all the time it was another.'

She had evolved a theory based less on facts than on certain emphatic morsels of conversation she happened to have overheard while dusting and tidying – for "they" never picked up a duster nor tidied anything – and now believed whatever we had thought about the Denham-

Lucie marriage plans was wrong. 'It was the other way round,' she said.

Aunt and I were not clear as to what she meant.

'It's a bit complicated,' she admitted, 'and I've never been good at puzzles,' but after some frowning thought she proceeded step by step with her analysis.

'At first we thought he was the mother's,' she said.

Aunt nodded.

'But, when it turned out as it did, we decided he must have been after the girl all the time.'

Aunt looked thoughtful.

'But she hadn't wanted him so the mother encouraged him to keep coming while she worked on the girl – not wanting to lose that money.'

Aunt agreed.

'And when the girl came round they still went on as if it was the mother who was his intended – I don't know why – perhaps they were ashamed because he was old and the girl so young.'

'Lucy Denham was always devious and enjoyed mystifying everybody,' said Aunt. 'If there was a roundabout way instead of a straight one she'd take it.'

'I've given it a lot of thought,' continued Charlie's mother, 'and it's my belief we weighed it up wrong. He *was* the mother's at first, I'm sure of it. I saw the way they behaved together. They meant it, I'm certain. He was content enough with the old one and she was thankful to have him.'

'Old one!' cried Aunt. 'Lucy D. would have a fit if she heard that.'

'Then, what nobody expected,' Charlie's mother prepared for her dramatic thump, 'the girl stepped in.'

'What!' cried Aunt.

'She stole him,' said Charlie's mother. 'She took him from her mother and her mother made the best of it.'

Aunt had never thought of that but was willing to consider the new slant of the story. 'It could be,' she said, 'it's unnatural in a girl to want an old man like him, even with all that money, but she isn't a natural girl, though she is Lucy Denham's natural daughter.'

'Perhaps that's something to do with it,' said Charlie's mother, 'and the girl had a grudge against her mother for it. I've heard plenty of rows.' She hesitated, then said, 'They had high voices, you see, and I've got good ears, they can't help hearing, and I've heard 'em, mother and child, going on at each other. "You keep out of it, mother," I heard the girl say, "if it isn't me he wants it soon will be." I was a bit slow at putting two and two together at the time. I thought she was thinking of our Charlie, but there was so much talk of money, then it came to me they might be thinking of what Charlie'll get when we've gone, because the girl said something about him not lasting for ever and I thought she meant my poor hubby. "He won't last for ever," she said, "then we'll have everything as we want it, as I want it, for I'm the one who's going to have the say over it." She promised her mother she'd always be comfortable and I think she said she would repay her for everything she'd done, then I got the idea she said pay her out for everything, but what was there to pay her out for?' Charlie's mother stopped but went on again without waiting for a reply. 'Yes, she took him from her mother, thinking he's so old he'll die soon, then she'll be free and have his money for herself.'

'And the power of his money, and power over her mother too,' said Aunt.

'I was scared it was Charlie she was after,' said his mother, 'when I found 'em together and pretended I didn't.'

'She's a minx,' said Aunt.

'She's a young monkey,' said Charlie's mother, 'upsetting my Charlie with her teasing ways.' She glanced at me.

'Kate knows,' said Aunt.

'The things that went on this summer,' said Charlie's mother. 'I've had my eyes opened. I can tell you,' and her round eyes opened wider. 'The times I've lain awake in the night listening for Charlie to go to bed, wondering if I should go to that boudoir, as they called it, with a walking stick, but I always thought better of it, there'd only have been a row between him and his father. But to think of it all going on between Charlie and her, like that, in my own house.'

Perhaps she wouldn't have been so outraged if it had gone on in a hayloft.

'But it's the way of the world,' she said, 'and I suppose Charlie's got to learn it, but he went off his food and I didn't like that.'

That night I kept thinking of Zoë's words to her mother, whether they were "repay you for everything" or "pay you out for everything", gratitude or revenge? I almost decided it was better to have sprung from a source, ordinary but known, than from a romantic but mysterious origin which could leave somebody unsure of who she was.

Chapter Twenty-one

I hardly saw Charlie that autumn. Perhaps he caught the 8.3 in the morning. As usual I took the 9.13. He may have taken a later train at night. Our paths never crossed. I knew he hadn't left school and I knew he was giving trouble about it at home. After his emotional upheaval in the summer he was making ever more desperate demands to leave and had fought a battle with his father which had achieved such a pitch of fury on both sides the old boy had threatened to take a stick to end it and Charlie had put up his fists and defied him to do it.

One morning, well into the term, I found myself in the disagreeable situation of being on the 9.13 with several girls who had missed the earlier train. I was displeased about sharing a privilege I regarded as mine alone and was dodging the usual impertinent questions as to why I was allowed to travel later than everybody else, when I happened to look out of the window and saw Charlie rush past it. In one lightning glimpse I was aware of a difference in him. Though not noticeably taller he was more stalwart, more mature, his face had harsher lines and I thought, 'I bet he's shaving.' Having produced him once Fate decided I should see him again that day.

It was because of hockey which I was more adept at dodging than playing. Between the cloakroom and the bicycle shed I was caught – skulking was the word used by the games mistress – and reproached for conduct unbecoming in a member of the matriculation form. I paid for my lack of *esprit de corps* with a session in detention and was on the station later than usual that evening.

I was the only High School girl on the platform, almost the only traveller. The train came in with lights on, the dining-car had tables covered with white cloths, each table a rose-shaped lamp. I wished I could eat there, and travel through the night, anywhere, everywhere, sleep on the train and wake somewhere else.

I sat in a corner seat staring at the damp station, thinking of nothing in particular then, as usual when my mind was vague, thoughts of St Orbin came to fill it. I was wondering which of my fancies about us I should engage myself with, the one in which we met after I was rich and famous, or the one about us meeting in the woods and he being immediately fascinated by me, a superior ME certainly not in school clothes; then the whistle blew and Charlie rushed on to the platform. He didn't see me but when the train moved I looked out of the window at the same moment he poked out his head further along and we stared at each other until a smut flew into my eye.

As I was leaving the station at Welham he overtook me and asked if I were bussing or biking, for there was a bus service several times a week between the station and our village. When I said biking he replied, 'Same here, we'll go home together,' and I felt a return of our old friendship as we walked into the yard of the Railway Inn. He must have felt the same for he said it was like old times and I said it was and it wasn't.

'Such a lot has happened,' I made haste to explain, 'it can't possibly be the same.' He groaned, 'There you go again, dotting all the "i"s and crossing all the "t"s, always so precise. You're just the same in that, anyway.' An argument might have begun but we both laughed, got on our bikes and began our journey in a friendly mood.

Presently I asked, more for the sake of conversation than for the answer which I knew already, if he still hated school. He exclaimed impatiently, of course he did, it was a pity I hadn't anything more sensible to say than that, and went faster, but I soon caught up with him.

It was good to be cycling with him again. Once we had left the street lights it was dark, but not pitch dark. A watery moon sent gleams between the clouds on to the wet road. The bicycle wheels whirred, evoking memories of our rides together in the past. Companionable sensations awoke strongly in me and again I was aware of a difference in him. I couldn't define it. I could sense a manliness in him which I hadn't noticed before. Whatever it was it was pleasing to me and I expressed pleasure in being with him again and asked if he too was remembering the miles we had shared. What a pity our friendship had become so tangled in other people's emotions and actions it had almost become lost in them and – 'Still warbling on,' he said, 'still the same old Warble-lip, I bet you'll never change. You'll be warbling on your deathbed, trying to put everything into words with your last breath,' then added that my lamp was flickering and would soon go out. 'You should have one like mine,' he said, 'it runs on an electric battery.'

The wind blew dead leaves around us as we rode in the swift, efficient style of those earlier times when, keen with hunger and the desire to reach home, we raced tirelessly against each other. Once more we were together, joined in the old familiar rhythm, wheel against wheel whirring amiably on the damp road, and remembered with benign amusement our past arguments about who could ride the furthest with no hands, who could ride faster, who went downhill at greater speed. We were in perfect agreement, perfect rhythm, perfect accord. After a time I mentioned the latest crisis at school. A girl in a parallel form to mine, a B form to my A, older than I was, though not much, had run away with a married man. The upper school was in such a ferment about it the Great Orb had called us together for a cooling talk. She had been grave about the offence, had stripped it of any romantic aspect and while not disparaging real love – she herself had once loved, we heard with astonishment – was contemptuous of the tawdry emotion which had sent the errant girl flying off to ruin, and here the Great Orb had made the famous gesture of distaste with which she handed back an unsatisfactory essay.

Charlie listened in silence then made it clear his sympathies were with the girl. 'I bet she hated school,' he said, 'I don't blame her for doing a bolt. In fact I'm thinking of doing one myself.'

'Not to Gretna Green,' I said, and annoyed him so much that when I repented of my frivolous remark and asked seriously where he was going he said he wasn't such a fool as to tell a warble-lip. I was hurt. When had I ever disclosed his secrets in the past?

'What secrets?' He denied he ever had any.

What secrets? The summer had been full of his secrets, most of which seemed to have become mine. I was too delicate to mention Zoë but what about him and Ivy Holt? He told me to shut up about her so I returned to the subject of his premeditated bolt. Forgetting the unwisdom of telling secrets to a warble-lip he said his plans were made. He would take plenty of provisions on the back of his bike and make for the caves on the moors round Sheffield. He paused so long I wondered if he were brooding upon evocations from the word "Sheffield" but he said it again as calmly as if he had never heard it in connection with Zoë or the Undertaker.

'It's a long way on a bike,' I said, then tentatively suggested the wood near home as being more convenient.

He had thought of the wood, naturally he had thought of it first. He knew every hollow tree and hole in the ground. 'But so do you,' he said, 'and I don't want you nosing around, trying to persuade me to come home before I've stayed long enough.'

'Long enough for what?'

'To get expelled of course,' he said, 'what d'you think I'm going for? I've got to make folks realise how much I hate school.'

'They realise it now,' I said, 'and it hasn't made any difference. No matter how you grumble you're still there.'

'That's why I'll do it. That's why I'll bloody well bolt.' He thumped the handlebars so that the bicycle bell rang. 'Something's got to happen, something drastic.'

Something did happen, a puncture in the back tyre of his bike and he responded to the inconvenience with such a string of maledictions against the world for its misusages of him I lost my patience and told him off. A puncture was nothing, we could walk home, we had walked further many a time.

'Clear out!' he cried. 'I'm sick of your preaching. I'll walk by myself,' then was so dejected at the way life was treating him I offered to let him ride home on my bike while I walked with his, but he said I was too bloody noble.

We trudged on without speaking until my bicycle lamp went out and he said, 'I told you so!' That broke the ice and gradually we drifted into conversation again, but into dangerous zones. I thought he had recovered from the crisis in the summer but he said only a fool would think he could ever get over Zoë. He had been thinking about the affair at school I had told him about and said old men who hung around young women should be shot. He hoped they'd catch the bloke and hang him. I wasn't sure which bloke he was talking about, the one in the school affair or the Undertaker.

'That tapeworm!' he cried. 'I can't believe she ever liked him, I can't believe that all the time we were together, she was thinking of him. She couldn't be so cruel.' But I believed it.

I remembered something Mrs Denham-Lucie once said to me when Zoë had been unkind to Charlie and I was indignant. I was to think of a cat playing with a kitten, pouncing and patting, purring but sometimes scratching, the scratch never did the young one any harm, the cat was being cruel to be kind, giving a lesson in survival. I regarded this simile as not very complimentary to Zoë, and seeing I was unconvinced by her bit of philosophy, Mrs Denham-Lucie smiled and excused my inability to understand on the grounds that I was very young.

'We all are,' I replied, meaning Zoë, Charlie and me, 'but I don't see why we can't be honourable to each other,' and Mrs Denham-Lucie laughed and warned me not to be a prig.

I had often thought of the affair since then and understood it better.

As Charlie and I plodded through the autumn night I

tried to enlighten him from my superior comprehension saying nothing hurts so much once it is understood, but he said that was rot, even if he understood why his leg had to be chopped off it would hurt just as much.

'You think Zoë was unkind,' I began and wouldn't be stopped, 'but you've been just as unkind as she was.'

'Me? Unkind? To Zoë?' He was astounded.

'I didn't say to Zoë. To Ivy Holt.'

'Shut up!' he cried. 'I've warned you.' We faced each other across my bicycle and I went on, 'Zoë treated you in the same way you treat Ivy. As Zoë was to you so you were, so you are, to Ivy Holt.' He began to speak but I hurried on, 'You pick her up whenever you feel like it, then drop her when somebody better turns up, never considering how she feels. Zoë treated you the same and you didn't like it but Ivy – '

'Be quiet,' he shouted, 'I told you never to mention her name again.'

'Which name?' I asked. 'Ivy or Zoë? They've both been the same to you. You don't like the truth but Ivy Holt – '

He hit me. By a sudden intuition I had moved my head or his blow would have caught me full in the face. I reeled back and my bike fell on top of me. As I scrambled to my feet he shouted, 'I kept telling you to shut up, serve you right if it hurts.'

'You shut up!' I yelled. 'It serves you right if you're miserable. I hope you'll never be happy again. You don't deserve to be. You've always been selfish and cruel. You drowned my chickens,' I bawled.

A thin moon came from behind a cloud. I saw his astonished face. 'You drowned my chickens, my little yellow chickens off the Easter egg. You held them under the pump, until they drowned,' and I sobbed, pain from the past suddenly rushing from where it had buried itself within me since I was three. I experienced that grief again and at the same time for the small me who had felt it, a maturer sensation of pity.

'It's no good saying you're sorry,' I wept as I dragged my bicycle on to the road from the path where we had been walking, and flung myself on the saddle and rode away as fast as I could.

I heard his voice above the wind and the rain. 'I won't say I'm sorry,' he shouted, 'I'll never say I'm sorry, because I'm not.'

But he soon was. A few minutes later, going full tilt downhill in the dark I rode over a broken bicycle which was lying at the side of the road and was thrown.

Chapter Twenty-two

I stared at the ceiling wondering why I was in the best canopy-bed, gave up puzzling about it and dissolved into the void again. Later, I realised the reasons for the honour – a crack on the head, some bruised ribs, scratches and cuts and a wrenched arm. I was lucky. I could have been dead.

After a few days Charlie came to see me, bringing some things from his mother and a bunch of flowers which he lay on my chest as if I *were* dead, then, settling himself on one of the wobbly chairs which haunted our bedrooms, he said I looked like a spook and asked what on earth had made me fly off like that the other night and land myself in such a mess, I almost apologised. It was good to see him. I was weak and peaceful and didn't mind what he said, his voice was so manly and resonant. Even Mrs Denham-Lucie had described it as a good voice and had admitted its depth and resonance. It wasn't well modulated, 'But you can't expect that from a grammar school.'

Without thinking I touched the side of my face where he hit me. He asked if I had toothache, and I spoke of something else. He didn't stay long. When he had gone Aunt came in with the local paper. On the centre of the front page was a wedding photograph, the bride in a white gown, the groom – 'It's him!' I cried, the shock reverberating around my cracked ribs. 'It's St Orbin.'

Aunt was pleased to have gained such attention. 'I

thought you'd be interested,' she said, 'you seem to have had the name on your mind. That trip we made to Orbin Old Hall must certainly have made an impression on you I never knew about.'

I was alarmed and asked what I had said. 'Nothing much but the name,' said Aunt, 'you just kept on about St Orbin and asking if he was here.'

St Orbin never would be here, not where I was. He had gone, escaped from his place in my private world. I hid under the sheets, trying to collect my thoughts. I had come a cropper again, this fall was as hard as the one from my bike, the shock even more painful. Now I was passion without its object, a mirror without its image, I was in a void amongst a million little pieces.

After a time I came from under the bed things and read the paper with the surface of my mind while underneath it seethed with protest and disappointment. It wasn't fair. Life had forestalled me, letting him get married, not waiting for me to grow up, not giving Fate a chance. 'She isn't pretty,' I said.

It was a society wedding. The guests were County. What was that? Aunt was vague. We lived in the county. County people belonged to old families. Our family was old, donkey's years old, as church records proved. Aunt searched for a definition. Perhaps it had something to do with owning land. Hadn't we owned, didn't we own, land? That wasn't enough. She grew impatient, what did it matter? She liked being what she was. What about the bride, I persisted, whose family name was famous in connection with pork pies, was she County?

'She is now,' Aunt was tired of the subject, 'and she's rich so it doesn't matter if she's not.'

She went downstairs. I looked at the photograph long and earnestly, then threw the paper to the bottom of the bed. Solemnly I expelled St Orbin. His place was empty but the need of emptiness is to be filled, somebody must come to occupy the void. My mind went round the circle of my world. Who? I had another look at the photograph. No she wasn't pretty. Serve him right.

When Charlie came again I was being miserable by the bedroom fire, and he asked if I were still mad with him. He touched his cheek with his fist and said, 'I never meant to be sorry, but I am.'

I didn't understand him for a moment, my head being occupied with more poignant matters than our quarrel, then I told him it wasn't important and we were friends again.

I was having trouble with my wrenched arm so when Aunt brought tea and went away it was Charlie who poured it. We became more cheerful and animated until our firelight idyll was broken by Nurse who blamed her late visit on the wretched Holts, whose youngest member had been squashed under a tree which his father was illegally chopping down in the wood. She apologised for spoiling our "tate-ah-tay", it did her good to see friends being so innocent and nicely behaved together. When Charlie got up to go she amiably gave him permission to stay by the window with his back to us, though all she did was count my pulse and look at my arm while beaming at some mysterious joke only she was aware of. She assumed her professional voice, soft and intimate, as if everything connected with me were unmentionable except in low tones, then leaning even closer, in deference to Charlie's presence, enquired if the innards were behaving as they should. I wasn't going to discuss my innards with her and answered with an indignant stare, then Aunt came in and invited her downstairs to tea.

Nurse straightened her back. 'I was saying how it heartens me to see these two such good little friends again – ' there was an all-round beam from her teeth and specs – 'I'm sure we shan't have any funny rumours about them,' and she followed Aunt downstairs.

'The place stinks of carbolic. You can tell who's been,' said Charlie coming back to the fire. 'I can't forget it was her who spread those things about Zoë.'

'It was she,' I said.

'That's what I said.' He frowned.

To change the subject I plunged into another almost as disagreeable. When he groaned I comforted him by saying my school affairs, which for so long had been disappointing, would no doubt because of the accident be even more so and a thought came from the dark into the open part of my mind and made itself clear. Now I would have an excuse.

'You're clever compared to me,' he said, 'in some ways, that is. You can put thoughts into words, mine get stuck, and if you don't know things you can make 'em up. I can't.' Noticing some textbooks he said, 'Ask me anything you like. I bet I won't know it.'

I chose a book at random and in a few minutes he had proved his claim.

Planes droned across the sky and he dashed to the window to count their lights, saying what he really wanted to do was fly. He had never enjoyed anything so much in his life as that aeroplane flight – he broke off, and I suggested he'd better get on with some hard work at maths if he wanted to do anything with aeroplanes.

'Bloody education!' he exclaimed. 'You can't dodge it. Every damn thing you want to do you've got to be educated first. They even have colleges for farmers now.

The old man's daft enough to think I'll go to one though he knows how much I want to leave school and work in a garage.'

He lapsed into gloom but showed a spark of interest when I said he should begin a new life with a different object in view. 'Think about aeroplanes,' I urged, 'then begin doing your homework. Begin tonight. Bring it here and I'll help if I can, as long as it's not maths.'

'It's maths I need, you chump,' he said, but didn't turn down the offer. He even said it would be due to me if a bit of education did "get into" him.

Suddenly he burst out, 'I'm sorry about Ivy Holt.' I was startled at the intrusion of her name. 'I never see her now,' he went on, 'well, I see her, I can't help it, she's too big to miss, but you know what I mean, I don't *see* her.'

I made it clear it had nothing to do with me if he saw her or not and he was disappointed. 'I thought you didn't like me going with her,' he said. Choosing his friends was his own affair, I told him, though some friends were a better choice than others, he would do well to remember that, anybody must be blind to see anything attractive in Ivy Holt, poor girl, deaf too with a voice like she had, and when one had heard voices which were as voices should be with every cadence and modulation in its proper place – I stopped, moved by the memory of the two exotics who had recently flown away. Deep water lay ahead but he only shrugged and said, 'She can go to China for all I care now,' and I wasn't sure who he meant, one or the other, the high or the low.

Nurse had gone. Aunt was downstairs playing the piano and singing, practising her part in a chorus from *The*

Messiah. As the sound came to us we stopped talking. Even Charlie was affected, and I fell into a reverie permeated by the music. Thoughts of St Orbin flowed through me for his exit was not yet accomplished. He would not be exorcised until his place was filled by someone else.

'I like the way she sings those twiddley bits,' said Charlie.

Grateful for his appreciation of Aunt's talents, I smiled at him then experienced a sudden startled throb. He had aroused a similar feeling in me once before when we were hiding in the barn during a game. It was after the Ivy Holt episode, that hay and horseradish Sunday, and I had wanted to say, 'Here I am, Charlie, I'm older now and surely as good as Ivy Holt,' but I said nothing and he did nothing. We lay side by side in the straw listening and waiting, I could hear his heart beating, and my own. When I began to speak he told me to shut up, somebody would hear. Somebody did hear and there were jokes about our hiding together, but we had nothing to hide. I was sorry about that. We had nothing to hide at all.

Now we were almost grown-up. My thoughts began to drift towards a future with Charlie in it. He saw me looking at him and gave a mellow smile which caused me another leap of the heart. Was I, but surely I wasn't, falling in love with Charlie?

Aunt came in and he made ready to go. He had stayed all afternoon and we hadn't quarrelled once. Charlie! Could he, was he fitted to be, the new occupant of my inner scene? I looked at him as he spoke to Aunt, for the first time dream beginning to merge with reality. When he gave me his hand I took it eagerly and got up from my chair, and up, up and up, past his shoulder, over his head. I loomed above him, then sank into mortification and embarrassment. 'Good God,' he said, 'you've turned into a telegraph pole.'

Aunt said I had been as tall for a long time but nobody noticed until I was thinner, then to my horror advised him to grow a bit more himself or he'd be left behind.

'I'm left behind already,' he said, 'by the look of it,' and went to the door. When I reminded him about bringing his homework later he said, 'Oh, that! I don't think I'll bother. I've remembered something else,' and clattered downstairs.

Later, Aunt expressed her pleasure that Charlie and I were friends again. We had always been fond of each other as children, she had once hoped, so had Charlie's mother – 'He's short,' I said, 'and I don't think he'll grow.'

But I would. He was right. I was a telegraph pole. 'What does it matter?' Aunt said.

But it mattered to me. I was sure it mattered to Charlie. Tall women, little men. People laugh at them when they're together.

As I got into bed I thumped the pillows. Why did he have to be so bloody small, and worse, why was I so bloody tall?

Chapter Twenty-three

One evening half-way through December I was in the boarders' common-room wondering at the irony of Fate. I had pitied the plight of those who were martyrs of the Great Orb's private boarding venture. Now, because daily travelling was too much for me after my accident, I was one of them and spent every night from Monday to Friday in her house next to the school.

I had little in common with my fellow boarders. Even those of my age were not in my form. There was no likelihood of matriculation for them, and no desire for it. Their first ambition was to leave school, and their second to be married. Farmers' daughters, they boasted of farming mates waiting for them and of the times they enjoyed together from Friday night to Sunday night every week – but here laughter and gossip descended into undertones and excluded me who stuck my head in books when I didn't have to and was cut out to be a teacher like the Great Orb and all the other freaks.

Suddenly I heard a scrap of conversation which made me look from my book. Somebody mentioned the Grammar School. A boy had run away, had left home to go to school, had not arrived, had disappeared. The train girls had heard about it that morning. Of course I immediately knew who the boy was.

The next morning I sought some Welham girls. Yes, it was Charlie. He had been in a row at school, a worse one than usual, and had bolted in the classic manner, leaving notes about having been persecuted. Persecuted! He couldn't even spell it. I was considered heartless for laughing and when suicide was mentioned and I laughed again, the girls were shocked. Rivers and ponds were being searched and there was talk of bloodhounds.

The upper school seethed with rumours about Charlie's home life, school life, love life. Was it true there was a girl in it somewhere? If so, who was she? How many times I was asked that question, yet nobody thought she might be me. I had a pang of disappointment about that.

Several days passed. Holly and ivy went up. There was no news of Charlie. I was sorry for his mother. In her imagination he would be a starved corpse before the week was out. I began to worry about my secret knowledge of his whereabouts and wondered if out of loyalty to him I should keep quiet about the cave on the moors, or tell what I knew for the sake of his family? I became increasingly annoyed over the burden of this moral problem.

Winding ivy round picture frames I imagined Charlie's lonely Christmas in a hole amongst the heather then, perhaps because of the green leaves in my hands, a name came to my mind. Ivy Holt. Had she gone with him? But no, she hadn't a bicycle and he was supposed to have taken his.

Charlie certainly disrupted upper school education that week, particularly mine just when I had begun to pay some much needed attention to it and fancied I was being noticed in high places for doing so. I became more and more irritated by the rumours about him and was on the point of disclosing what I knew about his plans, but it wasn't necessary. He had told half the world about hiding on the moors, had let his secret drop into many different ears, had been seen buying a ticket for Sheffield at Welham Station, had brought attention to what should have been done discreetly by making a fuss about the cost of taking his bicycle on the train. Suddenly I knew he was not where he was supposed to be. He was in the wood near home where he knew every hole in the ground and hollow tree. I knew them too, and I knew I would find him, and I knew he expected me to.

On Friday night Uncle was waiting at Welham Station. Yes, Charlie had disappeared. No, he hadn't turned up. Not a clue had been discovered on the moors. Some bones had been found, old bones, sheep's bones. He might have gone further north where the Pennines were riddled with caves and underground channels in which he could hide for months if he didn't starve to death, or drown. Those channels were notorious for filling with water.

Aunt was as delighted to see me as if I had reappeared after years on a desert island and listened with fascinated horror to my stories of deprivation on porridge and bread and jam, then decided I was exaggerating as usual. But she took me seriously when I confessed my arm hurt and put on her pince-nez to examine it and was sure it looked different from the other. I promised not to make a fuss about going to the doctor at Christmas as long as she didn't fuss about it now. My private arrangements for the time being were with Charlie, though I kept my thoughts and plans to myself, and soon went to bed.

When I was sure Aunt and Uncle were asleep I got up and went outside. It was eerie being alone in the wood in the middle of the night, wind-tossed branches overhead, dry sticks snapping underfoot, splinters of moonlight in the darkness. Suddenly there was a touch on my shoulder, a hand covered my mouth, a dirty hand, and Charlie said, 'You've been a long time coming. I've been waiting for ages.' When I was able to speak I reminded him he was supposed to be in a cave near Sheffield – that was where the clues had led – and he laughed.

'That was my blind,' he said. 'Clever, wasn't it? Put 'em all off the scent. All that messing about with my bike on Welham Station, as if I was going to Sheffield,' he laughed again, 'then I nipped back home, hid the bike, and here I am, nobody knows where.'

'I know,' I said.

'Oh you!' he said, then asked, 'What about food? Don't say you haven't brought any. Just like you not to think of the obvious. If I'd been you, if it'd been the other way round, food would have been the first thing I'd have thought of. But not you, oh no, I suppose you're ready to deliver a lecture.'

I was, and I delivered it. I told him about the police searching all over the place, and bloodhounds.

'Bloodhounds?' he was partly flattered, partly scared. 'Are you sure?'

I wasn't sure, and spoke of his duty to his parents.

'Have they learned their lesson?' he asked. 'Are they sorry?'

I explained I had been out of touch with home affairs as I was boarding for most of the time, and he groaned in sympathy. School all day was bad enough, but school at night!

'I come home Friday nights,' I told him, 'or I wouldn't be here. Anyway, it's not for long.' I wished him a Merry Christmas in the wood and asked if he would hang up his stocking.

'Very funny,' he said, then his stomach rumbled and

he said it was screaming for food, and wondered how long a body could stay alive without being fed. 'I shan't die of thirst,' he said with gloomy pleasure, 'because it's always bloody well raining.'

I heard myself offering to go home for food and he hugged me.

'Just what I was hoping you'd say,' he cried, 'but you've been a long time getting round to it.' Even as he spoke I was being shoved in the direction of home. 'Grab as much as you can,' he urged, 'I'm not coming back till they've given in about school and I'd rather not turn into a skeleton.'

At the edge of the wood we stopped. There was a bright moon, a poacher's moon. Suddenly the sky was crossed with moving beams of light. I wondered if war had broken out but Charlie was calm and knowledgeable.

'It's searchlight practice,' he said, 'from that old aerodrome outside Welham. They often do it. I've seen it before.' We watched for a time, then his stomach rumbled again and I was reminded of what I had promised to do. My heart sank at the thought of crossing the moonlight space under the searchlights, and of going into the house and coming out again.

'I suppose you're backing out,' he said, 'and once you've gone in that's the last I'll see of you.'

Without another word I set off at a run, the searchlights weaving overhead, turning a familiar scene into alien landscape, arousing sensations of fear and distraction, as if in rehearsal for some indefinable terror in the future, but soon I was in the house cramming food into a bag, into my pockets, then returned to the edge of the wood.

*　　*　　*

Charlie had gone. So had the searchlights but the calm moon shone. At a slight movement in the undergrowth I stepped forward, then shrank into the shadows as two figures came out of the wood and made their way, shadows themselves, along the fringe of trees in the direction of the village. Poachers. I decided to leave the food on the ground, go home and try to forget Charlie and the complications he caused in my life, then he appeared.

'That was close,' he said. 'I was sure you'd scream.' Without waiting for an answer he grabbed the food and began to eat, saying bread and stuff was all very well but what he needed most was meat, his muscles were withering away.

My errand of mercy now accomplished I was ready to go home but he begged me not to be a spoilsport, I wasn't a schoolmarm yet – he had long decided on my destiny – and invited me to see his dug-out. The word immediately evoked memories of our trench digging. I hesitated and soon was being led into the darkest and most private depths of the wood, the Orbin wood where trespassers were regarded as vermin and threatened on recurring dilapidated noticeboards with dire penalties, where keepers, according to Charlie, would as soon shoot as look.

I was pushed over a bank, through a tangle of briars and weeds into a hollow made by the roots of a fallen tree where they were wrenched from the ground. The hole had been overgrown by brambles and small bushes, and he shoved me in. 'Make yourself at home,' he said.

He had been preparing it since the summer in case of emergencies, but its amenities, revealed by a lighted candle, were few. He had deepened the natural hollow made by the fallen tree, had carved holes for storage places in the clay walls, and had made a fireplace with stones. There were empty tins which had contained sardines and condensed milk, a kettle and saucepan. Water trickled in a little channel outside, when it wasn't trickling inside, he said, which was often. The place was damp and cold and he was becoming tired of his own company.

I said Ivy Holt would drop in and keep him company if he asked her. He was disgusted. 'Girls are all the same,' he said, 'they never get that sort of thing off their minds. What I've been thinking about is food.'

There was a bed of branches placed over a waterproof sheet, a sleeping bag and a blanket over the branches. He invited me to sit, saying my back would ache from stooping. 'It's not so bad for me,' he said, 'I'm only half your size.'

We sat side by side on the strange bed with the sounds of the wood around us, and my mind drifted from Charlie and his troubles to a scene not far away where St Orbin lay with his pork-pie heiress, out of my life for ever while I sat in his wood with shivering bones and chattering teeth and I was suddenly furious at the inequalities of life, and jumped to my feet in a bad temper and said I was going home.

'Keep your hair on,' said Charlie, 'nobody's stopping you.'

It was a long way to the edge of the wood and he went with me, glad to be doing something to pass the hours of the night. I noticed we were walking out of the wood without the exaggerated stealth with which we had walked in, and it occurred to me he wouldn't have minded being caught, but nobody saw or heard us.

Before we said goodbye I tried once more to persuade him to come out of hiding.

'I'll come out when I'm sure of being expelled,' he

said. 'I don't want to be excused and given another chance.'

He was dirty and bedraggled and I was tempted to be sorry for him but I hardened my heart, told him he was a fool and needed a bath, and said goodbye.

'Come again tomorrow,' he called as I left, but I didn't answer.

When I returned to school for the last week of term Aunt, who had been delighted by the spectacular improvement in my appetite, played into my hands by giving me a large bag of food to take with me.

Of course I managed to leave it for Charlie.

Chapter Twenty-four

My boarding life finished a few days before Christmas and though I left it with joy I realised to my surprise there had been some advantages. I had found it easier to concentrate on homework every night and the Great Orb had been unexpectedly affable. Our relationship had mellowed while I lived under her eye, yet I was wary. Long adapted at school to an existence without tutorial warmth I was confused by the sudden rays of approval and did not immediately bask.

When, sailing in her billowy gown, she saw me drifting school's breezy corridors, hands in pockets, *dolce far niente* in my notorious slouch, and instead of censure gave me that humorous twitch of an eyebrow which like a secret sign from a high priestess to her acolytes was reserved for those in her good books, I was tempted to believe I could enter in, but the price was continued boarderdom, and I wasn't going to be smiled and eyebrow-twitched into that, so I left the uplifting regimen of small meals, hard bed and extra study and was soon at home, lolling in front of rich fires, having baths with scented soap and reading in bed by a light I could put on and off as easy as winking – electricity had come to our house.

'Charlie's back,' Aunt said as soon as she saw me but had nothing more to tell which I didn't know. She had been keeping away from next door to give things time to settle and recommended me to do the same. What with the gossip in the village and the rubbish which had been written in the papers about his home and school and the curiosity of the police who had been here, there and everywhere except in the one obvious place near home – but I kept quiet about that – there was plenty to be settled. 'I wouldn't like to be in his shoes,' said Aunt, 'when he has to face his father.' Then she left the subject of Charlie and began to worry about me.

Boarding school had not apparently agreed with me. I was thinner, my face was pinched, I must have been half-starved in spite of the extra food I had taken, and that my arm was no better was obvious from the way I winced when I moved it.

As a first step Nurse was summoned next day. She came at once but pretended to be run off her feet over more important indispositions than mine and implied I was wasting her time over a mere arm which probably had nothing worse than a twinge of rheumatism in it.

'Well! Well! How's things?' she began in her usual way. 'What are we fussing about now?' and pulled my arm and looked pleased when an involuntary Ow! escaped me before I could set my teeth, then still smiling said, 'Doctor. Hospital, x-ray I shouldn't wonder, the sooner the better if the nerves are damaged.' She paused and I searched in her spectacles for her eyes. Aunt grew pale.

'Yes, we'd better get something done straight away,' said Nurse, 'and not waste more time if we don't want any withering.'

'Withering!' repeated Aunt looking shaken, 'but it's Christmas tomorrow!'

'I can't help that,' said Nurse, 'I don't arrange the calendar. It won't be Christmas for me, I'll be lucky if I can find time to sit down to a mince-pie.'

She picked up the black bag she hadn't opened, asked what we were looking so miserable about, patted the arm saying, 'It won't drop off you know – not yet,' then stood at the door for a minute in contemplation of the dismay she had wrought. 'You'll have to grin and bear it,' she said, then as a passing shot wished us a Merry Christmas, and went.

Christmas morning came with a present from Aunt and Uncle, an expensive pair of trousers, the last word in fashion, bought by Aunt in the smartest shop in Sheffield after she had seen a picture in *Vogue*.

'Trousers!' said Uncle, 'a funny sort of present.'

'They're called slacks,' said Aunt, 'and they're all the rage in Paris and London.'

'They have been for a long time,' said Uncle, 'and in other places as well,' but we took no notice of him. I was delighted. They fitted perfectly. I was ultra modern, the girl of the age.

'Women seem to be aping the men, these days,' said Uncle, 'they'll be driving trains and buses next.'

'Why not?' snapped Aunt.

'And going down the pit and into the army,' he added.

'Then let's hope they do better than your lot has done,' Aunt said, 'the world may be better for the change.' She looked at me as I walked about admiring myself, and remembered the miles she had ridden with long skirts which got into the back wheel of her bicycle in spite of a contraption called a dress-guard.

'Girls were hampered to death in those days,' she said, 'always being called fast if they did anything out of the ordinary. If I were young now I'd show 'em. I'd go so fast you wouldn't see me for dust.'

'There's nothing to stop you from wearing trousers,' said Uncle, 'if that's what you want, though there's some would say you wear 'em already.' But Aunt ignored him and told me I didn't realise how lucky I was.

'This is the time for women,' she cried. 'Make the most of it, make sure you don't waste it, and never, never let 'em push you back to what it used to be.' But I had gone before she finished speaking, into the orchard to look for holly and ivy and Charlie and to wear my slacks.

As of old, as if he were expecting me, he was sitting on his wall looking excessively well and cheerful, all signs of recent deprivations obliterated from his appearance. He grinned as soon as he saw me.

'Done it!' he cried, 'I've got the boot, been chucked out.'

'Home or school?' I asked, with an immediate pang of disapproval for his thriving looks.

'School, you fool,' he said, 'I've been expelled, just as I planned.'

My muted congratulations did nothing to dampen his glee.

'There was a time,' he went on, 'when it began to look as if they'd take me back, through Dad interfering of course, and promising to guarantee my behaviour in future and all that rot, but they thought better of it, thank the Lord, and chucked me out.'

'What about the police?' I asked.

'Police?' He looked blank.

'I don't suppose they liked chasing around looking for you. I expect they've got it in for you, after all that trouble.'

'Trouble?' He opened his eyes, wide and innocent.

'Yes, trouble. If you're not in it you jolly well ought to be.' I was irritated by his complacent looks and the irrepressible way he had bounced up again. He wanted to know what crimes he had committed. Had he stolen anything, murdered anybody? He hadn't set anything on fire, had he? Anyway, everything had been settled, smoothed over one way or another, and he shrugged away the episode.

When I began to tell him how selfish he was, how self-centred and careless of other people's feelings, he broke in. Hadn't he tried to do everything the proper way, the reasonable way? Hadn't he begged and prayed – he paused to consider the word then said it again – yes, prayed to leave school, but nobody had listened. Nobody had cared about his suffering, he could have gone insane. He paused to consider that word too. 'Yes, I could've gone stark staring mad,' he said, 'for all anybody cared. They called me idle and stupid when I was the one with common sense and consideration, trying my best to save Dad spending a lot of money for nothing.' He waited for me to speak. I supposed he wanted me to admire him so I said nothing and he went on. 'You can't deny I was pretty smart. Nobody found me, you know. They had to wait till I came back volun – vol – when I was ready.'

I reminded him I hadn't been fooled by his false clues. I hadn't believed in the cave on the moor theory, at least not for long.

'The way I bought that ticket for Sheffield,' he boasted. 'You should've seen me making sure I was noticed, fussing about the bike – then I nipped home and hid it in the old stable.'

'Very clever,' I said.

'So I was,' he grinned, 'making a false trail, like a spy. I wouldn't mind being a spy in the next war. Look at the way I holed up without getting caught. That's what spies do. By the way – ' he looked around and lowered his voice, then had the impertinence to ask me not to mention his dug-out to anybody as it might come in useful again.

'You never know,' he said, 'when I might need it. I'd bolt all over again if I had to go back to school, or do anything I really hate doing.'

His gleeful looks clouded. There was one disappointment. All his plans were not successful. He wanted an apprenticeship in a garage or somewhere he could work with motors but no, he had to be stuck on a farm, not their farm, but one in Lincolnshire. 'Dad's got a friend there,' he said, 'who's a big pot with thousands of acres. That's where I'm going after Christmas, but it'll be better than school.'

His story at an end, I refrained from expressing more disapproval because it was Christmas morning, and I was pleased to see him. So far I had kept my lower half out of sight. Now I stood on the wall.

'Good God!' he cried, 'what've you got on? Are they your uncle's?'

'They're a Christmas present,' I told him and walked on the wall.

'You're more like a beanpole than ever,' he said. 'What a sight!'

'They're the fashion,' I began.

'They always have been,' he echoed my uncle, 'for men.'

I realised I was not going to be admired for my new fashion and asked sulkily if I could have some yew, I was looking for evergreens.

'I thought you were looking for me,' he said, 'that's why I was here, but come over and get what you like.' So, agile as a monkey in my slacks, I jumped from one wall and climbed over the other and he said I'd better join a circus, people in circuses were always looking for freaks. I let that remark go by and he soon picked up the threads of his important reflections. There was some idea of a farming college, in a year or so, if he could manage the qualifications. 'But there may be a war before then,' he said, 'and if there is nobody will keep me on the land. I'll join up.'

'Same here,' I said.

He laughed and called me a silly ass but I reminded him women had done war work in the last war and would do it in the next. He agreed about that but, 'I can't see you being a nurse,' he said. 'You'd faint at a spot of blood. You could work in a canteen, I suppose, or go on the land, though you'd soon be sick of that, it's not much fun. Ask Ivy Holt if you don't believe me.'

'I wouldn't do it for fun,' I said.

'You're too noble to have any fun. You could work in a munitions factory, there's not much fun there, I should think, with all those explosives about. No, you'd better stick to teaching. That's more in your line. Girls like you always end up as teachers, though nobody'll know you are a girl if you dress up like that.'

He was breaking branches of yew from the hedge and had his back to me. I wanted to kick him. I wanted to knock him down, this dunce who had abandoned all effort to be educated, this duffer who hardly knew a book from a bus ticket, this donkey, this self-satisfied dolt who was relegating me, ME of a matriculating future, to the boring routine of canteen or factory or school because I was female. I made inarticulate sounds of rage. Surprised, he turned his face to me. I smacked it.

Equally astonished, we stared at each other. I could see the marks of my fingers on his cheek then – 'You great lanky virgin,' he shouted, 'that's what you are and always will be, so you'd better get used to it, you and your trousers.' He thrust branches of yew at me. 'Take your bloody evergreens, and a Merry Christmas.' He walked away, his back shooting out rays of fury.

I gathered the fallen evergreens and hid in our orchard, huddled against the wall, crying inside myself at what he had said, frightened it might turn out to be true.

It was awkward having a row with him because Aunt, Uncle and I were to go to his house for a grand Christmas supper, a prodigal's return supper with, as he had mentioned with anticipatory gleam, a fatted calf, or in this case, a goose. We had been looking forward to the spree, even Uncle who hated putting his legs under other people's tables. Now it was spoilt for me before it began.

The scene was not as Mrs Denham-Lucie would have arranged it. Instead of bottles of wine there were jugs of cider and milk and tankards of beer. There were no lobster patties and confections delivered express from Sheffield, no bottled and potted delicacies from Harrods or Fortnums.

Everything on the table had been prepared by Charlie's mother whose culinary effects were substantial rather than exotic but looked festive enough to be regarded as a feast by the company who sat to enjoy it. Only I held back, remembering the delicate rarity of that other table in the summer and saw myself a being in the wrong world and didn't know how to find the way out of it.

Charlie and I ignored each other. Our mutual coldness was like a chill breath surrounding me. Inside it I was frozen and still, seeing everything from a point of ice, a ghost watching ghosts. The familiar had become strange, the living like the dead, everybody was old except Charlie and me and we were in hate with each other.

Suddenly my leg was kicked under the table. Nobody was looking at me and Aunt was at the far end of the table. I was puzzled but took the anonymous gesture as a hint to dispel my morose reflections. I looked round the table. There was Nurse. What a liar she was. She who had said she was too run off her feet to have any Christmas was certainly having it now, great plates and tankards full of it. She had cast off her starched blue and white uniform and wore a dress, a human female dress and it gave me a shock to see her in it, and was glinting and gleaming at a white-haired old farmer who beamed returns at her. It was weird to see her smiling and nodding at a man, even an old one, and even more weird to see one taken in by her and smiling at her.

And there was Uncle who never went to parties, seemingly forgetting his principles and prejudices and the ills of the world and the doom-laden future, sharing a joke with the chapel lay-preacher he had always called an arch hypocrite. I felt deserted.

Half-way through the evening we went to the kitchen and saw mummers perform the decayed remnants of an old local rigmarole. Some of the farm boys in disguise dragged in Frankie Slack who was half-hidden under a rug, pretending to be a ram. T'owd Tup, they called him. He wore a ram's head made from two pieces of wood joined by a hinge so that they moved up and down like jaws, a red flannel tongue hanging between, glass marbles for eyes. A lot of sheep's wool was stuck around it and kept falling off. Frankie was too old for larking about, he looked a fool and the general opinion in the audience was it was a pity he hadn't more sense.

I sat on the dresser and watched. The Tup was killed by the Butcher, then was restored, and the renewal of life assured for 1935.

Charlie's father called for a toast to the New Year and Charlie's fifteenth birthday. We must bury the bones of the old year, not a good year but bygones must be bygones. Everybody looked at Charlie who apparently had now shrugged off the peccadilloes of his past and was handing round glasses and bottles, smiling at everybody, and my mind came back from wherever it had been.

Aunt was sparkling over the rim of her wineglass as if champagne were in it. 'Is it real champagne?' I asked.

'I don't know,' she said, 'but it's quite real enough for me,' and gave a sudden giggle and asked for more.

Charlie came to us and offered to clink glasses and we smiled at each other for the first time that evening. I was sitting on a low stool so he could look down on me, which, no doubt, made him feel better.

For me the fun was just beginning and I dared him to smash his wineglass into the fireplace, and he did. The glass had been an heirloom, one of a few handed down from his great grandmother, but how could I have known that?

After New Year's Day he vanished, respectably this time, with a packed trunk in his father's car, in the direction of Lincolnshire and the great farm.

We forgot to say goodbye.

202

Chapter Twenty-five

One wet Saturday afternoon early in 1938 I put on a dilapidated raincoat and one of Aunt's old felt hats then, dressed to suit my mood of crashed hopes and chastened pride, went for a walk in the woods alone, the next-door dog having recently been run over by the bus which raced through the village once a day on its way from Doncaster to London.

My Fulford days, which had seemed so endless, were over and I was now in the second term of a year's student teaching with Mr Pinder before taking my place at a training college in September.

Charlie's fault, cried my tortured aunt when my matriculation, or rather my non-matriculation, results arrived. If my accident had never happened, if I hadn't lost months of study because of my arm and its various treatments – different doctors, different hospitals, then finally, desperately and successfully, a series of visits to a man in Sheffield who was considered a miracle-worker by some people and a quack by others – if it hadn't been for my taking matric a year later than I should have done, if everything in my life hadn't been thoroughly disorganised by the wretched accident which was caused by that wretched boy, I would now be eligible for university. But I was a next-best, with a mere school certificate and the promise of a place in a training college.

After a time Aunt disguised her disappointment,

staunchly refused to give up her idea that I was clever and took comfort in blaming Charlie and the accident. I absolved Charlie and was secretly grateful to the accident, having the uneasy suspicion that I might have done just as badly without it as with it. I had no intention of going to college, however, and of becoming a teacher like Aunt and my mother and hordes of cousins.

Under my bed lay a bundle of ardent scribble, visible result of a pastime turned into a passion, and that, not college, not teaching, was the refreshment of my hopes.

Charlie's new life in Lincolnshire had kept him away during the past years. We hardly ever saw him. His appearances were so brief we had no more than a few casual words with him before he dashed away to more excitement than our dull background would ever provide. Nobody could call him a Watcher Bee. He was a partaker, if anybody was, an eater of life, he gobbled it. No dreaming on the side-lines of other people's lives for him, watching but not content to watch.

Without noticing, I had walked far into the wood and had stopped where a grassy ride led into the heart of Orbin territory. Changes had happened, the Old Hall and estate had been sold, "changed hands" was the term most frequently used and nobody in the village knew whose the new hands were, nobody knew what was going to be done with the Hall or who was to live in it, the strongest rumour was that it would be pulled down. I leaned against a small gate and looked up the long drive, but everything was dripping with rain, mist and moisture blotted out the vista between the trees. The sensation of privacy was intense, deepened by the repetitive darkness of many yews, and exacerbated by notice-boards bearing newly painted threats to trespassers.

This was the place of my imagined meeting with St Orbin. This was where, I had pretended, he would ride down the glade for our meeting which never happened, which was never likely to happen now the estate was sold and he was gone, yet by force of habit, as I looked up the wide and mossy track, I listened for the sound his horse would make on the soft ground if he were to come now, if I hadn't given him up, or tried to give him up even as a fantasy. If I had ever met him it would have been here. If I were ever to meet him it should be now. This was the right place, now was the mood, this was the time, I was so utterly ready, this was the waiting point for the drama to strike, if life would only follow the rules.

I couldn't forbid the old fantasy, but it was not the same, I had grown away from it and both disdained and pitied the naïveté of my younger self.

I was still leaning on the gate, looking up the drive when I heard horse's hooves splattering on the soft ground behind me. I held my breath, hearing at last what in fancy I had heard so many times before, only half believing what I heard was real. The sound became louder, there was no mistaking its reality and I turned round. Out of the mist came a swiftly moving horse, a real horse with a real rider and they stopped beside me with a rush of sound and wet air and a shower of mud. Sitting high above me, blooming with vigour and confident reality was Charlie, not in the least dreamlike, very much his old self, laughing because his huge horse had splashed me with mud from head to foot.

'Hullo, you!' He beamed from his superior height. 'I thought it was you looming in the gloom.'

I said, because I had always imagined the rider

coming down the path towards me, 'You're coming the wrong way.'

'No, I'm not,' he said, 'I'm going there, on business,' and pointed up the drive with his riding crop. He grinned, 'I see you've got your Greta Garbo togs on.'

'And you your Cheshire cat grin,' I replied, disappointment at having reality instead of the dream beginning to wear off.

He was full of himself as usual and hardly bothered to ask about me but laughed at the idea of me as a teacher in our old school. I didn't explain I was only a student but let him go on about his life in Lincolnshire and the marvellous time he was having.

'I'm glad,' I said, though I wasn't. I was thinking, why can't I be the one having a good time, why does nothing interesting ever happen to me, then I realised he was saying he was engaged. Still busy with my own envious thoughts I asked, 'What in?'

He laughed. 'In what being engaged usually means,' and gave an impatient twitch to the reins which made the horse dance. 'My God! You're just the same,' he said, 'you never change. You're still so green I can't believe it.'

'Believe what?' I said.

'You don't know you're in the world,' he said. 'You'd better wake up before it forgets you're alive.'

It was uncanny how his words echoed my own mood of doubts and fears and I stared at him without speaking.

'God! You do look wilted.' He twitched the reins again. The horse did its little dance then gently but firmly put a hoof over my right foot. I should have spoken immediately but the moment slipped by.

I had been alone, deep in cogitations about my private disasters, ruefully contemplating an out-dated fantasy, being a problem only to myself, now I was under attack, and a great horse had put its hoof on my foot.

'I'm going to be married, you idiot.' He began to spell married but changed it to W-E-D.

The pressure on my foot wasn't exactly painful but wasn't exactly pleasant, more like the warning of pain to come than pain itself. I felt inert and helpless under this latest injustice of Fate. Words slowly formed in my head – would you mind moving your horse off my foot? Then I realised what an idiot he would think I was.

'Are you struck dumb or something?' he asked.

I sent up a confused prayer that the horse should move then turned what was left of my mind to his marriage. 'You're too young,' I said.

'You always say that,' he replied.

'You're only eighteen.'

'Well, she's twenty-one,' he said. 'Don't you want to hear about her?'

What I wanted was his horse to get off my foot but it was too late to say it now. He would have laughed himself out of the saddle.

'Is she nice?' I asked.

'She wouldn't suit me if she's not,' he said.

'Is she pretty?'

He hesitated, looking me up and down as if making a comparison. 'She's not as –' I had the mad idea he was going to say as "pretty" as I was, then in a flash realised the comparison would be with Zoë, not me, but he said "tall". 'She's not as tall as you, and not as clever,' he said, 'at least she doesn't stick her head in books.'

I didn't tell him I was far from being considered clever, recent events in my life had spoken for themselves, but asked more questions about the girl. She was the Big Pot's daughter, he told me, the rich farmer's only child. She was a good sport and had a marvellous seat on a horse. The word "horse" went through me from toe to top.

There was another stab when he said I should have learned to ride.

'I know I should,' I said, 'I always wanted to, but I hadn't a horse. You had it.'

He laughed. 'Poor old Moco, the milk pony. You never forgave me for owning him, you were always going on how he should've been yours.'

'So he should,' I cried. If life had been fair. The horse gently pressed my foot deeper into the soft ground. I drew in my breath. I must speak now.

'The trouble with you,' said Charlie, 'is that you think things should be yours because your family had 'em once but you're wrong. Nothing is yours unless you've got it.' He opened his hand and closed it again.

His horse gave my foot a final squeeze, then moved.

'Good old boy.' Charlie patted its neck. 'Quiet as a lamb but goes like the wind.' He hesitated, then said, 'I did give you rides on old Moco, you know, but you were always falling off.'

'No, I wasn't,' I said.

He patted the horse again. 'Of course, he's hers really, not mine, but I ride him whenever I like. I rode over this morning. Back tomorrow. I'm going into Orbin village now, with a message from Dad.'

I asked what was happening over there and he said nobody knew, even his dad couldn't find out, but, one thing was sure, there would be a lot of changes. He shook the reins, and touching the brim of Aunt's old hat with his riding crop, laughed as if I looked funny and said, 'I pity the kids you teach.'

'Don't pity them,' I said.

He was ready to go. 'By the way,' he said, 'talking of

school, were you ever found out about going on the late train, all that time?'

'Only at the end,' I told him, 'just before I left.'

He beamed. 'I'm glad about that. Good for you,' then rode away while I stood with one foot in the air and wriggled my numb toes.

Suddenly angry I yelled after him. He turned the horse round. My anger went. 'Are you getting married?' I asked for something to say. 'Truly?'

He nodded. 'Truly.'

'When?'

He grinned again. 'When I'm grown up,' then he danced the horse around and laughing rode up the long drive towards Orbin land, the place where the dream had come from. I looked and listened until I could see and hear him no more.

As I went home I was haunted with thoughts and memories of school, of the one I was in but mostly of the one I had left, and I thought, shall I ever really have left Fulford, or shall I be there for the rest of my life, and remembered about the late train, and saw the Great Orb as plainly as if she were beside me.

Just before the end of my last term the 9.13 was late by a few vital minutes and my form was in session when I went into the room. A new teacher was presiding and demanded the reason for my late appearance. I said my train was late and expected the matter to stop there but she was a new broom, intent on sweeping clean, and would not be put off by my usual explanation of "special permission" though I said it with the innocent look I kept for such occasions. 'Whose permission?' she asked. I told her the headmistress's permission, and some aggravating spirit made me add, 'Ask her if you like.'

She retorted 'I certainly shall,' and went on with the lesson while I gave myself to exasperated thought.

Later in the day the Great Orb sent for me. She had been given to understand I travelled every morning by a late train. I nodded. Might she ask why? Certainly she might, and my innocent look was employed again as I explained about the special permission. To save her the trouble of asking whose, I said hers. She was puzzled. I know I looked honest. I felt honest. I was honest. She failed to recall having given me permission. I expected her to fail to recall it and reminded her.

'It was when I was ill.' I spoke softly as if I were in a sick room.

'With your arm, do you mean? But – '

'With my eyes,' and I opened them wider hoping they looked as guileless as I intended them to look.

Hers looked baffled. If only I could have stopped there, but I murmured about cold winds, early mornings and conjunctivitis.

'Conjunctivitis?' She paused. 'Wasn't that years ago?'

I made a non-committal sound, hoping the question would go away.

She asked it again. Bafflement had no rightful place on her perpetually lucid brow, but it appeared there now I explained, 'That was when you gave me permission.'

'But it wasn't for ever,' she cried.

'It was never withdrawn,' I said. 'You never told me to stop coming late, so I didn't.'

'Years and years ago,' she said. 'You've been coming late for years.' She pressed the tips of her fingers to her forehead. 'You realise of course, now – ' there was ironic emphasis in the "now" – 'the permission is withdrawn. It seems to have lasted rather longer than was intended. Years and years.'

She was still murmuring "years and years" as I left the room.

I was annoyed at having lost my treasure but gratified because I had kept it so long and it was a comfort to me when I thought of my unfulfilled promise at Fulford, that nobody had twigged. I had been one up on them, and the privilege I had given myself, though not much of a prize, not much of a distinction, though only a poor thing, had been my own.

Chapter Twenty-six

Aunt was worried about my lack of social life and tried to manoeuvre me into village affairs of the lighter kind. There was to be a Grand Dance at the club and she wanted me to go but I refused with the excuse there would be nobody worth dancing with.

I almost regretted my lost chances with Frankie Slack who was now paying serious attention to a girl who worked at the post office, and had no time for me. Whenever I saw him with her he was leaning over her, breathing down her neck. If he saw me watching he leaned closer and pressed tighter. I was shocked. I thought he loved me.

'But you didn't want him,' cried my aunt.

'You didn't want me to want him,' I said.

'I never disliked Frankie,' she replied, 'I only thought you should look a bit higher in the world.'

'Well, I'm looking,' I snapped and moped about with the exasperated feeling of having lost something I hadn't known I wanted until somebody else had it, and was only half sure I wouldn't want it if I could have it.

If I saw him with the girl he gave me a mixed look, embarrassed and proud, with a touch of defiance. If he were alone except for the few mournful cows he was tending or the tired old horse of the family one-horse farm, he looked friendly and ready to talk, but I always rushed on, polite yet distant, to show I didn't care about him or his post office girl.

In the evenings he went about the village on wireless business, pushing hard on his bike and at his prospects. In his spare time – the adjective was ironic when describing the time Frankie managed to salvage for himself from his over-burdened days – he made and repaired wireless sets, having discovered in himself an extraordinary aptitude for understanding their parts. He made a set for us better than the one we had bought in Welham years before and Aunt frequently rejoiced in perfectly received music from London and abroad though it drove Uncle out of the house.

Yes, everybody agreed, there was something in Frankie after all. He began to do well – for a Slack. Dammit, people said, he would soon be saying goodbye to his bike and the half-dead horse and buying a van, but Fate had other plans for Frankie. One slippery night when he was fixing an aerial he fell from a roof and put himself out of action for months while his rosy prospects, and the girl, faded away. Just like the Slacks, said the village, no matter how they tried, they always ended up in the same place – at the bottom.

I refused to go to the Grand Dance and reminded Aunt of a former disastrous occasion when, several years before, she had tried to bring me out. The scene shot into my mind with forbidding clarity. To an onslaught of complicated sound from the band we had pushed through a group of village youths hanging round the door, my head higher in the air than usual to make it clear none of them had better ask me to dance.

Girls were everywhere – in a solid wedge near the ladies' room, hanging about in front of the band, talking to each other in restless groups. Some with desperate bravado, danced with each other, all the time darting anxious glances towards male territory by the main door.

Sulky and shy, I sat by Auntie, dreading being asked to dance, dreading not being asked, and began a morbid pastime of counting the men who were shorter than I was, short, short, short. Those who were not short were old. At last Aunt lost patience, sprang from her seat and cried, 'Dance with me!' then at my horrified look sat down again. After a time she was relieved to see Charlie and waved her handbag at him though I begged her to lie low and shrank even further down between my shoulders. I knew he would hate dancing with me. I was taller than ever and he seemed not to have grown at all. But he saw us and dutifully came to pay his respects. Seizing my hand, probably in reply to a mute appeal from Aunt, he said, 'Come on, Warble-lip, let's get it over,' then with a push from Auntie and a pull from him I was on the floor, shuffling backwards as he butted me into a quickstep.

It seemed not to bother him that his head was lower than mine and that he had to peer round my shoulder to see the way we were going. He was a good dancer and we went round the floor several times without mishap. When we passed Aunt I was rewarded with a reassuring smile and began to feel easier, then I saw people looking amused. Suddenly I realised Charlie was giving a little hop and kick at every turn. He was clowning. Even the band were laughing and blew their saxophones at us as we passed. I tried to walk away but he grabbed me and said, 'Laugh, you fool,' and kept a firm grip on me until I smiled and tried to look as if I liked being made a fool of. The end came with a crash of cymbals and some good natured clapping and whistling. I dug my heel into Charlie's foot, by accident I thought, but wasn't sorry when I saw how he hobbled away.

214

Surely that was enough to put me off dancing for ever but Aunt went on about the Grand Dance and the specially augmented jazz-band from Sheffield till I began to think she must be jazz-mad herself, and gave in. She made me promise not to be stand-offish so I accepted several partners and had a few dances which, though nerve-racking to me because I didn't know many steps, were not disastrous. If I saw a prospective partner I considered too ridiculously short I fled to the ladies' room before I could be trapped.

At midnight, over refreshments, I sat with Aunt for a breathing space and we took stock of the evening. I had dodged several dwarfs, danced with a few middle-aged husbands, including Charlie's father, had talked to a "rather nice" boy from Welham and promised him the next waltz. I was even looking forward to it, waltzing being less hazardous to me than quicksteps, and easier to "follow" than foxtrots.

Charlie's mother was serving refreshments. To our surprise she was wearing her yellow satin dress with the pattern of red flowers. It was her best dress, she was fond of it and reserved it for occasions of pomp and decorum. Certainly it was not for wearing while pouring tea and coffee and washing pots.

She gave us a glum look and agreed. 'They say everybody's good at something. Well, I'm good at getting landed with other folk's jobs.' Mopping up a mess of spilt coffee and crumbs she went on, 'I came here in me best dress, thinking I'd enjoy a look at the dancing and p'raps have a randy round meself, and now look at me – ' rebellion broke out of her in glistening drops – 'here I am, washing up, as usual. I'm getting a bit fed up with it.' She slapped a cloth into a puddle of spilt tea and untied her apron. 'But I'll be with you in a minute, I'm coming out for a breather.'

I hadn't expected to be, but was, impressed by the evening with its music and coloured lights and intricately moving dancers. Nobody could say these sophisticated quicksteppers and foxtrotters were clodhoppers. I didn't recognise most of them. Perhaps they were from Welham or had come with the band from Sheffield where, I supposed, this was how they did things, and when streamers and confetti whirled about, and showers of paper rose petals fell from the ceiling, I marvelled that I was in our village club and not in London or Paris.

Suddenly out of the swirling sound I heard the name St Orbin.

'It's true,' Charlie's mother was saying, 'I wish it wasn't, poor chap.' Both she and Aunt looked solemn and I asked what they were talking about.

'That young St Orbin,' said Charlie's mother, 'the one who married into the pork family.'

'What about him?' My heart was thumping.

'He's dead,' said Charlie's mother, 'we've only just heard.'

Aunt nodded. I stared.

'In Spain,' said Aunt, 'in the war.'

'I've never known what they're all fighting about,' said Charlie's mother, 'and I don't know what business it was of his, but he went.'

'Leaving a wife,' Aunt said.

'And a fortune in pork,' said Charlie's mother.

And he was dead.

The music changed, the nice boy from Welham appeared. I wasn't what he hoped for as a waltzing partner and he soon began to look ruffled. We trod on each other's feet, or rather, I trod on his and put mine where he couldn't help tripping over them. 'Listen for the beat,' he kept saying, 'can't you hear the beat?'

*   *   *

Hear the beat, one, two, three, listen to the beat, St Orbin's dead.

The music changed again and people began to dance the tango. Three steps forward, turn and swoop, three steps back. 'Let yourself go!' cried the nice boy from Welham, 'like they do in Spain,' and clicked his fingers and stamped his feet.

They kill each other in Spain.

'Pardon?' said the boy. Perhaps I had thought aloud. Soon I made an excuse and he found another partner, a girl in a flounced dress who swayed when he swayed and swooped when he swooped, and they stamped their feet and clicked fingers and danced the tango as if they were both in Spain.

I hardly knew anything about the Spanish war. I had been too busy with matric and leaving school and beginning my grown-up life to bother about it. The world had gone on by itself and got into a mess without my being interested and now I was ashamed.

I had tried to stop thinking about St Orbin after his marriage but there was nobody else to think of and the fantasy had run on. I had written a story about us. The guilty pages were under my bed. After the dance, as I lay awake thinking of his death, at times it seemed as if I were in some way to blame for it, and it was to punish me he was dead, and at times it seemed nonsense and a voice inside me said it isn't real, none of it's real, not the love, not the sorrow, only the death, that's real, or is that too only another part of the story?

At last I fell into a half-sleep, dreaming half-dreams confused with hot images of Spain where St Orbin and I were dancing the tango until it turned into a bullfight and he was killed, while I sat in a corner scribbling madly to write a story before I forgot it.

In the morning I looked in the glass to see what ravages were written on my face. There were none, and I was amazed.

After guilt, expiation. The next day time was ripe for an ameliatory sacrifice and, like an eastern widow accepting suttee, I was ready for the renunciatory fire. I saw it at the bottom of the orchard where Uncle was burning twigs on an incense-wafting pyre, noble enough to receive my offering, however rare.

Suddenly I knew what it must be, though I flinched as even the most dedicated martyr surely must at the flame's first promise. As a gift of flowers, useless to the dead, comforts the living, my gift would ease my grief and prove the truth of it.

With my bundle of writing, the only treasure in my store of poverty, I went to the orchard. Uncle was raking twigs into the fire and said, 'More rubbish eh? Well, chuck it on.'

But I couldn't chuck it on. I failed to perform the rite. I looked into the fire's pure heart and quailed, then returned to the house, a betrayer, unfaithful, tried and found wanting. I couldn't make my burnt offering. I put my story under the bed again and buried it under a rug.

After this the mood at home was not cheerful. Nearly eighteen, I was miserable at finding myself in the same place where I had been at eight, in the Big School with Mr Pinder, and though I was still fond of him, I was desperate to get away.

I saw an advertisement in *The Times*. A young English person, preferably a student, was offered a post in a language school in Brussels. No more than English conversation was required, the salary was described as modest. I didn't care how modest it was. I wrote, sent a photograph as requested, then nervous and grumpy, waited for an answer and became more and more depressed at every post which failed to bring one.

Uncle, too, was going through a strange phase. Aunt said his moods were almost as difficult to live with as mine. Perhaps I was affecting both of them with my morbid looks and gloomy habits. Certainly Uncle was more than usually irritable and Aunt more than ever irritating.

By way of delivering a reprimand since I was small she had exasperated me by tapping the top of my head with the back of a spoon if she happened to have one in her hand, in much the same way as she tapped a boiled egg before taking its top off. Sometimes she treated Uncle's head in the same way and as he was bald he felt the tap more than I did, though he put up with it.

One morning however, at breakfast, when my Brussels plan was in the making, I was more than usually on edge because there had been no letter. Aunt, responding to tension in the air, gave his head a more than usually sharp rap as she passed behind him. He sprang from his chair like Jack out of the box, then rushed from the room saying it was time he had a place he could call his own and he was damn well going to have one.

I went to school so Aunt was left alone to consider her ways.

I wasn't happy at dinner time and instead of going home went to the wood, which was now surround by a high fence. There were many new notice-boards, some with information that the property now belonged to the Ministry of War and was strictly private, and others with the simple message in red letters, KEEP OUT.

According to Charlie the whole of Orbin land and most of our woods were being turned into a training ground for spies, but the War Department wouldn't keep him out of his wood, he had seen to that by making a secret entrance at a convenient spot near the two orchards. By merely loosening a few boards he had made sure that we – he was kind enough to include me – could go in and out of the wood as we pleased.

I sat on a log and didn't care what the War Department did with the wood. Thoughts of St Orbin mixed with my awareness of the beginning of spring and I couldn't believe in being dead, only in being alive, and in going away.

In the evening there was a heap of recently delivered timber at the bottom of the orchard. When Aunt asked Uncle about it he said it was for a hen hut, though we hadn't any hens. There was something about his manner which forbade more questions. After a pause he said he intended to build a bolt-hole, a private place for himself, though it could be turned into a hen house afterwards. After what? I ventured to ask though Aunt kept quiet, and he said after things were different but he doubted if they ever would be, and Aunt lifted her chin as if she had a retort ready, but said nothing.

The growing asperity between them disturbed me. I wondered if it was my fault. There was certainly a snake in the garden and though ours wasn't the garden of Eden it was a garden of trees, and I wondered if it were through me the serpent had found its way in.

'He'll never finish it,' said Aunt, 'I know him. All that wood will end on the fire.' She laughed but was mortified.

With some paid help however, the hut was soon raised at the bottom of the orchard between the fruit trees and the high fence which bounded the wood. There, amidst unaccustomed peace, he would read, think and, like Kate, write.

'You write?' exclaimed Aunt. 'You won't even write a letter unless it's to order new fruit trees.'

'I'll write my memories,' he said, and went back and forth with his personal possessions while Aunt grew more and more disturbed.

The shed was neat and cosy inside with a paraffin stove, a storm lamp, bookshelves and an old desk picked up in the village for five shillings, and a red rug on the floor.

I was curious about Uncle's memoirs, not understanding how he could have any, nothing had ever happened in his life as far as I had noticed, every day had been the same for years. He read my thoughts and said, 'But you don't know what's in here,' and touched his chest.

I was abashed, seeing the comparison between him and me. Nobody knew what was in me, and there'd be an awful row when what was in, was out.

Chapter Twenty-seven

Aunt was quiet but wary. Though she noticed the gap
left on the dining-room bookshelves by the disappearance
of *The Story of the Heavens, The Autocrat of the
Breakfast Table, The Origin of Species,* and *Erewhon,*
she made no comment on discovering they were in the
hen hut (her status-reducing name for Uncle's bolt-hole)
but the appearance of a truckle bed down there wrung
from her an exclamation of alarm. She complained of
being treated like a landlady, she and Uncle only saw
each other at mealtimes, were leading separate lives more
or less. Now it looked as if they'd soon be sleeping in
different beds and that, as everybody knew, was the thin
edge of the wedge.

Uncle, though elusive, was as genial as ever and kept
his calm appearance in spite of the small crisis which had
happened between him and Aunt. It must have been
small, nothing big ever happened in their lives, their
storms were easily contained in tea-cups.

As time went on, however, relations between the three
of us deteriorated. Aunt's nerves were the more on edge
because Uncle refused her the satisfaction of open
argument, smiled when she tried to quarrel, turned the
other cheek when she struck at him, then disappeared
into his hut. I was harrowed day by day as I waited in
vain for a letter from Brussels and raced so dramatically
to the door at morning and teatime that Aunt began to
look suspiciously at me as well as at Uncle, and asked if I

was expecting a love letter. Uncle said, what if I was, it was a pity some people couldn't mind their own business, and thus directed more suspicious looks to himself.

I thought I should go mad with the tedium of school and the staleness of home, the wearisome procession of uninteresting week days punctuated by long boring Sundays. Monotony sank into my being until I was incapable of anything but getting up, going to school to do a vague performance of helping Mr Pinder, then going home to mope till bedtime. Dashing for the letters twice a day was my only excitement and disappointment always followed it.

There was a little Holt at school, the last of the brood. The wild energy of the stock must have dwindled away, there was none in him. He was pallid and passive, with a tiny ferret face under tangled dark hair, Holt hair, and sat silently hour after hour, seeming to take nothing in, giving nothing out, his expression perpetually blank except when, as if at some surprise known only to himself, he looked suddenly astonished. Tiny sparrow in a nest of cuckoos, perhaps he sensed the difference between himself and the rumbustious older occupants of the Black house. He touched me. We were in the same predicament. Trapped.

At teatime one afternoon raised voices within the house warned me of trouble ahead. I was late from school and the post had already arrived. Aunt was reading a letter. I wondered, with an inner thump, if it were mine from Brussels, but it was from Lucy Denham.

As always when that name was mentioned Aunt spoke with a satirical edge to her voice. It was no different now. The Denham-Lucies were in South Africa, far away from the stress and strain of Europe. Whatever was in store for us in the coming months they would escape. Lucy as usual had fallen on her feet, though how she stood on them in those ridiculous high heels she always wore – Aunt's lip curled to match the sarcasm in her voice as she read on. Zoë was having a wonderful time of course, being made a fuss of and going absolutely everywhere. Everything was perfect, though the Undertaker was alive and kicking. Aunt's paraphrase. Lucy's expression was "quite well" but the word "though" was there and Aunt made the most of it.

I read the letter, smiling calmly, though I absorbed from Lucy's careless passionate scrawl a sense of glamour and exhilaration which was almost unbearable to me by contrast with my own arid state.

'They all seem to be having a good time,' I said.

'I don't know about ALL,' said Aunt, 'but two of 'em are and that's what matters.'

As Uncle demurred she went on, 'The world's troubles don't mean a thing to Lucy. We can be blown to bits but she'll never know nor care as long as she's enjoying herself.' She picked up the letter. 'Scented. Just like her.'

It was like her. No doubt about it, Lucy's scent was diffusing over the scones and jam like breath from an aromatic paradise.

'I like it,' I said.

'So do I,' said Uncle.

'It's common,' Aunt glared at us, 'common and vulgar.'

I was up in arms now, full of hatred for plain teas and plain people but ready for plain speaking. 'Lucy isn't common,' I cried, 'and she isn't vulgar. Lucy is – '

Uncle clattered his chair back from the table. 'Can't we forget about Lucy?' he asked.

'You can't,' Aunt said. 'That's always been the trouble.'

He went to the fireplace and with his back to us, began to clean his pipe. 'If I were you,' he spoke slowly, 'I should let sleeping dogs lie.'

'I don't know if I'd call Lucy a sleeping dog,' said Aunt. 'Dog isn't the word I'd use about *her* – ' it was impossible not to realise what she meant – 'but she can certainly lie, in more than one sense of the word.'

It wasn't the time for me to acknowledge her subtlety by an appreciative smile. Instead, I tried to smooth troubled waters, and to encourage the return of pleasant and safe conversation, recalled the story of Zoë's mysterious origin, saying how romantic I thought Lucy's midnight ride into Sherwood.

'Romantic!' Aunt scoffed. 'Ride into Sherwood! You can believe that if you like. I believed it myself at the time. I was young, remember, and romantic too, though nobody noticed it.'

'But she was out all night. You said she didn't come home,' I reminded Aunt, not wishing to give up the pleasure of believing in Lucy's fabled expedition.

'She could have slept somewhere else,' said Aunt. 'She had other friends, if you can call 'em friends. I'm not as simple as I once was. Just because I believed what she said when she said it doesn't mean I have to believe it now. I think it was a lie.'

'It wasn't a lie,' said Uncle from the fireplace. 'It was the truth. She did go to Sherwood.'

'How do you know?' asked Aunt.

'Because I was there,' he said. 'I went with her.'

There was silence. I watched Aunt's face grow white.

'I'm sorry,' said Uncle, 'I shouldn't have spoken,' and he looked as if he wished he hadn't.

I broke the silence. 'It was you! You were the one. Zoë is my cousin!'

They stared at me. They had forgotten I was there. 'Of

course she isn't,' said Uncle. 'Don't be ridiculous.'

'Why not?' I persisted, 'if you and Lucy, if you were the one – '

'He's going to tell you,' Aunt spoke slowly, 'he's going to say they rode round the forest without once getting off their bikes.'

'No, I'm not,' said Uncle, 'I'm not going to say anything of the kind.'

Again there was silence. Suddenly I asked, 'What about the child?' then was abashed, but Uncle answered calmly, 'She didn't mention the child for some time, and when she did she swore it wasn't mine.' He paused. 'She didn't want it to be mine.'

'Why not?' I asked. Aunt was silent. He looked at her.

'She wouldn't have me,' he said, 'didn't want me. She said I wasn't going far enough in the world for her.'

'She was right about that,' said Aunt.

I looked from one to the other. They were in the past, ignoring me.

'She wanted to climb,' said Uncle, 'and I suppose she thought marrying that chap Denham was a step up from a farmer like me, him being a captain in the army.'

'He was a major,' said Aunt.

'There you are then,' said Uncle, 'she'd think that was well up.'

They were quiet for a time, considering the class distinction, no doubt. I broke in. 'But, Uncle, if you and Mrs Denham-Lucie, I mean, I still don't see why Zoë isn't my cousin.'

'She's not your cousin,' he was beginning to sound irritable, 'because she's not my child. I ought to know. I wasn't the only one who went for bicycle rides with Lucy, at night or any other time, in Sherwood or anywhere else, in Orbin woods, or our woods, or any other woods.'

'She was fond of woods,' said Aunt.

Uncle turned to her.

'I'm sorry, it should never have come out, and it never would have if you hadn't gone on and on.' Suddenly he went to the garden and disappeared into the hut.

I went out too and mused for a long time about what I had heard, partly disappointed, partly pleased that Zoë's origins, about which there had been so much interesting conjecture, might not after all have been more elevated than mine. I thought how nothing was exactly what it seemed and, remembering Mrs Denham-Lucie's dulcet manner and diffusive scents, put them against the plain and honest ways of my aunt which sometimes embarrassed me and made me ashamed of her. I knew Aunt was ten times better than Lucy Denham, and was glad I had enough sense to recognise the difference between the true and the false, then my mind's eye saw Uncle cutting roses for Lucy and leaning into the sphere of her fragrance and, in retrospection, I was charmed again.

At nights I had the habit of getting up when I couldn't sleep and going for long rides on my bicycle and I thought, as I flew along the empty lanes, of Lucy Denham and her loves and of me and mine, my empty love for dead St Orbin, and by a sudden lightning switch of thought which made me start as from an electric shock, I put her and the name together and wondered if ever in her amorous woodland wanderings she too had met a St Orbin lover and made of the meeting more than I had made of mine. Once when I had been describing a part of Orbin woods, she stopped me, and said with a sigh and elegiac smile, 'Ah the woods of St Orbin. How well I knew them once. How much they meant to me.' My mind hovered over a tangle of questions. Could Zoë be a St Orbin? She and my St Orbin, when he lived, were

227

similar creatures of grace and glamour. Suppose they shared lineage and the same ancestral root. Suppose Lucy – but Lucy's past was too remote and complex for me to unravel and eventually I gave up puzzling over its knotted strands.

No romantic episodes occurred for me in my nightly excursions, but I matched my speed with the wind's and hardly knew if I were in flight from my Fate or rushing towards it. Nothing happened, except that I returned home in the early hours purged by the privacy of the night and purified by speed.

One night, I found Aunt with desperate look, as one in a myth, barring the way out of the back door. As we struggled she cried, 'She's thousands of miles away but she won't let us alone. She influences even you.' I began to explain my midnight rides had nothing to do with Lucy's influence, they were my way of coping with restless nights and the mad discontent which possessed me but – 'It's because of her,' she said, as if all the discontent in her life were Lucy's fault.

It wasn't the time for arguing, I felt compassion for her. She had been much disappointed lately, often through me. A glimmer of a thought came to me that her whole life might have been a disappointment. It was a wonder she hadn't gone into the dreaded Haggard mountains weeks ago. She would go when I told her about Brussels. I was sure of that.

Fortified by my secret I went meekly back to bed where, unshriven by speed, I lay awake and thought of St Orbin and what he had meant to me and what I had built around him. I thought of Lucy Denham and Uncle and of secrets undiscovered, trying to find my way between reality and pretence, wondering what was true and what was false, and why one was so much more attractive than the other, and I wondered who I would rather be, if I could choose, Aunt with her honesty and worth or Lucy with her attitudes and charm, and with the most guilty pang I knew the one I would be.

The arrival of the letter from Brussels came as a surprise after the long time of my waiting. Usually, when books, pens and pencils were put away I was ready to dash out of school at the first tinkle of the bell but the little Holt was in trouble. He had waited his chance until the classroom was empty at playtime, then with an efficiency and speed he never showed at anything to do with learning, had destroyed most of the papers in Mr Pinder's desk, even laying sacrilegious hands on the class register, emptying ink pots over the red strokes for attendance and the black noughts for absence. He showed no sign of regret, displayed not a tremor of guilt as Mr Pinder loomed with the face of judgment above him. I was the one who was upset. I was fond of the wretch and had, I vainly thought, won a way into his inscrutable heart.

As I saw the letter on the tea-table by my plate my heart at once gave a leap of recognition but I showed no surprise.

'Who's writing to you from Brussels?' Aunt was pouring tea. 'You don't know anybody in Belgium.'

Didn't she remember one of the girls at Fulford, a rich girl, who had gone to a finishing school there?

'I never knew you were friends with her,' Aunt said as I went out of the room with the letter. Before I opened it I ran to the bottom of the orchard, then across the wasteground to the old stable where I hid until I had read the message. I read it again and again. I could go to

Brussels. The post was mine. I had won something at last.

Instinct told me to act quickly, so that evening I wrote several boat-burning letters, to Brussels agreeing to be there at the beginning of May, to College resigning my place for the autumn, to the Education Authorities in Nottingham abandoning my student teachership, and to the managers of the Big School giving notice of leaving. I would tell Mr Pinder in the morning, and the last phase of my battle would begin. Should I tell Aunt and Uncle now, or later, or let them find out? I decided to leave them in peace for as long as possible. Late at night I pretended to go for a walk, though it was pouring with rain, and put the letters into the post.

Chapter Twenty-eight

Soon, replies came in stern official envelopes addressed in typewriting to Mr Pinder at school, to me, and worse, to Aunt and Uncle. College was in touch with County Education authority, that in touch with school, and school, in a gravely cautionary visit by Mr Pinder, with home. Squire and Rector, dropped upon me from time to time for serious converse, admonishing on their side, stubbornly uncommunicative or truculent, on mine. A third school manager, our butcher, whose chief claim to intelligence, according to my uncle, lay in an ability to make large profits out of short weight, upbraided me publicly in his shop over a pound of sausages, saying I must be daft to give up a cushy job with long holidays and short working days to go traipsing amongst a lot of foreigners when war might break out any minute. Winking at his other customers, he declared he would know what to do with me if I belonged to him, then slapped the sausages on the scales and into a bag which he smacked on to the counter. I left them and walked out of the shop.

One day Nurse called to me as she cycled past school at playtime, 'Hullo, Kate, I thought you'd gone to join the Hun.' The same day Charlie's mother came into the house with only the slightest tap on the door and cried, 'Is it true Katie's run away abroad?' and was offended by my derogatory remarks about people who stuck noses into other people's business, and went away in a huff. I was sorry because I wanted to know when Charlie was coming home, thinking I might need his co-operation as he had often needed mine.

I was impervious to warnings of danger and appeals to common sense and became adept at dodging, or enduring without being affected by, censorious confrontations which were likely to happen with anybody, anywhere, at any time.

My greatest ordeal was one afternoon when I was trapped by officialdom itself in the person of a middle-aged widow representing the County Education Committee, "Notts" as we always called it. She supervised student-teachers' affairs throughout the county and regarded my defection so seriously she had come in a taxi from Nottingham to have a heart to heart talk about my future. Soon Aunt appeared, and I realised the meeting had been arranged behind my back. There was much affability between the three grown-ups in the shelf-lined hole which served as Headmaster's office, staff-room and stockroom, but I was in a bad mood and sulkily stared through a window at the children who were having a long playtime. An excited group was clustered near the railings through which the little Holt had stuck his head to get a better view of the taxi in the street. Neither the teacher in charge of the playground nor the taxi driver could set him free and both were visibly becoming more exasperated every minute.

'Do pay attention,' said the widow from Notts, 'and try to realise we want to help you.' I muttered that I didn't need any help, and she said, 'Oh but you do, my dear, we all need help and must help each other. That's why I've come such a long way today,' and I thought, I bet you've enjoyed it, riding in a taxi miles and miles from Nottingham, through Sherwood, and remembered the forest and certain powerful experiences there.

She opened her spectacle case and shut it again with a snap which recalled me to the present.

At headquarters everybody was being reasonable and understanding on my behalf, and would regard my foolish letters as not having been written, College would wink its eye and accept me again, the principal was a personal friend. At this, I rewarded the widow with a stony look so she concentrated on Aunt for a time. For the sake of my family connections with the profession and the impeccable reputation of my teaching relatives past and present, and supported by the good words of Mr Pinder and the three, well two, school managers who had known me since I was a child, and because I had won one of the County's treasured scholarships and had once been regarded as a flower in the garden – she smiled, 'a flower in the garden of Notts' – she would approve, she would personally contrive – she broke off, hesitating over the word as if she didn't like it so I helped her by offering another, "wangle," which she ignored with a slight frown and substituted "organise". My mind became busy with alternative words – plot, intrigue, scheme, influence, manipulate, pull strings, fiddle, until I heard her say, 'Well, thank goodness that's settled. I'm so glad you're going to be sensible.'

'But I'm not,' I cried in alarm, 'I mean I am, but I'm not, not in the way you mean.'

She smiled and patted my arm. She understood girls, her students were under her wing like daughters. Girls had nervous indefinable moods sometimes, even sound predictable girls sometimes did unpredictable things. One made allowances, perhaps the prevalent mood of the world in general had something to do with the tendencies of modern youth towards impetuosity and instability. These were dangerous times, and looking at everything sensibly, where would I have been if war had broken out and the school in, where was it? Belgium? – closed, if indeed it was a school and not a façade for something less respectable. I saw Aunt nod, pleased to hear her fears spoken aloud by someone else. Where would I have been, asked the widow from Notts getting her tenses wrong and speaking as if my affairs were in the past and not the future, I would have been in a mess.

I struggled to save my future from being buried in the past before it happened but not a word came out.

'You would have been stranded,' said the widow, 'perhaps, no almost certainly, without money, in a foreign land, unqualified, inexperienced, untrained.' She shuddered, picked up her handbag, and thanked goodness I had seen sense.

'I am going to Belgium,' I said, 'and I'm not going to college. I hate teaching and I won't be a teacher, at least not an ordinary teacher, in an ordinary school like this.'

The sound of the children outside grew louder and wilder. Aunt gave me a despairing glance. Mr Pinder looked at his watch. The widow did her best to stifle a yawn. It had been a tiring session. She began to assemble the various personal possessions she had disposed around her. She had tried to save me from my foolishness but apparently I wished to persist in it. She shrugged. Mr Pinder offered tea at his house across the road, but she refused saying she had a call to make at the next village where another student was in need of personal advice, no trouble there, this girl was very keen.

The taxi went away, and Aunt went home looking dejected. My head ached but I hadn't faltered. I had been a stone in the midst of the whirlpool.

The teacher in the yard blew the whistle, the children formed lines and said prayers outside, school was dismissed. I dodged Mr Pinder and went for a walk to calm myself before going home.

234

Aunt told me later the widow had said I was a rude and intractable girl.

I went over and over my plans, knew every detail of my journey. A year ago I had nearly gone to Paris on a school trip which fell through because of an epidemic of measles, so I had a passport, but I had no money. My fare to Brussels would be refunded when I arrived, but I had to find it first. I had my salary to collect at the end of March and again at the end of April, a few pounds for each month. Half was due to Aunt for my board so I would still have some money for myself, almost enough; then I remembered I owed a girl in the village for making a blouse and skirt, I had taken books from a second-hand bookshop in Welham and promised to pay at the end of the month. Bad ways! I had saved nothing, had spent my new income with abandon. I had taken Aunt to a performance of *Carmen* at a theatre in Sheffield, had bought a coat in a sale for thirty shillings. Now I could see the error of my spendthrift ways and had only myself to blame for my penury. I couldn't blame Aunt who had claimed part of my earnings more as a moral duty than because she wanted it. She had been pleased to see me buying things for myself and had been so generous in giving me impromptu half-crowns I thought I had discerned in her the tendencies of a secret spendthrift.

Though hard-up I was not despairing. I was used to having my own way and, expecting to have it again, began delicate negotiations.

Aunt was blunt. 'No use asking your Uncle and me for money,' she said, 'the answer is no.'

Half-joking I said if I couldn't get what I needed any other way I would have to steal it and warned her to hide her cash. She looked at me steadily. 'Never since you were born,' she said, 'have I found it necessary to hide money from you, and I shan't do so now. You must do as you will.'

Oh damn! Oh blast! She knew I would never take any. She had always been careless with small coins, now more often than before, little piles of silver were left here and there on shelves, on the dresser top, or in little pots. Of course I never took any. After a time no more appeared. She had made her statement. I had made mine.

I had nothing to sell, nothing was mine but my books, clothes and bicycle and nobody would buy those. I ground my teeth. If I could be financially helped through two years of college why couldn't I have a fraction of that help now? To me it seemed a reasonable request, to Aunt madness. 'Don't expect us to pay for your ruin,' she said, 'get your training first, then we'll see.' How I hated, had always hated, those delaying words, "we'll see," which meant not yet, or sometime, or never.

'Nobody understands me,' I wailed, and prepared the knife for a deadly blow, 'it would be different if I had a mother and father – ' here I struck – 'you are only an aunt, and uncle only an uncle, and even a double aunt and uncle aren't as good as parents.'

She was hurt but obdurate. I had to think of other tactics. She was the one I must concentrate on. I could twist Uncle around my finger about anything but cash. It was no good badgering him. I hardly saw him to talk to. He was absorbed in the orchard as spring advanced, waiting for the fruit buds, ready to guard them from every frost with old lace curtains which he draped over the trees, making the orchard seem full of ghosts at night. There was a wireless in his hut now and when he wasn't among the trees he was listening to the news or discussions of foreign affairs and made it clear he wouldn't be drawn into arguing about mine.

* * *

The month dragged on. I refused all overtures at reconciliation and never smiled, determined to make life at home unbearable until I won my own way.

I was astonished at the strength of my will, and recalled only one other time when I had shown a similar capacity for obstinacy. It was in my first summer at Fulford in the days when Charlie and I cycled to Welham. I refused, one morning, to go to school and arguments raged. Charlie waited, then went to Welham alone and I locked myself in the box-room with the used linen. No matter how Aunt raved and banged on the door and Uncle coaxed outside it I stayed where I was, even when the time for going to school was long past. Hot summer droned outside. The window was stuck so no fresh air came into the room. At intervals Aunt came upstairs to renew her attack, threatening to break down the door but I was rooted in a mood as unyielding as iron and never spoke. Late in the evening when Uncle forced the lock and Aunt rushed in to wreak her vengeance they found me in a stupor on top of the washing basket. I had been too deep in my mood to come out of it by myself.

Sulks, said Aunt, she had never seen such sulks. She was seeing them now.

Moping about the house one day I heard her going on to Uncle about me.

'She'll get over it when the right lad starts hanging around,' he said, and I could hear the reposeful puffing of his pipe.

'She won't look at anybody,' said Aunt.

'Because there isn't anybody,' I pounced on them with a yell. 'There isn't anybody worth looking at in this hole, that's why I'm leaving. And I don't want a lad, I want men, exciting men, foreign men, wicked men,' and I whirled out.

*   *   *

I began my midnight rides again. Nobody stopped me,
and I was disappointed, having developed an appetite for
rows. Catharsis. I discovered the word. The rows in some
measure assuaged my insatiable discontent. They didn't
soothe Aunt.

I noticed how thin she had become and her gaunt
expression told me she was now in the Haggard
mountains, but I didn't care. She was weak. I was strong.
I knew I would break her. I would break her down into
the ground and step over the wreckage, free at last to
discover what was waiting for me, the life labelled mine,
but I had to go looking for it, the search would ensure
the discovery, the act of going was the magic which
could change me into one who would do, not watch.

Even the sight of my aunt and uncle was enough to
start my resentment boiling. What I wanted was little to
them, but they wouldn't give it, they were so stubborn, so
rustic, so sure their ways were right, so rooted in one
spot, so restricted, so hemmed in by custom, birth,
environment, so blind to the enticing vista I could see
opening before me. I filled with implacable resolve never
to become as they were.

Aunt said, 'I never thought you could be so sly . . .
making your plans behind our backs. I've never been so
shocked. Such secrecy wasn't like you.'

Oh Aunt, poor old Aunt, it was like me. I've been full
of secrets all my life, always. A wave of sorrow washed
against my pride, then receded and pride grew strong
again. My will hammered against theirs. Go to college.
Give me money for Brussels. Demand against refusal,
denial against longing. Why didn't they give in?

I became deliberately cruel to Aunt. I accused her of
being against my writing, of having always been against
it, though I knew it wasn't true. She had always

238

encouraged it, had been proud of it, had never grumbled about it even when I persisted in writing my novel when I should have been swotting for matric.

I prepared my most hurtful stab. 'Lucy would understand,' I said.

'Lucy?' Aunt, momentarily off guard, looked surprised.

'Lucy Denham. Mrs Denham-Lucie. She'd help me if she was here. I could ask her for anything, even money. She wouldn't refuse.'

Aunt stared.

'Because she's generous,' I cried, 'not mean like you, and she's kinder and prettier as well. No wonder Uncle loved her more than he ever loved you.'

She rushed at me. I seized her wrists and easily held her off. I was a lion fighting a feather. Even in her passion she was weak, but I was full of power and laughed. I was still laughing when Uncle came in and separated us.

Next day she was ill. Half-sorry, half-excited I wondered if my evil thoughts were killing her. For the first time in my life she stayed in bed. I was shocked when I saw her lying on the pillows and had an impulse to say I was sorry but crushed it.

Confident of victory I could afford to lighten the atmosphere with witty remarks, but she took no notice. She was deep in the Haggard mountains, so deep I wondered if she would ever come out.

I had a day off school and did the housework, carefully as she would have done it. I took her meals she didn't eat, novels, newspapers she didn't read. I made a bunch of spring flowers and, giving them, avoided the haunted look in her eyes. I wondered if she would die. Would I be sorry, or pleased? Or would she survive and try to be as secretive as I had been, and write behind my back to spoil my chances in Belgium? I resolved to be unceasingly vigilant. My battle was not yet won.

She soon recovered and got up to register a birth. I was pleased to see her downstairs again and helped her by making a copy of the birth certificate. She gave me a half-crown.

Peace, at least on the surface, was between us, and continued so for some time.

Chapter Twenty-nine

Aunt came into the sitting-room where Uncle's entrenchment by the fire was a declaration of his immobility for the evening.

She spoke to him twice without receiving an answer and absentmindedly lifted her hand to rap the top of his head. I held my breath, but the danger passed and she only tapped his shoulder as she reminded him of his promise to go with her to eat a dinner in aid of the war effort.

'Oh Lord!' He lowered his newspaper. 'You're not going to keep me to that. You know I never go calling.'

'This isn't calling,' said Aunt, 'it's duty, and it's sure to be a good dinner.' But Uncle had eaten one good dinner that day and wilfully refused to understand how eating another could be regarded as a duty.

'It's paid for,' Aunt told him, 'and I can't get the money back.'

It didn't matter. Let the money be kept for the war effort and the paid-for dinner sold again. That would be even better for the cause.

'I've ironed your best shirt,' said Aunt, 'and been half the afternoon pressing your good suit. All you have to do is to go upstairs and put them on. I've lived like a widow long enough, always going out by myself, but I'm not going by myself tonight,' and she sat opposite to him looking resolute. He gave in with less of a struggle than usual, perhaps trying to make up for the revelation of his

Lucy Denham affair years ago.

The excitement of going into society with Uncle brought an agreeable lightness to Aunt's appearance, and there was a subdued sparkle about her when she was ready, which touched me. She wore a lace blouse which I hadn't seen and glanced at me, looking for a compliment, but I was still unfriendly and didn't give one. Uncle, who had resigned himself to an evening wearing his good suit, posted himself at the front door to wait for Charlie's parents who had offered a lift in their car.

Continuing my course of self-immolation until I had won my own way about Belgium, I had refused the outing, saying I couldn't afford it, and when Aunt had offered to buy my ticket I had been quick to ask for the money instead. She had refused to give it, and I sulked.

It was stalemate now at home. I didn't know the next move. Easter had gone, so had my eighteenth birthday, and it hadn't brought me extra funds, but my will was as strong as ever to go abroad, war or no war. Abroad was different. To go abroad was to get out of the rut. There was a rut in our family from one generation to the next, teachers on one side, farmers on the other. University might have moved me off the track. Going to college would fasten me to it. I thought of my teaching cousins. Some of them had never married, never would marry. They clung to school year after year because teaching was safe and respectable and meant paid holidays. They became grey people dreaming of pensions, watching life waste. If I went to college, my life could be like theirs, set deep in chalk and ink like a fossil in stone. I suddenly smashed a lump of coal in the fire and willed something drastic to happen so that the mould would be broken and life could rush in, and said aloud, 'Let it be soon, let it be now.'

The clock's tick was louder. Rain trickled down the windows. I imagined the scene at the dinner. There would be a lot of old fogies eating a solid meal they didn't need. There would be nobody for me to talk to, not even Frankie Slack who was elsewhere, encased in plaster. I gave a commemorative turn to the knob of the wireless set he had made. Sound came out, fading and crackling. Something was wrong with the aerial, but Frankie wouldn't be able to put it right.

I hadn't seen Charlie for ages and wondered if he had secretly married the rich girl with the marvellous seat on a horse and the hundreds of acres. He would get on well with her. She wasn't as tall as I was and didn't stick her head in books.

Suddenly I was alert. Hot water gurgled behind the fireplace but I thought I had heard something else and opened the back door. Nobody was there. I peered into the rain, then shut the door, put more coal on the fire and was idle for a time but sick of idleness, bored with doing nothing, yet with nothing to do.

I went through my little hoard again, clothes, passport, money. Not enough money. Dismally I put it away.

In its grave under the bed was my novel. That could change the pattern and set me free, but how long would it take to finish it and send it away and have it published and be rich?

The water was raging hot in the pipes so I had a bath to get rid of it and kill time. There wasn't much time left till the end of the month yet tonight it crawled and I wanted to kill it.

After my bath I roamed undressed through the half darkened house, posing before one dusky glass and another until a sound outside sent me flying to my room. I opened the window. I could see no one. Enchanted air flowed to me from plum trees shrouded in white, adoring the rain. I leaned out, open, receptive to the message from the night, of love, tenderness, longing intertwining and mixed with the impulse of spring.

A gust of wind struck the trees. Moisture and petals fell in mingled showers. Suddenly I thought of the little Holt and his destruction of the things in the desk. The same sort of pent-up life struggled in me. I looked round my room, was stifled in it, wanted to smash it. I wanted to shatter the glass and scribble in red on the walls and leap through the window and run naked through the orchard in the rain.

I rushed downstairs, took Aunt's old coat from a nail on the back door, pushed my bare feet into her rubber boots and bolted through the trees. In what seemed one winged swoop I was at the boundary fence and leaning against it and listening to sounds from the wood.

There was a key in one of the pockets of Aunt's coat, Uncle's key to the hut. She must have been peeping. I felt sorry for her. Between Uncle and me she had been having a rotten time lately.

Rain ran down my face, my hair was wet. I didn't care. After a time I sensed a presence but wasn't alarmed. Before the new boundary was put round the wood poachers often cut through the orchard. I wasn't afraid of them. Perhaps Charlie had come back from Lincolnshire. I missed him. Even quarrelling with him was better than nothing. I realised I had been longing to see him, and wondered if longing were love. Sometimes it felt like love, especially when he wasn't there. Thinking of him I had found my way to his secret place in the fence. It was open, the loosened boards pushed aside. Was he in the wood? But he would never be so careless as to leave the gap unclosed. Rule number one, made specially for me, it was to be closed immediately after use on pain of my being excluded for ever from his confidence. I put the boards in place, turned for home, and fell over a body.

Again I thought of Charlie, but soon saw it wasn't Charlie who lay in the wet grass, unconscious, perhaps dead. It was useless to look for help, though I did look and called out. Nobody was near, nobody at home. If the stranger were not dead, if he were not to die, I must move him, then go for help. I began to drag him towards the hut, unlocked the door with Aunt's stolen key, and pulled him inside, then lit the lamp and stove.

He showed no sign of life, his face glistening with rain was chalky-white, strange and death suggesting. I stared at him, scenes from half-forgotten films jerking through my mind in moving pictures of violence and death. The hissing and flaring of the stove recalled me to reality and reminded me of the open door. I closed it. As the flames steadied my nerves calmed and I dragged the stranger nearer to the warmth.

He lay motionless, yet I was sure he wasn't dead. He wore a knitted helmet which was wet through. I took it off, and with a sheet from the bed, dried his hair. One side of his face was bruised and bleeding from deep scratches. I pulled off his wet clothes, all soaked and marked with clay and stains from the wood, rubbing his damp skin as each garment came away.

The air grew warm. I threw off Aunt's coat and sat on my heels expectant yet self-forgetting, then for the first time looked with full consciousness at the man who lay helpless and naked, beautiful and piteous as a fallen god, and the fog of half-truth and half-knowledge dispelled from my mind. Here was the revelation of the mystery.

He was young, pale and cold like sculpted nudes I had

sometimes seen in museums. Like, yet not like, for hair was damply clustered on this body, making perfection human and its flesh more tender and appealing than any marble statue.

He was not perceptibly breathing. Even when I bent close to his mouth I could feel no breath. Perhaps because the beat of my own heart was so loud I could hear no tremor from his. Moved by the same impulse which impels the hands of worshippers to touch their idols, I touched him, and a miracle happened. Imperceptibly at first, the part beneath my hand quivered then stretched, grew strong and filled with energy, proclaiming life. At the same time, matching this wondrous change, there was an explosion of sensation in me, and I was caught up on a wave of astonishment and delight.

Something I had heard or read came to me, how the dying can be revived by warmth from the living, how death can be made to give way to life. I knew what to do, dragged a blanket from the bed, rolled him on to it, pulled the stove nearer. Breath is life. The name Elisha spoke itself to me. I pressed my body over that of the stranger, opening his lips, putting my breath into his mouth with such an intensity of tenderness and the power of giving I forgot everything except the act of breathing myself into him.

There was a rush of cold air and a voice said, 'My God! Sex! It's here! It's come at last.'

Aunt and Uncle were at the door. I noticed how strange they looked in their best clothes, and wondered what they were doing in the hut. Aunt said again, 'My God! Sex!'

I heard my voice, 'He was dead. I'm making him breathe,' and saw Aunt hold her hands to her head.

'It's all right. I'm making him breathe.' I spoke

soothingly, 'I've given him breath, like Elisha. Elisha and the dead child.'

'I never knew Elisha took his clothes off,' said Uncle.

'Get up,' said Aunt, 'get up,' and threw the old coat over me.

I stumbled to my feet. 'He was outside in the wet,' I said, 'I brought him in here to make him warm and give him my breath, at least I didn't think of that at first, I only – '

'Be quiet,' cried Aunt, but I was humbly persistent and wouldn't be quiet. 'I wanted to bring him back to life,' I said, and a thrill went through me that he was St Orbin come out of the woods into life, 'and I love him,' I cried, 'I've made him live and I love him. I love him because he's alive.'

'Sex!' moaned Aunt. 'She's crazed with it.'

Uncle had wrapped blankets around the stranger. Aunt was picking up the wet clothes from the floor where I had spread them round the stove to dry, and I babbled about old stories of prophets and wise men who restored their waning powers against the flesh of virgins.

'I've read about it,' I said, 'in books about old times.'

'Disgusting,' said Aunt, 'if that's what reading's done for you.'

'Stop bickering,' said Uncle, 'fetch some brandy, then we'll get him to the house.'

'Are you mad?' Aunt was horrified. 'Get rid of him. Put his clothes on and put him outside – ' she flung the wet clothes at Uncle – 'or everybody will know she's been naked in your hut with a naked man.'

I wailed, 'Don't put him outside or he'll die and I love him,' and Aunt grabbed my arm till it hurt and asked if I knew the man and had been meeting him in the wood and I laughed and cried and said I wished I had.

'Get help,' said Uncle. 'I think he's dying.' Aunt shook

with anger. 'I don't care if he is as long as he doesn't die here.'

I never knew she could be so cruel. 'The damn war,' she cried, 'it hasn't even begun and you've gone demented,' and pushed me out of the hut and rushed me over the dripping grass to the house and all the time I was weeping, 'Don't put him outside in the rain or he'll die,' and she grumbling that it served her right for going out to enjoy herself, she ought to have known she should have stayed at home.

From the window of my room I saw lights moving and heard the sound of voices at the bottom of the orchard. Cars arrived and went away. Aunt and Uncle came into the house. I heard them moving downstairs, and Aunt talking. They climbed the stairs. The door of their room closed. Still Aunt's voice went on. At last there was silence. For a long time I crouched on the floor going over and over the confused events of the night, then it came to me with the anguish of unbearable truth that the stranger was dead and I wept for the waste of breath and warmth and love I had poured out, and because something precious was spoilt. I wept most because of that, because something which had seemed so noble was making me ashamed.

I dreaded going downstairs in the morning and stayed in my room. Nobody called me to breakfast. After a time I heard a car stop at the front of the house. Somebody came through the front door. I heard voices. Uneasily I roamed from one bedroom to another while people talked downstairs. Were they talking about me? Was I a criminal? I felt nervous and guilty. Doors opened and shut, the car went away. Still nobody called me. I supposed the shadow of disgrace was upon me. I was an outlaw in hiding, skulking from one place to another. Instead of being in charge of the emotional situation in the house I was now uncertain and timid.

Eventually hunger drove me downstairs. Nobody was there. I cut some bread and took it into the orchard. Every tree was fragrant in the sun and alive with the songs and wings of birds, but I heard and didn't hear, locked in a mood of sadness and loss, grasping after the sensations of the night as if I were in the aftermath of a dream whose delight and pain had vanished at morning.

At the bottom of the orchard marks of wheels spoilt the grass. I sat on the step of the hut, my back against the door, wondering at the unique event whose imprint upon me was already fading as the most vivid kiss fades from the skin. I was sad and dull and my head ached.

At the other side of the orchard Uncle was poring over his newest treasure, a little peach tree which had not yet bloomed. Each spring he waited for its first blossom, each spring was disappointed.

After a time he came to me. 'Don't be unhappy,' he said, 'it'll all blow over.'

I didn't reply and he went on, 'He's been taken away. It's no use looking.'

'I'm not looking,' I said.

'An ambulance came last night, after you'd gone. I don't know where he was taken.'

'Did you put him outside?' I asked, 'like she – like Aunt said.'

Uncle shook his head. 'Of course not.'

I didn't speak and he said, 'After you'd gone into the house I went to telephone. I was away a few minutes and when I came back – '

I put my hands over my ears then took them away. 'He

was alive,' said Uncle, 'he opened his eyes.'

I took a deep breath.

'It's no good, child,' said Uncle, 'you'll never see him again.'

'I know I won't,' I said.

'He was alive,' Uncle repeated. 'He opened his eyes and looked at me. I think he wanted to say something and couldn't. But he was alive. I thought you'd like to know.'

'So it wasn't wasted,' I said, 'nothing was wasted.'

'The ambulance came,' Uncle went on, 'and the police, then he was taken away. I don't know where, I don't know who he was, somebody important I reckon. When they asked questions I said he'd been found outside in the wet. I said the same when they came again this morning. I'd taken him into the hut and made him comfortable then telephoned for help. What else could I have done? They said I'd done right.'

'I'm glad he's alive,' I said.

'It's war department – none of our business.' Uncle went back to the peach tree.

None of our business.

'But he's alive,' I said and everything around me was alive again and the orchard burst into joy.

Uncle had said, 'You'll never see him again,' and I knew it to be the truth. The stranger had gone from me for ever without knowing I lived. I hoped he would keep the life my breath had given him, but it no longer mattered to me if I should never see him again. He was both more and less than a person to me, he was omen and prelude. The intimacy of our closeness the night before and my involvement in his plight had revealed to me the power of my own tenderness and passion and I was glad.

The veil which had deadened me fell away. Every

joyous tree was singing, tender and lovely, beauty was everywhere, in blossoms and pointed leaves, in songs of birds and cries of nestlings, in Uncle stooping over the peach tree and Aunt who came out of the house to join him. The hatred and anger of the past weeks melted from me.

Aunt looked and hesitated, but Uncle beckoned and I went to them. I put my arm round Aunt's poignant shoulders. 'I'm sorry,' I said, 'sorry I've been so awful.' Our voices spoke one into the other. In a passion of self-denial I offered to give up my plans for going to Belgium, though with a pang at such a renunciation, but to my surprise Aunt didn't immediately accept it. She said, 'We'll talk about it later, without any rows,' and we went into the house.

What we said we had said before, but now the scene in the hut was behind our words and though it wasn't mentioned I knew it had frightened Aunt. She seemed puzzled and wary when she looked at me as if wondering what new catastrophe was waiting up my sleeve. At last Uncle said, 'She's ready to try her wings.' I thought of the fledgelings in the orchard. They were ready to fly, from safety, even into danger. 'And she'll have to go,' said Uncle.

Charlie's mother dropped in with the news that our doctor's daughter was going to Germany that very week and Nurse, stopping to gossip at the front gate, said the Squire had taken his villa at Le Touquet for the summer as usual. People were going abroad as if the world were in no immediate danger of coming to its end. All very well, said Aunt, if other people put their fingers in the fire, do we have to do the same? But she was influenced.

A letter came for her. She had managed to find out

that the school in Brussels was a school with a respectable academic reputation and its Principal an Englishwoman married to a doctor, a Belgian but a doctor. That was the deciding point for Auntie.

'It'll be like a finishing school,' she said, 'part teaching, part study. You must work hard at your French. You'll be studying French in Brussels, quite a distinction!'

She became busy with plans for my departure – though I had made them myself I allowed her to make them again – and was affected by the excitement of packing. 'There was a bit of a wanderlust in me, once,' she told me, 'but living with your uncle took it out of me and I never went anywhere.'

There were no more problems about money.

'I won't take a penny of your salary,' she said, 'and there'll be a few extra pounds from your uncle and me as well.'

What she asked in return was that I should buy return tickets on bus, train and boat so as to be able to leave Belgium quickly if necessary. I must promise to tell the Englishwoman my problems and listen to her advice – as she was English it would be sensible – and write home every week.

I relaxed into a mood of puzzled tranquillity. I had been ready to sacrifice my will, yet such is the contrariness of life, I was, after all, to have my own way.

Chapter Thirty

On the day I left school the children brought me gifts of spring flowers and sweets. From the little Holt I would have been pleased with a smile but he remained impervious to the valedictory mood in the classroom, except that in his dilapidated cap there was one wilting primrose and I wondered if it were intended for me. The day wore on, the cap stayed with him, rolled under his jersey or in his trouser pocket or stuffed beneath him like a cushion. When I last saw the primrose it was dead and he stuck it in an inkpot.

When my goodbyes were said I stayed to have a last look round the main classroom. It had strong associations for me. Here I had read my first Shakespeare, here had recited *Lucy Grey* and learned *The Ancient Mariner*. That very morning, in turning out a cupboard, I had found one of my composition books of ten years before. Now I was leaving I looked round lovingly and saw, with my books and bag, a rusty cocoa tin full of acorns. I was sure the little Holt had put it there and ran outside to look for him, but he was gone and I went home with my posies and sweets and acorns.

The next morning there was a red two-seater sports car outside Charlie's house and Charlie's head was under the bonnet. Without preliminary politeness or bothering to find out if the shadow on the ground belonged to me, he said, 'What do you think of it? I made it myself from bits and pieces and a few old tin cans,' then lifted his head and

grinned. Of course I expressed surprise and congratulations.

'It didn't cost much – ' he was twiddling screws – 'but
it's gone wrong. I managed to get it here this morning,
then it conked out. I'll have to work on it all day. You can
give it a shove now you're here.'

So I helped to push it downhill between the two
orchards to the waste ground near the old stable which
was now a garage for his father's car then, rattling the
cocoa tin, I said I was going into the wood to plant an
oak forest.

'Good,' he said, 'just what I feel like doing. I'll come
with you,' and we went to our secret entrance into the
wood. The boards had been implacably nailed together
and swirls of barbed wire curled along the top of the
fence giving sinister emphasis to the notice-boards. It was
obvious no outsider was meant to get in, perhaps no
insider to get out. As I thought of what had happened
there a few nights ago the memory must have showed on
my face for Charlie said, 'Don't look so grim, nobody's
going to keep us out of our wood. I've made another
place further up.' But I didn't reply. My mind was with
the stranger I had found, who without knowing me, had
changed my life or at least had made it easier for me to
change it.

'Don't look worried,' said Charlie, 'nobody will know.'

'Know what?' I was startled.

'Know we're here,' he was deftly loosening nails, 'or
that we're planting oak trees.' He made a gap in the fence
and we went into the wood.

Here lay our old familiar path, here waiting for us were
long-remembered sounds, sensations of childhood as
creatures, leaves, sunlight and shadow all moved in the

stirring life of spring.

Something of the glee of those old days came to us and we laughed as if we had no knowledge of discontent and disappointment and only knew of pleasure. After a time I said, 'I'm glad we've seen each other to say goodbye.'

'So you've heard.' He sounded pleased but surprised.

'Heard what?'

'I'm leaving.'

'So am I – ' not the reply he expected – 'on the London bus tomorrow. I'm going to Belgium.'

'Belgium!' he exclaimed. 'What on earth for?'

I explained and he said, 'If there's a war that's where trouble will start, you'd better be careful.'

I said I wasn't worried, I'd be sure to get out in time, if I wanted to, but perhaps I would want to stay and do something useful or noble. Of course, though I kept the last word to myself, my confident attitude annoyed him. 'Typical!' he said, 'just like you, always so sure of yourself, knowing better than anybody else,' then went on quickly to say before I could argue, that he had joined the Air Force.

'So we're both leaving,' I said and added without knowing why, 'never to return.'

'Oh I don't know,' said Charlie, 'it's not so bad here. I won't mind coming back now and again.'

I asked about the farmer's daughter. How did he feel about coming back to her?

'That's finished,' he said, and when out of politeness I offered sympathy, he laughed. He was more relieved than sorry, he didn't want to be stuck in farming, it bored him. I was impressed by the light-hearted way he was giving up the magnificent acres and the horseriding and the horse which had put its hoof on my foot. When I told him about that he stared at me, then burst out laughing as I knew he would, and called me an idiot.

Presently I said, 'Ivy Holt has a baby,' and he replied quickly, 'Well, it isn't mine, if that's what you mean.'

I had meant it. 'I'm glad it isn't yours,' I said.

Our grove was brilliant with sunshine, so many trees had been felled. The bright ground was covered with green. Bluebells were tight closed but getting ready to be blue.

'Remember how it used to be,' said Charlie, 'now there's hardly any trees left.'

I rattled the acorns. 'Let's plant some more,' so we crawled here and there making holes in the soft earth, and planted acorns, giving every one space to grow into an oak, and were absorbed as we used to be when, years ago, we made gardens in the wood by sticking fir cones and flowers into the soil and making paths with the white pebbles we thought were pearls.

'They say it takes five hundred years for an oak to grow,' Charlie said, 'so in five hundred years' time this will be an oak wood.'

'Our oak wood,' I said, 'though nobody will know.'

Random words flew softly between us as we worked with our hands in the earth. What would the world be like when we were not there to see it? What a strange world it would be without us. How impossible it seemed that some day we wouldn't be alive. We laughed in the certainty of our existence. The sun was strong upon us, we drew in familiar scents and sounds almost without knowing we breathed and heard, and for a time were as much a part of the life around us as were other beings of the wood.

The last acorn was in the earth. We brushed soil from our hands and knees and sat on a fallen tree where moss and tiny fungi were growing in patterns of green and brown and yellow. Birds swooped and flew, ignoring us. This was our charmed playground, our own place, the place of the beautiful bird which people said we said we had seen when we were children, the bird which had led us deep into the wood until we were lost.

Could we really remember it? I closed my eyes to recapture a pristine vision of blue and golden flight.

'I can remember.' Charlie's voice was low.

'Sometimes I think I can,' I said, 'but perhaps we're not remembering. Perhaps we're only imagining something we've been told we said we saw. Perhaps we only imagined it then. Perhaps there never was a beautiful bird.'

'There was.' Charlie spoke in the same low voice, 'There was, and she led on and on until she flew away.'

I knew who he meant but, to lighten the moment, only said, 'Now you're the one who's flying away.'

'And you.'

'I'm only going. You're flying.'

'I've got to have my training first,' he said, 'I won't be allowed off the ground for ages, but some day, perhaps, I'll fly.'

I thought of the special summer we called Zoë's summer and remembered my fancy of the mythical kingfisher's nest. The village, the meadows, this wood, our youth together, for Charlie and me these had made our nest on the sea of time, we were leaving it, had to leave, whether we liked it or not it was floating away, and coming apart whether we stayed or went.

Charlie was saying something about Orbin Old Hall and I came back to the moment.

'Nobody knows what's going on,' he said, 'even I can't find out, and Dad doesn't know. I bet I'd find out if I stayed, but I'm going so it's none of my business now.'

I was indignant. 'None of our business! That's all anybody says. But suppose – '

I broke off.

'Suppose what?'

'Suppose there's something wrong, something we wouldn't like to find out.' Again I thought of the unconscious stranger, the mystery of his coming and going, the secrecy and the barbed wire and the notice-boards but I only said, 'It's a bit weird. Too many secrets.'

'It's Ministry of Defence,' said Charlie, 'and they can have as many secrets as they like, do anything they like in a war.'

'But we're not in a war, yet.'

'Soon will be,' he said, 'and it's none of our business whatever they're doing. Tell you what,' he changed his tone, 'let's go and look at my dug-out.'

I didn't want to leave the sunlight for his dismal grotto and he went alone while I sat on the log and looked into the intricate pattern of moss and lichen and watched the purposeful wanderings of ants amongst cracks in the bark.

When he came back he was frowning. 'Somebody's been in,' he grumbled, 'perhaps it was that character they found in your place the other night.'

My heart jumped. Lights at the bottom of the orchard in the middle of the night, cars, voices, an ambulance . . . of course people must have heard.

'But why should I care?' Charlie sat beside me, 'I won't be using it again. It'll fall in soon. All the same – ' he gave me a serious look – 'I'd rather you didn't tell anybody about it.'

258

My thoughts were still with the "character", my stranger, and I said, 'I haven't told anybody. I'll never tell anybody. But how did you know?'

He stared at me. 'Are you dotty? I made it, didn't I? I don't suppose I'll need it again, but you never know. Promise you won't mention it.'

I promised.

'I can depend on you once you've promised,' he said.

'Even though I'm a warble-lip?'

He smiled and patted my shoulder. 'You're not so bad.' He was standing with one foot on the log and poked the bark with the toe of his shoe until startled ants rushed over it. He watched them for a time, then shook them off. 'I always got on with you better than almost anybody.' He looked down at me. 'Pity isn't it?'

'Why?'

He shrugged, then took off his sock to chase out an ant. 'I've been such a long time waiting to grow,' he said, 'I've been bloody well waiting to grow.'

He gave his gap-toothed grin.

'I hope you meet a chap who is six feet three.' He touched my face with his fist as if commemorating an action made in anger years before. 'I'll have to go,' he said. 'I've a lot of work to do on the car.'

I wanted to stay in the wood so we said goodbye. He trod carefully through the acorn grove then turned, his smile gleamed in the sun. 'I'll meet you in five hundred years' time,' he said, then went through the bushes and disappeared.

That was the last I saw of him. He was shot down somewhere a few years later. I never saw him again.

One of the acorns had fallen unnoticed. I made a hole for it away from the others, giving it plenty of room because it was special, having nearly been left out. 'Grow,' I said, as I pressed it into the soil, 'be here in five hundred years' time.'

The breath of the opened earth came to me, familiar and assuring. Everywhere bright pointed leaves were vibrant and thrilling, sunshine shone through them, birds moved amongst them. Near me a bee alighted on the log, paused then flew away.

Suddenly I saw life all around me, spread like a feast, and I was partaking of it.